GIA'S SECRETS

GIA'S STORY, BOOK 1

LUCY H. DELANEY

United States, 2018

To the men and women and boys and girls who suffered at the hands of an abuser and kept your secret in silence.

To those who faced the fear and shame and told and stopped your abuser and saved others by your courageous act of telling.

To those who told and weren't believed and had to learn to survive not only the abuse but the lack of validation.

And to those suffering and struggling with your secret now... take heart! You are not alone. Do what you must to survive.

PREFACE

"WHY ARE YOU here?"

"I'm here because you asked me to come."

"Right, but why did you? Why are you here today?"

She sighed deeply, lowering her green-eyed gaze to the floor. Did she say why she was there? The next second their eyes re-connected and she knew what to say but not how it would be received.

"It's a long story," she said looking away again, suddenly nervous.

"I've got time."

"OK… but to understand why I'm here, you have to understand where I've been."

"That's the story I'm looking for." The questioner nodded at her, almost imperceptibly, "Gia Gianelli, tell me why you're here."

CHAPTER 1

MY STORY IS nothing special. I'm just one of millions who suffered sexual abuse and survived, one of many who battled addiction and won (with some help), and one of billions with a story full of light and love, tragedy and triumph. The only thing remarkable about my story is that's it's completely mine. There's no one else quite like me and no other story quite like it. On that note, I have to say that perception plays a vital part in this, and all stories. I see things my way, because I'm me. Ask my Nonna, mom, dad or the evil man, Brad, and they would tell things differently. This is simply my version of the story of my life.

According to me, my story starts like this: I was born on November 11th in the late seventies, into a close-knit Italian family. My parents, Mike and Peggy Gianelli, had a lot of promise and potential. They got married young (some say too young) and did the family thing, complete with dog and white picket fence. My dad was a charismatic high school athlete who dreamed of going pro, and a small town Evangelical pastor's son who swore he would at least escape the Bavarian tourist town of Leavenworth, Washington if the whole pro thing didn't turn out. Then my mom changed everything on him, or so I was told, by his mother, Cecilia Gianelli, from here on out lovingly referred to as Nonna. My mother was an absolutely beautiful woman, with thick flowing chestnut hair, and emerald green eyes that sparkled in the right light, and long, slender piano-playing fingers. She was not athletic but rather musically inclined and I don't remember a time when thinking about her didn't also conjure up melodies from Beethoven or Chopin.

The best I can gather from various family members is that Mom played piano at an old gospel church camp in the woods, about twenty miles out of Leavnworth, when she was in high school and met Nonna there. They took a liking to each other and Mom started filling in when the regular piano player couldn't make it to Gramps' church. That's how she and my dad met. Mom says she slept with him for the first time on her seventeenth birthday, his gift to her, and got to have his first two children: me, Gianna, and my twin brother, Giovanni at barely eighteen.

The next part, I don't remember myself; but it's a story Nonna's told me so many times that it seems real enough. She's got a thing for keeping family stories alive. Keep in mind no one else has confirmed, or denied the facts Nonna told me. I threw it in both of my parents' faces at one point or another in my teen years and I'm sorry about that now that I've been through being a young adult myself. I'm confident, neither of them, if presented with the chance to do that time in life over again, armed with the knowledge of what would happen, would do it the same way; just as I would certainly not do mine the same way.

Nonna says my mother left when Gio and I were almost two years old. My dad came to Nonna and Gramps' (Samuel Gianelli) room in the middle of the night, holding me in one arm and Gio in the other and said, "Peggy left, what am I supposed to do?" While Gramps consoled my dad, Gio and I cuddled up next to Nonna and fell fast asleep, oblivious to how our lives would never be the same. What I know to be true is that my dad was awarded custody. Since it happened in the late seventies, when fathers seldom got full custody, I surmise it was because of one of two things. Either whatever my mom was into was bad enough for the courts to not let us stay with her, or the muscle that came with the good, God-fearing, prominent Gianelli name automatically made her the "bad guy" no matter what. Whatever the case was, she didn't get us.

My dad was a good provider, which was the Gianelli way of saying he was a workaholic, with a slap on the back and glint of pride in the eye over the hours clocked any given day. Since I don't know exactly what happened, all I can say is that being as young as my mom was, with a workaholic for a husband and two crying babies at home, I can understand why she maybe didn't like her life enough to stay in it. In fact, years later when I had a crying baby of my own, and a man that stayed out drinking, drugging and partying until the wee hours of the morning, I actually called her and told her I never understood why she left until that moment. It was the first time I ever remember my mom dropping everything to be with me (the story of that night is actually a turning point in my life for many reasons so, out of necessity, I'll come back to it later). Whether my dad used having to provide as an excuse to over work, or as a way to avoid being a present husband and dad, or because it was the work ethic he was raised to believe was right, I do not know. All I know is that he worked a lot; in my opinion, too much, and it cost him dearly in the things that count: family, friends, faith. The truth is, I follow in his footsteps and should check out that plank in my own eye and consider my penchant to work too much myself.

When he was around I remember that my dad went on a lot of dates and there was usually a pretty woman on his arm or he was hanging out with his buddies, laughing and rough housing. At that time there were also a lot of sleepy Sunday's in padded church pews listening to Gramps drone on about things I didn't understand from the pulpit. I also remember dark, scary spaces and yelling and screaming, chunks of pulled hair, fear of the rapture and not going to heaven because I was bad. And then there were Nonna's insufferable rules and restrictions and the piano that ever and always played the soundtrack to my life.

As I look through the memory mirror back at the event that probably defines my life, the most recent scientific studies tell me my recollection is skewed by my own interpretation and re-interpretation of the original happening. What science says doesn't matter much to me. The staccato memories are real. He did what he did and it changed me forever. Thankfully it wasn't my first memory.

My first was actually from when I was about nine months old, although science says children have no memories from the first couple of years. Again, I do not care what science says. I have always remembered it, and once about ten years ago, in passing conversation, I shared it with my dad thinking I'd been a toddler and the other baby I remembered was Gio, only to have him tell me it was my cousin Billy (who was six months older than us) and I was barely walking. He told me, with certainty, I was about nine months old at the time. The blue and turquoise shag carpet on Nonna's bedroom floor felt rough between my fingers and on my knees, so I must have crawled into her room. There was a mess in my cloth diaper, a poopy mess. I remember feeling frustrated that no one would get it off and somehow making my way into Nonna's bathroom with the other baby. I don't know how I did it, but I got that nasty thing off and plunged it up and down in the toilet the way I saw my mom do it. Fascinated, I watched the pancake of feces loosen with each dunk into the water and was so proud when, finally, it flopped off the diaper into the toilet. I tried to get Billy to flush the handle because he was on that side of the bowl. No, it wasn't like "Look Who's Talking," I couldn't talk and he didn't understand what I was trying to get him to do. All he was doing was holding onto the bowl, bobbing up and down. I pushed past him and tried to pull the flusher thing down, the way I'd seen big people do, but it barely budged. I was a weak baby, but finally the toilet flushed while I was holding the very edge of the diaper. I watched it swirl and tug with the water. I don't know if we laughed and that's what got the adults into the bathroom or if we'd been gone long enough to warrant a household search. Two pretty, long-haired ladies, my mom and Aunt Maria, came in to retrieve us and there is no more to that captured moment in my life.

Flash to the next memory, not cute and not at all happy. Gio and I were in a small closet, one of those closets with the bi-fold door that had slats in it. It was shadowy, but sunlight cut through the slats. I was terrified.

CHAPTER 2

AS I BREATHED in, the air would catch and convulse my lungs. I had been crying a lot, but wasn't anymore. Gio was snotty and sniffling next to me, his breath catching too, but I wouldn't let him cry. I rocked him and smoothed his hair and did my best to keep him still and quiet. Something bad was outside that closet, and crying would not be good. I think we must have been in the closet a lot or at least we were in it a long time, because the image is burned into my brain like I was in there this morning. I vaguely remember clothes hanging but do not recall anything on the floor like shoes. The door opened and in front of me was a silhouette of a thin, slightly muscular, probably white, man. I think he had dark hair, but I'm not positive on that. I know his name was Brad and he was naked. And I know he was evil. In his hand he had a zucchini, maybe a cucumber, but I'm pretty sure it was a zucchini. He completely ignored my sniffling brother and talked directly to me. I was intensely aware of both Gio and him and tried to listen very carefully to him while hoping Gio would be okay. It was difficult to give both equal attention, but I did my best. Brad told me he was going to let me practice on the zucchini so I didn't do it wrong and then I was going to do it to him. If I didn't do it, or if I bit him, he'd kill Gio. If I told anyone, he'd kill Gio too. Maybe he didn't tell me that, but I feared that, because he warned me not to tell.

As I did what he showed me to do, he either ejaculated or urinated on me. I remember the warmth and fluid and a smile on his evil face. For the longest time I'd assumed he urinated on me, but as I grew and came to understand how the male body works, I started to question what he actually did. I speculate now that he ejaculated, since he was making me give him head, but I can't be sure he didn't urinate. That's all I remember, thank God, but it's enough, isn't it? One tiny horrendous memory filled with fear and terror and an erect penis. One little fragment of my childhood fragmented me physically, emotionally, sexually and spiritually for the rest of my life. One evil, selfish, sexually deviant act defined my life. My fear and terror was for Gio's sake. I don't know why I wasn't more afraid for myself. I was focused on following Brad's directions precisely because I really didn't want little rosy-cheeked Gio to die. I couldn't imagine how he'd kill him, but I didn't want Gio dead because of me. Somewhere, deep down inside, I was afraid for myself too, but certainly I was more afraid of doing it wrong and being the reason Gio died. The sorrow over my loss of innocence and safety came later, when I better understood the gravity of what he took from me.

The memory has always been the same: same closet, same sunlight, same naked man, same vegetable and Gio crying. No piano playing in the background, it's a place too dark for music to live. Like the washing of the diaper, it's there, stuck inside me, part of the essence that is unique unto my fragile soul. I hardly think about it anymore; unless I see a man too uncomfortably close to a child for my liking, unless I hear a story about rape or sexual trauma, unless someone gets busted with kiddie porn. I thought a lot about it as a teenager when I grasped for details of the abuse. I don't remember telling anyone what happened until years later, as a pre-teen and teenager when the memories more than haunted me; they tormented me. I wanted his whole name and anything else I could conjure to help me deal with it, understand it. I tried to get others to confirm the abuse happened. Nothing … for years, nothing. But apparently, I did tell. I did rat on Brad when I was little. More to come on that later, years later.

A few other vague, terrifying, memories pop up and I think they must have been from around the same time, although I'm not sure. They're quick moments, flashes, snapshots with smells, feelings and sounds tied to them. For whatever reason I remember them so they must be pertinent to what I've become. Here they are:

My mom put either me, or me and Gio, into a dryer and shut the door almost all the way. She was afraid and wanted us to be so very quiet, like little mice, and tried to hum Beethoven's Moonlight Sonata, like she did to rock me to sleep, for a moment. Then I remember horrible yelling and screaming. I don't recall words, but I think it was Brad she was fighting with; or maybe he's always been my bad guy so I imagine it was him and it was really someone else. I remember her long, shiny hair pinned half-way back and how pretty she sounded as she hummed and stuffed me in my metal womb. She was beautiful, even though she was terrified and trying to act brave the way I did in the closet.

Another time, I remember feeling very sick and being on some sort of hospital bed or examining table with a big, bright light shining on me and my Auntie Maria, fingers pressed to her lips, looking worriedly over me. She was a veterinarian so for a long time I thought I'd made or dreamed that memory up. I'd spent so many uncountable hours through the years with her at her equestrian clinic, I knew her metal operating table, with a light shining down on it, like I knew my own room. But one night when I was fifteen or sixteen years old I asked her and Nonna, over a girls' dinner, if I had ever been in a hospital on an examining table, because of the memory. They both looked at each other, became uncomfortable and Aunt Maria confirmed that I had. Nonna's face pinched in disapproval and she glared at Aunt Maria, squeezing her jaw so tightly her lips turned white. A secret was going to come out, I knew it because that's how Nonna looked when secrets slipped out. Aunt Maria told me of a time that I'd been very sick after coming back from a visit with my mom. She said both Gio and I had been examined at an emergency room. That's all she offered to me, with a rebellious sideways look at Nonna when she finished the confession.

Later when I was twenty-two, I reacquainted myself with my babysitter, Meredith, who came into the picture sometime shortly after my dad and my mom divorced. She and my dad dated and were a thing for a while, but I remember her most without my dad around, when she was babysitting. In a long, emotional reunion over hot, bitter coffee with no sugar and only cream, she filled in a lot of the gaps in my memory, and mentioned that I did indeed disclose some sexual abuse to her. I asked her what, and she told me I said something about a closet, oral sex and a zucchini. I didn't know how to take it when she told me exactly what I remembered. Her tenure as our babysitter ended quickly when things fizzled between her and my dad and my family always called her crazy so part of me thought she must have brain-washed me to believe the story as a child. I suspected that's why she remembered what to tell me after all those years; but another part of me was overwhelmingly relieved to finally have someone validate what I always remembered happening.

Continuing on with preschool memories, I remember crying and begging and crying and begging to go with my dad when he said he was leaving for a night out. I loved being with him and his buddies and maybe a date, drinking the coffee creamers like a cool kid and begging for fish 'n chips. I can't remember if I got to eat fish 'n chips or not, but I know I got to go out with him, at least that one night. We sat in booths. They were blue and I was not very still, but I was probably pretty cute.

In one memory I have a yellow puffy jacket, brown, squarish, rough leather shoes and a white man, named Kevin with a stub of an arm below the elbow. I think we were at the zoo by the orangutans. His arm intrigued me. It looked round and smooth and more purple than fleshy colored and I wanted to touch it to see if it felt as soft as it looked. I didn't feel afraid or sad for him. I was simply curious about how it felt and why his hand part was missing.

I also remember a black and white newspaper photo of a blackened, burned-out vehicle and reassurance that *he* couldn't hurt anyone again. I don't know who the "he" was but in my child's mind, I wanted *him* to be Brad so that he couldn't hurt me again.

And then someone came into Gramps and Nonna's house... and maybe he could hurt me, hurt us all again...

CHAPTER 3

IT WAS CHRISTMAS. I was terrified. I ran down the shag-carpeted hallway at Gramps and Nonna's; away from him as fast as I could. He was coming! Coming down, down, down a ladder. There was "ooohhhing" and "aahhhhing" and I didn't know what was going on except that everyone seemed concerned. The grown-ups looked at Gio, Billy and I weird-like. Through the window, I saw a man in red coming down the ladder on the back porch with a bag. All I could think of was that it was Brad and he was coming to get me and no one could stop him. The closet fear overwhelmed me, but I forgot about Gio. I was afraid for myself and wanted to get away as fast as I could. Someone came to retrieve me, my dad maybe, and everyone was laughing in the living room. They were laughing at me, and when I whimpered or tried to run they thought it was very funny. I wasn't afraid anymore because they were all happy and because the red-dressed man was kind and had toys in his bag. Everyone took turns sitting on his lap. I liked the attention and laughs the little game gave me, so I played pretend afraid a while longer until their delight went away.

Another distinct memory is of my dad telling Gio to give him the jack handle while we were driving home from Wenatchee one night. He pulled the car into a parking lot and stopped abruptly at a gas station near the turn to our house in Leavenworth. He grabbed the metal pipe from Gio's little hands, pushed the door open and flew out of the car in a furious rage. I was afraid and hid on the floorboard and saw nothing of what transpired. My imagination always guessed he was beating up Brad to protect us, because my dad was my hero and took care of everything.

I only knew two evils at that time in my life: the devil and Brad. They were, and I suppose they still are, the same to me. Back then, I naively attributed anything that would cause fear or anger to one or the other of them. I don't know what my dad was actually doing or who he was standing up to, but knowing my dad's sense of justice I still imagine he was protecting someone from something bad, certainly not purposely offending anyone.

When I was a little older, I also remember being underwater, and not breathing and feeling terrified. At the time, I remember thinking the hand on my head, tangling fiercely in my hair was holding me under the water and trying to drown me. I would come up flailing, gasp, and then plunge down again scrambling to get up. All the while the hand pulled at my hair. As an adult, I assume differently. Best I can figure it, I must have somehow fallen off the dock I was on and into water and the hand on my head was grabbing my hair in a frantic effort to retrieve me from the water. I always assumed the hand was female and I knew her, even if I am maybe still a little unsure of what her hand was doing to me.

Then there are the vagina memories seared into my mind. I remember extreme pain in my private area being a constant source of anxiety. There were times I was swollen "down there" and it hurt to touch it or even wear underwear. Sometimes I was chaffed so badly I could flake off chunks of dried skin under my little fingernails. Other times, it burned like the very fire of hell to urinate. The burning was more of an outward pain, like a tear from an episiotomy, than the inside pain of a UTI. I hated going to the bathroom when I hurt like that. I would hold it until pee came without trying and dread the next time I had to go.

No one would look at my vaginal area, not Auntie Maria or Nonna and certainly not Dad. They told me to put Vaseline on it. Once, I was lying on my bed, in my most endeared childhood home, screaming and crying in pain holding my vagina in my hand trying to cool it because it burned so bad. Another time I sat over the toilet desperate to pee, but bawled because it stung. I had to go badly, though, so I knew I had to let it come out no matter how much it hurt.

Then like reprieve from a nightmare, it all stopped. I have no more painful vagina memories from childhood and I somehow

forgot almost all about that pain until the first time I had sex as a
teenager. I lost more than my innocence that night, I realized I
hadn't had it to lose in a long time. I ate the forbidden fruit, my
eyes were opened, and that winter night on a friend's cold porch,
under sleeping-bags and down comforters, I had a better idea of
what Brad had *really* done to me all those years before. I tried to
forget but no such luck.

I wish for the sake of my story and my sanity I knew more about
the exact time and circumstances of a lot of those memories, but then
again, maybe I should be glad I don't remember more and that my
family didn't speak of it.

My father's family, to this day, is masterful at looking good
and keeping secrets. It's probably one of the reasons I say more
than I should or than is socially acceptable at times, because I don't
want to keep things from people. Some of the secrets, I imagine all
the Gianelli's know, and probably half the old timers and gossips
in Leavenworth do too, but they only whisper them in the daylight
once or twice if ever. The Gianelli's are tough, and my paternal
family name is powerful in that small tourist town of less than
three thousand. When the vacationers go home, all we have to talk
about for the rest of the long, cold, dark winter is each other. The
Gianelli's were an institution in the town, and we NEVER spoke of
the bad. Gramps was the reason we were so respectable. Today the
town is bigger and there are more churches, but back in the sixties
they had one Catholic church, one Lutheran church and one lively
Assemblies of God church. Gramps was the pastor at the good old
AG of LV, his charisma, community involvement and genuine
compassion for the town and his fellow man grew him into a man
of great repute in the town. He was a leader in many of
Leavenworth's small town circles both community and religiously
based, but he wasn't the boss of our family.

The Gianelli's were dominated by Nonna, who we all whispered
about. All our family members have tried telling her to her face that
she's domineering and repetitive and sorrowful and guilt inducing.
But, the thing is, if accused of any kind of wrong, Nonna starts
praying in Italian and casting the devil out instead of considering
she may be wrong. She has never, to my knowledge, entertained the

idea that the complaints we bring against her may be true. As I said, no one speaks of the bad, except for our matriarch, Nonna. She allows herself the exception. She *always* speaks of her mournful childhood. There are several stories she tells that we, her family and friends, have memorized because she tells them so frequently.

Her childhood stories have had a huge impact on my life because of how often I heard and still hear them. For that reason I need to share them, though, I hate to give any more face time to the same old tales. They go like this...

CHAPTER 4

ONCE UPON A time, when Nonna was a baby, her mom abandoned her. She left her, literally, on a neighbor's step with a note penned to her blanket. I saw the note once when I was a teenager—not that it matters. Nonna's dad, Sergio, was a good first generation American and, in my opinion, spoiled her, probably to make up for her lack of a mother. He loved the Lord and with the help of a sister started a cowboy church in Wenatchee that Nonna says grew to a great number. Her dad was drafted into the army during WWII, when Nonna was but a *bella bambina* and became a contentious objector. The Army made him a medic instead of a soldier, somewhere in the South Pacific where bombs were dropped on bad guys by good guys and her Pops helped them all. Nonna was forced to live with a wicked step-mother, not unlike Cinderella's, complete with not two but three evil step-sisters, who made her do all the house work while her dad was serving his country.

Nonna's real mother, Mildred, didn't die like Cinderella's. It was much worse than that. She was an alcoholic and Nonna dreaded visits to see her, which is why she stayed with her wicked step-mother instead of living with her mom. When Nonna was fourteen, her Pops was wounded and was sent home from the war. But he was too hurt to come home and Nonna was too lonely without her dad. Her step-mom sent her to stay in a hotel in close to the VA hospital Pops was ailing in. Nonna says she spent every day with her Pops watching him get weaker and weaker. Eventually he died and she was forced to return to her sorrowful, lonely childhood. Nonna's only bright spot was Jesus and the church her Pops built, and her idolization of her father.

When Nonna was a grown woman with children and grandchildren of her own, her mother came to know the Lord in a miraculous way. The story goes that great-granny Mildred was officially pronounced dead for several minutes but woke up and was over her alcohol addiction from then on. Great-granny claimed to have died and gone to hell. She said that the smell was horrific. I remember her saying, or Nonna telling me she said, the screams of agony from others were excruciating to listen to. She would try to respond, or get them to hear her, to no avail. In the horror of it all she saw the tiniest of light in the blackness surrounding her. The light was small but it was the only hope she had so she fixed her eyes on it. The light grew into a rope of dots and speckles, and she realized it was a rosary wrapped around the hands of Christ. Jesus told Great-Granny Mildred that thanks to the prayers of her family, she was being given the chance to live again. Great-Granny didn't go to Gramps' church though, she lived in Wenatchee and, because of that lit-up rosary she saw when she was dead, she chose Catholicism. Of all the things Nonna held against Great-Granny, I think that was the one she had the hardest time getting over.

I guess it's a neat story to hear… once. Stuff like that doesn't happen to me but most people in my family have supernatural stories like that. As a kid I felt like I was the odd duck—well, I still feel like that—but back then, I wanted to see a lit-up rosary or angel, like others in my family saw. I got nothing, nothing but a burning vagina and Nonna's stories of how bad her childhood was. I wish I'd been older when Great-Granny passed the final time so I could have actually heard the story from her and not re-told in Nonna's style. And I would have liked to have had the privilege of meeting Pops this side of heaven. He always did sound like a wonderful man.

I'm not sure how the Nonna stories sound to someone on their first telling, but after hearing them hour after hour, day after day, year after year, the stories lose their tragedy and wonder. They start to sound more like fairy tales, which would of course make Gramps Nonna's knight in shining armor, and he was, but the stories annoy me. It is sad that her mother was a drunk and left her with a note pinned to her. It is sad her dad died a soldier's death in a veteran's hospital. It is sad she was treated like a Cinderella and that she missed out on a year of school to watch her dad die. It's sad I never met my great-grandfather. It is utterly amazing how Nonna's mom came back to life, but the stories are old and tired and only emotionally affect me when I force myself to feel them anymore. Her attempt to keep her dad's memory alive has worked tremendously; he is known to all our family and most of the town of Leavenworth. I wish I had been able to meet him here on earth, but then I'm sure, had he lived, things would have been very different than the tales Nonna told.

And now, back to reality…

CHAPTER 5

WE DON'T TELL our secrets so I had to infer and hang on to any whispers that slipped out and sort through them by myself and hope that in the process I didn't suppose things that weren't real. I heard whispers, lots of whispers, as a girl and I collected them into a jar of secrets that already held the closet secret. I knew not to talk about the closet because my brother would die, but I didn't know why we had so many other secrets too. I didn't really know what was okay to say and what wasn't. I knew it wasn't okay to talk about something that could get Gio killed, but I didn't know why no one would talk about my mother outside of whispers. Just because I didn't know what was okay to talk about doesn't mean I didn't. I don't think I've ever been accused of being tight lipped. I remember lots of warnings to be quiet as a kid, and I now try to warn myself to talk less and listen more, like in says in the *Desiderata* to "listen to others, even the dull and ignorant, they too have their story."

The whispers are almost as prevalent and fragmented as the memories. Admittedly, I don't know which whispers were really hushed truths and what I might have made-up to fill in unanswered questions. There were lots of whispers about my dad's doings. He was quite the ladies' man, I know that for sure. There were always rumors about him with any number of pretty girls. He preferred blondes. I know that because all the women, except my own mother, had blonde hair. There were whispers of a married woman named Vickie-Jean. He ended up marrying her, so maybe I misinterpreted some of the hushed conversations. Maybe the whispers were simply secret plans about how he was going to marry that woman, not that she was a married woman. Maybe he was scheming about a proposal, and Auntie Maria was his hot-headed partner in the plan, and Vickie-Jean wasn't married at all. Maybe I was confused by. Or maybe my dad and Vickie-Jean were caught up in an affair and I overheard too much.

Vickie-Jean wafted in and out of childhood memories. My dad would date nice, pretty ladies for a time, then Vickie-Jean would show up again, then she would leave, or fire season would take Dad away and when he came back, she would reappear too. In many ways she's been there from the beginning, always on the fringes of my life. Some whispers said she may have been pregnant before she and my dad were legally married, a major offense in our religion. I do not know which whispers were true but the secrets about Vickie-Jean and my dad simmered through a lot of my childhood and still leave me wondering what the real story is.

There were other whispers too. They abounded about what my reckless mother was up to or how badly she screwed up over and over again or how badly Brad or Lester, her second husband, beat her. There were really hushed whispers about me and Gio that I always supposed were about Brad, but as a mother myself I realize in hindsight they could have been about something as mundane as what we got in trouble in school for. I took everything to a sinister level. I honestly still assume the worst when people whisper or gossip because of all the secrets I grew up with.

There were, of course, the church and small-town whispers. Professionally, among church goers, these whispers are known as "gossip" and publicly, among church goers we call gossip a sin, but privately, gossip is the fodder the ladies live for. Even though everybody in church pretends to dislike gossip, most everyone in church listens to it and people are ostracized, mortified and crucified because of it. As a pastor's grand-daughter, in a small town, what I found was that, like vultures, gossips are always around, circling and waiting to find out the nastiest, juiciest tidbit. Then when they hear it, they like to plaster it into the ears of anyone who will listen. Church gossip always seems to find its way to the pastor, so I heard whispers about who was a drunk and how much they drank. It's especially bad to be pegged a "drunk" in the fundamental church culture because drinking is "of the devil." No one cares if someone is two hundred pounds overweight, but God forbid they drink too much. I heard about people not having enough money to keep their knick-knack store open, and people not getting paid. I knew who was not having sex and who was sleeping around. I heard about the secret cigarette smokers, the dead beats and whose sons or daughters were "backslidden" and what they'd done to slide backwards. That term always got me. I pictured someone on a slide, and instead of going down forward, they went down backward, but down a dirty mud-slide, not a shiny, polished metal one.

It was confusing to go to church Sunday after Sunday and see all these people looking so dressed up and good, and knowing how "bad" they really were or how bad their children were, or at least how bad other people told Gramps and Nonna they were. But inside the perfumed and coffee-infused AG of LV walls, they all looked put together and fake and perfect. They never talked about their secrets in church, but I knew what I'd heard, ear-up to the outside of my Gramps' counseling door. On top of that, I knew the secrets didn't always stay behind that carved oak door. Worse, I knew if I whispered to anyone about my secret, it would most assuredly get back to Brad, wherever he was. I accepted it. For Gio's sake, my secret was my cross to bear, in silence. Everyone seemed to have a secret hovering over them, a bad thing they tried to only tell Gramps or a bad thing they knew about someone else. We all had secrets and we all pretended we didn't in the light of day. I was simply doing what everyone else did.

Nonna always insisted I "be good" and would shame me and scold me for what seemed like any and all infractions. I couldn't breathe right, eat right, clean right, and like her stories of her father, her corrections to who I was and what I did, were relentless. Part of her insistence on us being good had to come from her knowledge that the vultures were circling, waiting to find something to pick apart, and who better to pick at than the pastor and his family? Nonna didn't express how much our family image and the gossip whores had to do with her desire for us to be good though, she made it mostly about Jesus. I had to be good if I loved Jesus, or at least that's how she projected it. She also made it clear I was far from good, with how I sat, cleaned, sang, talked, etcetera, etcetera,

etcetera. And she didn't even know about the closet. I knew the really bad things I'd done with Brad. I knew I was not a good girl and I knew I'd go to hell someday. Even though it seemed inevitable, I didn't want to burn in eternal fire, so I tried to do as Nonna said.

At the time, because of all the secrets, I made it my job to keep Gio safe. I never knew when or where Brad would strike. I was always waiting for him. Everything whispered in secret or in hushed tones made me perk up and take notice and collect whatever information the whispers contained. I have no idea how it is for other little children with more innocent lives, but I was sure that whispers were bad or sinister and I was confident there was a big bad guy around every corner and his name was always the same, and I feared him. I was always filled with a sense of uncertainty, anxiety, terror, guilt and shame and a budding knowledge that everyone had secrets to keep, but that most secrets didn't keep long. They contaminated things, like mold on old food, and that's when problems started.

CHAPTER 6

I KNEW FROM a very young age that I didn't matter. My opinion didn't count, what I had to say didn't need to be factored in, and I was an after-thought and burden to those around me. I'm sure it wasn't as bad as that, but that's what it felt like. I don't remember too many adventures or play times with anyone in the family, except for the fifteen minutes of fun that my dad used to give to Gio and me on the rare occasions he wasn't working. It was literally fifteen minutes, pomodoro-style. Pomodoro is Italian for tomato and our fun was measured in ticks on an old kitchen tomato timer set to insure the fun didn't exceed the set amount of minutes. But oh, how wonderful those fifteen minutes were when my dad played with Gio or I exclusively. I don't know how long the tomato timer dictated my play time with my dad but all my favorite childhood memories revolve around that worn red tomato timer and my dad shouting, "Fifteen minutes!" from somewhere in our little Bavarian bungalow. Nothing compared to our fifteen minutes.

My favorite times with my dad and Gio were in that bungalow, before Dad married Vickie-Jean. I remember him being there more than any other time in my life. I played with him more there and I had a generally less stressed existence. I think it was either because we didn't live right across the street from Nonna, or because by then Brad was out of my mom's life, or because Dad and Meredith were dating and she really liked me and Gio so Dad spent more time with us because of her.

Of course, the pomodoro kept our fun time in check. I loved that tomato timer; I can't walk past one for sale in a store and not touch it or turn it and listen for the familiar tick and ding. Our timer is long

gone. I have no idea where it ran off to. All the little white minute
marks had long since worn off and were frequently replaced with
black Sharpie hash marks at the most pivotal minutes, fifteen and
five. Five was for corner time, because the tomato wasn't just about
fun and games. Pomodoro kept naughty time too, and, trust me,
there was a lot of naughty time. I was keenly aware of the fact that
more often than not, I ought to have been ashamed of what I did or
said, and found myself in the corner. Many times I didn't know *why* I
ought to feel that way, but if someone, usually Dad or Nonna, said I
ought to be ashamed of something, corner time was coming.

I became a connoisseur of corners, preferring the shiny, latex
painted ones that smelled like stale air and were slippery on my
nose, to wood-paneled musty ones. I was a big fan of pressing my
nose hard into the corner then smooshing it down until my nostrils
flared on the cold wall. The timer ticked behind me but I couldn't see
how close to "ding" it was. I never watched the pomodoro tick,
always too busy playing or nosing around with a corner. Sometimes
when I was especially not good enough, kind enough, or quiet
enough, I would bang my head into the corner and call myself
stupid, over and over again, which usually got me in more trouble.
The corner times that confused me most were for masturbation. I
was little, and I didn't know what it was called only that some
movements or touches made me feel good. I learned to hide when I
did it, though, because everyone agreed I shouldn't do that. It was
guaranteed corner time if anyone saw me with my hands in my
pants or wiggling my hips a little too much. We never talked about
why it felt so good but was "wrong" to do. They just told me never
to do it again and put me in the corner if I got caught.

I don't remember being thought of as a cute or pretty little girl,
certainly not a good one. Everyone always told me I looked like my
brother, and, well, I didn't hear or see too much good about him
either so that further reinforced my "good-for-nothing" feelings
about who I was. Anyway he was a boy, so I figured I must look like
a boy more than a girl.

I didn't feel good about myself until I started school. For the first
time, I was good, real good! I was smart and clever and the teachers
would say things like, "Look at Gia's work," with pride splashed

across their faces as they showed my project to the other kids. I felt special at school and I loved it. People listened to me and recognized my good work. I shined in school, so school became my heaven. It was the anchor that kept me from floating away into shameful oblivion and the time-stamp I post on my memories from there on.

Preschool and maybe kindergarten too, I spent at the Immaculate Conception Catholic church in Leavenworth. That puts me and Gio around age four when I remember the first real fire danger. I can't say I recall the fire itself, I'm sure it was far enough away to be non-threatening, but in our region of the Pacific Northwest, fire season in the summer was as real as avalanche control in the winter. The God of nature could, and would, and did consume houses, lives and roads without a single human consultation.

My dad was a firefighter and was always busy dealing with fires. But that time he went away to fight fire in the mountains quickly and quite unexpectedly.

CHAPTER 7

ANXIOUS PANIC… RUSHING adults… demands, commands and orders, and of course, I linked it all with a certain bad guy. In reality, the fire was so close that we were on an evacuation notice. Auntie Maria told me to hurry and choose one toy to take and I cried and cried in my cozy bedroom, with the big red toy box, because I had two favorite dolls and didn't want to leave one behind. After those fires, the whole town, right down to the time-out corners of the church and houses, smelled of sooty ash and burned evergreens. In the mountains, trees lay where they fell, charred and chunked into scaly, squeaky pieces of solid, shiny black tinder that crinkled like Styrofoam under inquisitive fingers.

Luckily the fire never made it to the bungalow and my most favorite trees survived that dreadful fire season. In the front yard of our bungalow were big, huge planter boxes around two rough trunked Douglas Firs. To a grownup the boxes may have been fairly small, but as a kid those things were *huge* fortresses. Gio and I could climb into them, hunker down and make believe anything we wanted. We didn't plant anything in them. There was nothing but hard, parched summer-time dirt and pine needles but we made the most wonderful mud cakes and tree cakes and rock patties. We played war and zoo and any other number of fun, fantasy-filled childhood games inside the planters boxes. My other favorite game was *boyfriend*. I had one even then. His name was Terry. I don't remember ever doing anything with him, and I can't even recall what he looked like, but I remember I had a boyfriend and he played in the dirt with Gio and I quite often.

Developmentally I was learning a lot during preschool and kindergarten. I was fully potty-trained in the bungalow house. I remember the day I stopped wearing diapers quite distinctly. Meredith, the babysitter and Dad's girlfriend, was watching us. We were down for our naps, but I didn't want to stay in bed. I wet my diaper a little bit, got up, found Meredith, and asked her to change me. She changed me and I did it again. The next time she had me get my own diaper, which I did and she changed me. The process repeated itself until finally she took me to the bathroom, sat me on the toilet and told me to finish. I did and she said I was done with diapers! I felt liberated. Underwear really is the cat's meow when you're three or four.

I learned about procreation thanks to our gerbils. Maybe they were named Adam and Eve, but whatever their names, they were fruitful and boy, did they multiply! We must have had two full tanks of little rodents. They were such a joy to watch... I don't know what happened to all those little guys when we moved, but the only animal that came with us from the bungalow with us was Baxter, our husky.

Supposedly during this time my mom came from the resort town of Chelan, where she worked as a pianist in the bar for one of the finer resorts, to get us for visits regularly. I can neither confirm nor deny this. I don't remember any visits with her, except the closet times and dryer times until I was in second grade when Brad was gone and Lester was her partner. I suppose it's possible that Brad and the closet happened while she worked in Chelan but to know definitively would require key individuals sharing information. Unfortunately, this was one of the things the Gianelli's never spoke of, only whispered about and I could never quite catch their drift.

Visits or not, preschool was a great time for me. Immaculate Conception was a fabulous place to start learning. The church was old and ornate and had statues of saints and candles everywhere. All the good ole AG had was a piano and water fountain. Gio and I learned songs and games and brought them home with us to sing and play. The teachers told me I was SOOOO smart, and SOOOOO good, because I knew my ABCs and colors and shapes. I didn't think it was smart, I figured it was common sense. Shouldn't all kids know what an A was? But I was an attention seeker. I milked it and had the teacher hang on for a few seconds before I picked the right color or shape when she worked with me one-on-one because I learned quickly that if I always got it right they left me to myself, and worked with the kids having a more difficult time. I liked people *ooohhhhing* and *aaaahhhhing* over me, it made me feel like I mattered, so I stalled my responses.

Then one day the sameness of our preschool routine was broken up by a "special" smart test I got to take because I was "so smart" and I totally fell for it. Gio didn't get to go with me, neither did any of the other kids. Alone, I was ushered into an office. There were undressed dolls on a shiny coffee table and the two ladies administering the "test" sat on the distressed leather sofa opposite where I kneeled on the floor. If my dad, mom, Nonna, or Aunt Maria were there, they stayed out of the picture and out of my memories of the test. My gut tells me someone was there watching from somewhere. They asked me questions, I gave them answers. I thought I'd get to start kindergarten early if I did good. I really wanted to pass the test and tried my best. The only thing that bugged me was that the dolls weren't clothed. I may have commented on that fact. Well they oohhed and aahhed over my smartness too, and I guess I passed, because the next school I remember is kindergarten at the school with the big tires to play in. I suspect that the test was probably an interview to see if I could confirm any abuse suspicions, but again, the Gianelli's don't talk so I don't know.

All I have from kindergarten is a recollection of the sweet smelling paint and paste, wonderful kindergarten songs and the best snowman art project ever. Once again, I was a star student and my art project was used as a class example because I colored carefully inside the lines and put the pieces together so nicely. I even cut out the miniature sample picture at the top of the page and made a baby snowman. The teachers were impressed, and kids back then were too innocent to care about jealousy over whose work was better. I paid attention to what the teachers wanted us to do, I was careful to please them, I was smart and I was good in school.

If I had to name a first love, it wouldn't have been a boy but rather an institution. I fell in love with learning and following classroom directions because I was so good at it. Pleasing teachers was easy to do, and no matter what bad things happened at home, in the closet, or at church; school was always good.

Our school, Osborne Elementary, was situated in the heart of the residential neighborhood and back streets of Leavenworth. My first grade teacher, Mrs. McLennan, was thick and buxom and came to Gramps' and Nonna's church. She had tight curly brown hair, big round glasses and seemed old like Nonna, so she was probably only in her forties, but at six years old, forty seemed ancient! I remember our classroom window looked out toward the monkey bars, and the little boy in front of me always had very nicely done hair. His name was Adam or Andy and he had blonde hair cut like a Marine's, buzzed on the sides and slightly longer on the top. I always imagined touching his hair to see what it felt like. I spent plenty of hours in class imagining myself touching it. Always it was stiff and spikey, not smooth. I don't know if I ever did get the guts to touch it, but I did get his phone number and called him. I told him he was my boyfriend. Apparently we didn't work out.

First grade was the last time Gio and I were equals in school. He stayed behind one more year with Mrs. McLennan and I jumped ahead; and somewhere between making teachers proud and falling in love with school, our family of three, and Baxter the dog, moved from the bungalow to a tiny house across the street from Nonna and Gramps. I speculate that dad's break up with Meredith influenced the whole thing but I know for sure that the fighting between the two of them started before the move.

I grew up believing Meredith was a half crazy woman. I heard whispers that she abused Gio and I. I don't remember her ever spanking me either, but maybe she did. If she did, it certainly wasn't enough to register on my abuse-o-meter. The whispers said that she was "off her rocker" and that she had fits of anger... but isn't that any and every woman? As a child, hearing that Meredith was abusive and crazy over and over again by so many people, and having the Gianelli propaganda reinforced second after second by my new sitter and surrogate mother, Nonna, I believed it. I believed Meredith was crazy. I believed she abused my brother and I while she watched us. For the longest time, I believed that was the sole reason for the break-up and probably the most likely reason for the move.

There are always two sides to every story, though, and the side Meredith shared with me on that fated meeting later in my life, deserves equal attention. The truth, according to Meredith, is that my dad was, and always had been in love with Vickie-Jean, and it was that relationship that split them up. Meredith claims she answered an ad to be a nanny for Gio and me and she and my dad started dating not long afterward. Vickie-Jean and Dad knew each other long before Dad had hired Meredith and she admitted that she was jealous of their relationship. It's likely that all the fights and disagreements I remember sprung from the uncomfortable triangle. Who doesn't get a little crazy when jealousy rears its ugly head. Meredith said she and my dad parted ways on less than friendly terms and she wasn't shocked one bit when he and Vickie-Jean got together.

CHAPTER 8

THIS IS WHEN Nonna took over my life. Her grumblings and complaints, off pitch hymns and endless stories of Pops and her Cinderella childhood filled my before and after school ears and hours. Her stories invaded my life. She always had some tale to tell about Pops and even though I had heard every story before, and Pops was just some old dead guy to me, she didn't care. If I didn't listen and look her in the eye to show her my attention she went off about how disrespectful it was to not listen to my elders. She would tell me to stop what I was doing because she was going to tell me something important. I didn't want to hear it, my heart would race, my face would flush but I knew if I didn't stop, look, and listen, it would be worse for me. Then, when I looked her into her coffee brown eyes, and she knew she had my undivided attention, she would begin her tirade about her Pops and how her mama left.

She'd go on and on about how bad she had it, how horrible it was to see Pops go off to war, how lucky I was that my daddy only worked in the mountains and down the street in his shop. I wondered if she was ever in a closet when she was a kid or if anyone ever told her not to tell secrets. She didn't have a brother to protect so I guessed not. It was a terrible secret to keep and the anguish of it made me feel the way she sounded when she lamented. Quite often she threw in little nuggets about Jesus, how she was this lonely miserable little girl and her only friend was Jesus and she would walk out into the woods and cry on a stump and talk to Him. I always wonder why, if she had time to go out to a stump and cry alone to Jesus, she didn't go out and find friends to play with. Then the next thought I'd think was that if I saw a surly little girl like her, I would call that kid a whiny cry-baby and wouldn't want to play with her. So I guessed and still do assume, that Nonna wasn't the type of little girl that had many friends because people don't like kill-joys and she could suck the joy out of a room faster than Jack Frost could put a freeze on trees.

Truth is, despite my distaste for her historical recollections, I definitely preferred those to her futuristic, end of time speculations. Everyone and anyone who is acquainted with church knows about "The Rapture." Nonna believed, as is promised in the Bible, that there will come a day when Jesus will come back for His church—that is everyone who believes He is the Savior, God's son, and has allowed Him to be Lord of their lives. The Bible doesn't say when it will happen, but it does give signs to watch for, and tells of future events that can loosely pinpoint the era the rapture will happen in. It also says that it will be an awful, terrible, horrible time and we're to not want it to happen because it'll be so bad.

The Bible further says, the Lord is reluctant for the day because it means complete destruction and an end to this world. All the souls who go against God will no longer have a chance to repent, not that they would anyway. Those who believe in God get taken away in a split-second to heaven where there is no death or destruction. Nonna said we would get transported away from this wicked world and get to go home, finally, to Heaven where Jesus and Pops were waiting for us. According to Nonna that day has been late in coming since before I was born. She, like so many others, wait for the day, bank on the day happening in their lifetimes, and don't live or plan for the future because they're so sure the rapture will happen before they're old.

I had countless nightmares about the rapture happening and me being left behind on earth when all the bad stuff starts to happen. Nonna would blame the nightmares on the devil but I blamed them on Brad. The way I figured it, Brad made me bad and he was the reason I was going to go to hell. Maybe if he had been gentle in his abuse, had made it subtle or "fun" (if abuse can ever be considered fun) I might have never known what we did was bad. But I knew what he made me do was bad because he threatened to kill Gio if I told anyone. I knew what I did was bad because no one let me touch my private parts and when I did, they said it wasn't okay.

Bad people were the ones God would punish. I was bad. If that wasn't enough to make me a sinner ready to go straight to hell, Nonna told me everything else I did that was bad... not listening, not sitting still, not cleaning good enough. I knew I had nothing but hell in front of me. I didn't want the rapture, because that would mean I was going to hell. My insides filled with terror whenever I found myself unexpectedly alone at home or Nonna's or church. I'd be so afraid that the rapture happened that I frantically searched for, someone, anyone who believed in Jesus to be sure I didn't miss it. I was terrified the rapture had happened and I was left behind and going to hell. I'd panic as I hunted for saved souls.

Eventually, I would hear Gramps behind his oak door counseling someone, or Nonna singing an old hymn in her warbled way, or see Gio or my dad and would be able to breathe again. If good people were still around, I knew the rapture hadn't happened.

In the early years when Nonna started in on one of her old time stories or rapture rants, I tried to tell her I had already heard that story before and could she please tell a different one. But then she would berate me for interrupting and being rude to an elder and that lecture, about how bad and naughty I was, would be way worse than learning about the lake of burning fire. In short order, I stopped telling her I already knew what she was going to say. I decided it was far better to hear the same old worn-out story than to hear all over again how bad I was.

I became a master, or at least I thought I had, of looking but not listening. I could look at Nonna, fixate on her light brown eyes, nod my head, even repeat a word or two to make her think I was with her, but in my head I traveled far, far away from World War Two when her mama left her on the door step and her daddy went off to the South Pacific. I thought about school and coloring in the lines, about Gio and climbing down into the pine tree boxes in the old bungalow, or a Tom and Jerry episode, where Tom could squish into the shape of a frying pan if he got hit with it. Being rescued was a favorite escape too. I would sometimes imagine being kidnapped and day-dream that a hero came to rescue me. All the while off in the distance, in the real world, Nonna would drone on and on about a life I knew nothing of, sad things that didn't seem so sad to me compared to the closet, and seemed less sad with every retelling. Maybe disappearing into their imagination is a talent all kids have, or maybe it's a special gift I developed to escape Nonna's stories and Brad's closet. All I know is I couldn't stay there with Nonna day after day listening to her same stories. I had to escape the monotony of her past, the endless lectures about how I did something wrong again, and scary times when all the good people disappeared.

I felt sorry for her because she always told the same stories and complained about what everyone did wrong. Her life ended when her Pop's life did and ever since, all she did was keep his memory alive. She missed out on my dad and Aunt Maria growing up, she missed out on me and Gio being born. She lived and died in the 1940s and was a shell of who she could have been. To say I always tuned out isn't exactly the truth. Sometimes I paid careful attention because the stories evolved over the years. When she would change or embellish her stories, I never called her on it, but I took special note of different versions that sometimes popped up. She would ad adjectives to describe the depths of her loneliness, to try to keep the listener hanging on to Pops too, to make the stories sound all the more tragic. They were fish stories, really, bigger and bigger every time. I started wondering how many of her old stories were embellished before I first even heard them. I wondered if she tweaked them before they got to my ears. I had seen the penned, pinned letter from her mother so I knew that was real, but I wondered what it was really like, those stories of her life before they became fables. Was she truly Cinderella or did she make herself feel that way because she was a whiny baby her step-sisters didn't want to play with?

I started to question the Bible too. If Nonna's stories were embellished and they were only from the forties, could the Bible stories of walking on water and pillars of fire be sensationalized too? Were any of the stories in there real? Was God real... Or was the Word just a collection of told and retold fantastical stories?

CHAPTER 9

IN SECOND GRADE I met my favorite teacher ever and my first true, for real, boyfriend. My teacher Mrs. McCutchen was soft and sweet with the most melodious voice I had ever heard. She sung as good as the ladies on the radio. I could have stayed in her classroom and listened to her sing the ABCs for the rest of my life if she would have let me. I wanted her to sing while my mom played the piano. I wanted her to be my mom and play the piano while she sang. I wanted my mom to be her, to play the piano with her beautiful long fingers and sing so sweetly and never put me in a dryer again.

Good teachers are everywhere, but the truly great ones are few and far between and Mrs. McCutchen was one of the best. When she spoke, she said "we" and her laugh was more of a giggle than anything. If we didn't understand what she was teaching she didn't talk down to us like she expected us to know it already. She would come to the struggling student, settle herself down on her knees and work one-on-one with said student until comprehension was achieved. And then we got a pat on the back, ruffle of the hair or a lovely hug that enveloped us in her fruity perfume. Needless to say... I played dumb a lot to get her attention.

I started to notice how different I was from other kids at this time too. I was invited to my first slumber party and felt completely out of place. It seemed like the other girls were all better than me or more normal than me or somehow different than me and I couldn't quite fit in with them. I isolated myself, away from the giggling gaggle of girls to play alone with some dolls, probably like Nonna had done as a girl. Every time the other girls laughed I was sure they were laughing at me. I tried not to call home to have Dad come and get me, but the later it got the more convinced I became that I couldn't spend the whole night there and asked the mother of the house—always these girl parties included mothers—if she would call my dad to come get me. I'm pretty sure I cried until my dad got me. I didn't fit in. I don't know why I felt that way other than I was sure they saw how wrong or bad I was. I don't remember any of the girls there actually doing anything to make me feel bad. I did it to myself by shying away from them, by being sure I was less than what they'd expect of me. It was a terrible feeling and I wanted to get away from it so badly.

Then there was the boyfriend, Jeremy. Our affair was completely innocent as any second grade love affair should be, but, oh was I devoted to that little boy! He wore a red, silky, quilted jacket and I think I loved that jacket as much as I thought I loved him. Every recess we climbed to the top of the big metal dome toy and held hands in his pocket, where I could feel the silkiness of the jacket. He would push the boys off the top of the toy and I felt like his princess. I don't know why we played the game together, and I've never seen any other set of second graders so devoted to each other, but it was my life then. We also held hands in class as much as possible. Since we didn't sit next to each other, though, this was pretty rare. During times when we were allowed to choose our places, I would sneak over to the desk next to his and hold out my left hand to his left hand and we held hands while writing or reading. I think maybe once I remember the teacher asking us to stop and maybe, no not maybe, *definitely* one time I remember throwing a big fit because some other girl sat in "my" seat so I couldn't hold Jeremy's hand. I'm pretty sure I actually threw myself down on the floor and cried my eyes out and thought my life was over because I couldn't sit next to him. I don't know if I got my own way or not, but I do remember being embarrassed of the fit afterward. I never talked to him outside of school either but inside my academic cocoon of safety he was my steady.

I don't think having an innocent relationship with a grade-school boy caused it, but for some reason I started to masturbate a lot more that year. There was no mental connection between those feelings and anything or anyone else. It felt good, so I did it. My preferred technique, and the only type I performed on myself until I was a teen, was always clitoral stimulation and muscle tensing and releasing. There was no penetration.

It started to concern me when I wanted to masturbate several times a day to the point of exhaustion. I'd sneak away to my room or a bathroom and find my way to an orgasm… but one was never enough. I knew what I was doing would get me in trouble because of all the corner time I earned in the past. So I hid from everyone when I did it. I started to think something was wrong about it because it involved my privates, and it felt like I "had" to do it, but it felt good, not scary or painful like the other stuff that had happened to me with private parts.

Since I wondered about it, I asked my dad one time why I liked to do it, and actually started to show him how I stimulated myself in the car, on the way to the grocery store. I had been feeling an urge to do it at that moment and thought it was as good as any time to actually ask someone about it. I knew touching my private parts was bad, and I knew I was doing it too much but I didn't know why it felt so good. I simply wanted to understand and satiate the building urge inside me. So there I was, seven years old masturbating in front of my dad…in a car… in a very populated parking lot and asking him to explain it to me. The poor man! I can't imagine how shocked he must have been, how overwhelmed with my questions and gyrations. He clearly became very uncomfortable. His face looked horrified, but not angry. I can't remember his exact words but they were something like, "That's not okay, don't do that ever, ever again!"

He exited the car as if it was on fire and we never talked about it again. I went from questioning what I'd been doing to being absolutely sure I was doomed to hell, because Dad made it clear that was bad, and Nonna made it clear bad people go to hell… and even worse than doing something I knew was bad… I liked it! It felt good to me and I was trying to share what felt good and, I guess in a way, see if it really was okay and my dad totally shut me down. No dialog, no age-appropriate explanation, no "private parts are for private places" speech, not even taking it as an opportunity to talk about not letting anyone else touch me there. We never talked about it again and left the car in stone cold silence.

Shame bubbled up, like water from an underground spring inside me. The overwhelming sense of being wrong boiled and percolated through my veins like never before. It burned my neck, tingled in my toes and knotted my gut into a horrendous side ache. In that moment, like none before it, I knew shame, and it wrapped tight around me like a boa constrictor with prey.

I don't hold how my dad handled the situation against him, he had to have been shocked. I do think a child compelled by sexual urges the way I was, may be in need of help or counseling. And I don't think a child should ever be shamed for doing it. The facts state that early and excessive masturbation is a sign of abuse; but some self-touching, exploration and stimulation is a normal part of development. I was masturbating a lot more than anything anyone could consider normal. I couldn't even hide it. It was a compulsion and I had been caught, and literally cornered, too many times for it to have appeared age-appropriate. There had to have been so many signs and red flags that I'd been abused. The adults in my life had to know something was off, but they probably didn't know what to do about it.

After Dad told me to never, ever do it again, I persisted in the practice and the shame of doing it burdened me a little more every time. I kept it my own little secret. Everybody had secrets. I simply added one more to my stash. I knew God was already mad at me because I was bad, but when I didn't listen to my dad, and didn't quit masturbating, I knew punishment was coming, just not what or when. So I bade my time in my Bavarian town, waiting for God to let me have it.

CHAPTER 10

OUR TOWN WAS a magical place where fears and frustrations were not supposed to exist, neither were calories or cares. It was an oasis, an escape from life in the very heart of the Pacific Northwest. Leavenworth started as a town of necessity, sprung up from the logging industry because it rested near the railroad tracks. As times changed and loggers left, the town neared death. People, in love with the area, came up with a plan to keep it alive. They strategically converted the village from a logging hub into a tourist destination. The faces of the buildings were reconstructed to look like old world Bavaria. From speakers hung on a blue and white May pole in the center of town, accordions played polka folk tunes while women in dirndls and men in lederhosen performed authentic dances. Feather capped men blew that long Riccola horn and Heidi played in the outdoor amphitheater. The scheme worked and in short order Leavenworth was a well-loved, not too close, not too far getaway destination.

It makes perfect sense that my famous-for-denial family would choose to settle there. The magical town I grew up in was nestled safely at the feet of the Cascade mountains. We had horrendously hot summers, complete with fire season and evacuation notices that made little girls choose between one of two favorite dolls. But, oh, the other seasons were worth the heat and fire! In springtime Leavenworth's mountains were awash in perfect purple, yellow and orange alpine wild flowers. The warming sun and singing birds awakened the city to new life and an influx of foreign and domestic tourists. Fall had colors of its own: rust, red, orange and yellow. Instead of springing up awake and vibrant, autumn colors fell from the sky, silently, aimlessly, drifting, bidding farewell to the heat, the life, the world as we knew it. Then came the best season and the most lucrative time for our town: winter.

Snow didn't drift in lightly, stay a few days and then bid a kindly farewell as the temperature rose again after a cold front. No, our snow fell in storms that were measured in feet not inches. One foot, two feet and sometimes three feet would fall in a single storm that could last a whole day and into the next. The snow, like glitter from heaven, would twinkle and fall. I would run outside at first sight to catch winter on my tongue and welcome the covering that was sure to come.

Everything in Leavenworth changed in the winter. We prepared for Christmas months in advance, an eager, expectant welcoming of the celebration of the Messiah. Of course as a tourist town we cornered the market on commercial Christmas as well as the religious parts. The town literally lit up in Christmas lights, carols and, yes, we even had chestnuts roasting on an open fire. Our little villa of no more than a few thousand, at best, would swell to ten, maybe fifteen thousand every weekend! Year after year more cars would be backed up on the highway for miles to come and see our celebration. The living nativity played out in close to zero degree weather, snow or stars, every year, every weekend of December until Christmas day.

Leavenworth was me. I was Leavenworth. By the time we were old enough to know our phone number, Gio and I were walking into town to the taffy store with our dollars from Dad for doing our chores. I didn't know bigger cities with muggers and barred windows existed. The closest thing to a big city I knew was Wenatchee, nearly an hour away, where we had to go to get linens or furniture because all our town had were trinkets and toys for tourists. All I knew was small town living and local life, complete with whispering towns folk and gossiping parishioners.

When it was clear the whole football/escaping thing wasn't going to work out for him, my dad did what he does best: he figured out how to thrive with what he had in front of him. Since we were Italian and we lived in Leavenworth, a tourist trap, what he had were affluent vacationers looking for niche novelties in exchange for their money. He had a proud Italian heritage and though there was already a German and Australian store, a French store and a Russian store in town, there was no Italian store, until 1985 when he opened one... and this is also Vickie-Jean's official step into the picture of my life.

Vickie-Jean was an art major with an insatiable love of light and dark, contrast and shadows and silhouettes and fine photography. She had traveled the world collecting landscapes and architecture through the lens of her clicky and windy super big camera. She gathered others' photos as well. She had an art gallery of sorts in Leavenworth that I remember well. Pictures hung from wall to ceiling in thick, matted, ornate oak, cherry or walnut frames, all of them lit with the brightest shop lights she could afford. Her gallery, a tiny little thing, maybe twelve feet wide at best, had a carved-out arch-way to the next-door store in the Obertal mall; a pink building a block off the main road. When Vickie-Jean learned that Bearly Purrfect, the bear and cat collectible store, through the arch was moving to Front Street in Leavenworth, she told my dad and all of a sudden my life became a mix of Dean Martin songs about Amore and pasta and oil.

I don't know how long it took to set up, but those little stores, in my little town, defined the rest of my childhood and kept my father away from us even when the fires finally relinquished him from their summer-time grasp. He was determined to run the best tourist shop in town. He joined the Chamber of Commerce, the Bavarian Business Owners, went to town hall meetings, even sat on the city council—still does—all in an effort to be the best.

Gio and I had to walk to Nonna's after school because Dad was either working in, or fixing up his or Vickie-Jean's shop. On the occasions that Nonna had a place to be, we walked to the shop and played, or fought together, behind the cash register. Sometimes Dad would let me dust the knick-knacks of the leaning tower of Pisa and the vinegar and oil bottles, but that was rare when I was young. Too much of a risk I might break something.

The burning mountains, the stores: "That's Amore," and "The Gallery of Light and Landscape," Vickie-Jean, and the magical town of great escape, owned my father. Things were never the same after the moon hit his eye like a big pizza-pie.

CHAPTER 11

THIRD GRADE ROCKED my world for so many different reasons. There was, of course, the store, but there was also Lester, my mom's new husband. I'm not sure when he really came into the picture. As best as I can do the math, it was around the time we were five. Lester's and my mom's first child, Trent, was born a month after mine and Gio's sixth birthday. So that would put his conception nine months earlier and give or take a few months that means I was around five. I really don't remember too much about Lester until the red house.

There were always big holiday gatherings on my mom's side of the family and one of these is the first place I think I remember Lester. He and mom moved into a little red house in the middle of an orchard in Dryden, an even smaller town than Leavenworth, about five miles toward Wenatchee. They lived over the rail road tracks and bumbling over them is always a part of any memory that has the red house in it. The timeline is sketchy and I only visited while they lived there, but it was probably around first through third grade; which means Dad, Gio and I had recently moved from the bungalow.

Mom started playing the piano in a jazz lounge in Leavenworth sometime after she moved back from Chelan. Lester did something, probably tending trees and orchardist stuff like that. They did not associate with the good local church folk in town, so even though there were only a few thousand people in our area, she seemed miles away from my world of heaven and hell.

Mom was an unusual kind of beautiful. I liked to simply look at her. I thought she was the prettiest lady in the world. I compared all the women my dad dated to her beauty. I hoped to grow up and look like her. Alas, Gio and I only inherited her stick straight chestnut hair, the rest of us was pure dark, olive-skinned Italian. Mom tried to be fun too. In fact, I don't remember her ever being mean: emotionally disconnected, afraid for herself, addicted to drugs and alcohol and wholly unfit to parent, sure, but she wasn't mean or vindictive. Most importantly, in my estimation, she didn't make me feel bad about always doing everything wrong. I was a kid who was used to feeling bad about every "no-no" or mistake I made, and for a grown-up to not make me feel like a screw-up, made her cool in my eyes.

When she lived at the red house she would get big cardboard boxes and show us how to stick them on our bunk bed and cut out holes for windows and doors. She helped us fix up the bed like a castle or bus, or fun things like that and play pretend in. She read to us in that house too. I remember portions of "The Lion the Witch and the Wardrobe," and she had the most fantastic reading voice! Her tone and inflection, like the melodies she played on the keyboard, made me hang on to the sheets whenever the book depicted danger. She put me inside the story! She was a great reader and I loved her, if for nothing else, because she read to me, but for so much more than that.

I can't say much good about my mom's parenting. She made a lot of mistakes, but who doesn't? She tried to be good and hit the mark on enough occasions for me to give her credit for her attempts. I know her neglect was never intentional, but rather a by-product of her mental illness or drug addictions, which like her hair, I would also inherit. I honestly had fun at the red house for a while. I liked the stability of a schedule and plan of visitation. Every other Monday through Wednesday after school (because when you live in a tourist town, weekends come on different days), Gio and I packed up our suitcases, his of He-man, mine blue, green and turquoise paisley and we got in the car to my mom's. No shame, no same re-told stories, no rapture, just make believe, terror, and a lot of unsupervised adventures.

Gio and I played outside a lot, with cats, with the other kids in the neighborhood, many of which we knew from school, and with each other. We rode our bikes around Dryden, which really only counts as a town in a rural place as small as small as our neck of the woods was. We were free to do what we wanted, with no adults to tell us how wrong we were.

Inside the house we played with more cats. Mom and Lester had a thing for cats. I forgot to shut the door once, and her special cat, Wednesday, with one eye, got out and got hit by a car on the main road at the end of the driveway. Mom was really upset about losing her, but unlike Nonna, I don't remember her shaming us about our mistake. She was heartbroken, and she stood outside cradling Wednesday's lifeless body in her arms, rocking back and forth for hours telling her how much she loved her. Maybe she was high, maybe she was really sad, I'm not exactly sure but she stayed out there with that dead cat until Lester came home and snapped her back into reality. We buried Wednesday by a bird bath in the tiny backyard and Mom kept flowers on it as long as I remember her in that house, except when it snowed. We must have gotten in trouble for leaving the door open, but when it was done, it was over. No shame, no guilt, no reminder of how badly we screwed up, but always- fresh flowers by a bird bath, so I don't even remember our punishment.

I do remember I was nervous about Lester because the last guy Mom had around was a very bad guy. At first, Lester didn't seem to be a bad guy and I enjoyed having fun with Mom so I tried to be nice but I didn't want to spend too much time with him either. He was nice enough, for a while. The closets in the red house weren't slatted so they were safe. Sun couldn't shine through the closet doors in either my room or Gio and Trent's. Mom and Lester's closet didn't keep children locked up inside it to do naughty things.

Their closet did have more than clothes inside; it was a garden! Big green plants grew inside their walk-in closet with bright lights shining like inside suns on the plants. They used black curtains hung over the door to keep the light in. I recall seeing the plants once and being in awe of a jungle inside a house. Mom told me there were baby pear trees in there that needed the room to stay warm and quiet to grow up big enough to be planted in the spring. I was supposed to stay out, and not tell anyone because they were special pears and people would want to steal them if they knew we had the most special kind. Obviously, they weren't baby pear trees, but other types of vegetable matter… At the time I bought it hook, line and sinker and didn't want anyone stealing their pears. Fortunately for them, I knew how to keep secrets like a pro! Their jungle secret was safe with me.

Lester was not like the foul-mouthed but soft-hearted firefighters my dad hung out with and not at all like the men in my grandparents' church, so he always made me a little nervous. I tried really hard not to let it show. I didn't want to be rude and hurt his feelings, but I wasn't sure of him. He was a hippy, a conspiracy theorist and not a quiet man when he was excited about something. He'd go into these long tirades pacing up and down the living room, shoving his horn-rimmed glasses up his nose, making eye contact and nodding his head at whomever he was lecturing or conversing with. I was nervous about not looking at him if he happened to lecture me, because with Nonna if I didn't look it was a sign of disrespect and she would extend the "talking to," and I certainly didn't what him to continue talking to me about things that made no sense to my elementary little mind like "sticking it to the man" and "multifaceted propaganda tactics perpetuated by the DuPont corporation." Again I became a master of looking at someone but going away in my head to somewhere else. It always worked with him because he never asked if I was listening. He didn't care if anyone listened as long as he could hear his own sniveling, nasal voice and no one tried to talk over him.

He had the most annoying belly laugh. I think it was almost like a tic or something because he did it at the end of about every sentence he uttered, like a Southern Baptist pastor bringing in the congregation, "Blah, blah, blah… HA!" I grew to hate that laugh, or whatever it was. It was so incessant I wanted to grab his stubbled face in my hands and ask him if he realized he did it, if he knew how annoying it was, and if he could please, for the love of humanity, never do it again! I can still hear the, "*Ha!*" in my head, pecking away at my sanity. His animated dialect was my alarm on the days I stayed with them. Whatever time it was when he started his talking was the time I woke up.

He wasn't an attractive man either. He wasn't ugly, not hideous or disfigured, but certainly not good looking. It was worse when he took his glasses off and his lazy eye wandered. He was balding and sensitive about it, but couldn't quite let go of his hippy days so he kept it under a ball cap most days and let his thin ringlet of a blonde ponytail hang down his back. It was long and graying and the strands hung out at all angles. I really couldn't tell why my mom picked such an aesthetically displeasing man as her mate. They didn't fit together; she was so pretty and young, he made her look bad... and he made her cry.

CHAPTER 12

LESTER STARTED TO hurt my mom in the red house. I know it went on all the time. We weren't there that often and he did it while we were there, so I know it happened when Gio and I were gone and Trent was left alone to deal with it. Gio and I only saw a few real knock-down, drag-outs. Lester would get on a rant about something she did wrong. My mom would try to defend herself, to fight back with him verbally, which no one could really do because of his tremendous vocabulary and ability to throw words like high-speed darts. She defended herself but she also groveled and apologized and let him treat her like garbage. It was so confusing to hear the sentences she'd string together. One second she justified her right to be treated fairly, the next she called him a foul name, then apologized saying he was right. One time, the door to my room was open and I was supposed to be sleeping, but who could with their shouting? I saw Lester storm down the little hall to their bedroom and Mom was crying, yelling...and following him with a huge wad of hair in her hand. She was saying, "Look what you did! Do you see this? You pulled this from my head, you! What a man, Lester! You're such a man, aren't you?"

She was mad, she was hurt and she was clearly no match for him physically but she continued to advance the fight, hollering back, not cowering unless he came too close. She was right you know, he had no right to do it, but I couldn't figure out why in the world she kept going to him instead of retreating. He would leave the room where she was, the bedroom, the living room or kitchen and she would be the one to follow and keep the fight going. The night she chased him with her hair, I snuck into Gio's and Trent's room and cuddled in with Gio.

When Gio and I got in a fight, which we did a lot, grown-ups always separated us; we weren't allowed to keep egging each other on. I knew Lester was wrong, way wrong, for hurting my mom, for yelling and calling her all those horrible names, but somehow, even though my mom was the one getting hurt, I started to feel like she was sort of wrong too. Mom never gave him a chance to get away or calm down. She kept antagonizing him and following him. I really felt like she should shut up. I thought maybe if she stopped, he would shut up too. I'd plug my ears and wish the fighting away. I'd chant rhythmically in my head, "Shut up Mommy, shut up Mommy, shut up Mommy." I'd cry for my dad, my Gramps and even sometimes Nonna. I started to get confused by the things my mom did and said but made a definitive decision that I did not like Lester and he was not safe.

For the longest time I kept my new secret to myself. I sort of felt like it was maybe my fault because of what I was wearing. The evening he touched me, my mom had let me play dress-up in her nightgowns. She had the prettiest, laciest, most colorful collection of lingerie and nighties. I loved the feeling of the silk and lace and the look of them. She let me go to bed in one of them. It was a light lavender and white lace negligee, and I felt so special and pretty. Snuggled up underneath the fuzzy, reversible Biederlack blanket, the silk contrast was smooth and soothing and easy to feel good in. I was warm, comfortable and felt like a pretty princess going to sleep for the night.

The creaking bedroom door woke me, but I stayed still when Lester came to tuck me in. He had done it before, and I had no reason to believe that night would be any different. He was quiet and stood still for a moment or two, presumably to check to be sure the coast was clear. Then he reached for me. He adjusted the fuzzy blanket, then his hand slid under the covers. My little head was confused. I couldn't think of what he was doing or why he was reaching under my blanket. I don't know why I reacted the way I did, but I think it was because of Brad. I think I figured if I pretended to be asleep he would leave as quietly as he came in. I thought if I was still, maybe he wouldn't be mean. If I didn't move, maybe he would stop. I lay there as stiff and still as I could, pretending to be asleep, painfully aware that my breaths were more shallow and tried desperately to keep them sounding normal.

His hand went to my privates and I was so afraid. I'm sure my breathing gave me away. My heart was about to break out of my chest. It was so scary. I knew it felt good when *I* touched my privates, but it scared the living daylights out of me to think of anyone else touching them. Privates were private after all! I didn't want him to touch me. It was my secret, not for anyone else. It was not okay. I was afraid, though, that it'd be worse and he would get mean or try to kill Gio like Brad if he knew I was awake; so I lay there and let him touch me. I let him do it. I hated it; I hated his smell, his breathing, his disgusting presence. I hated that house, and the stupid nightie. I hated me for being there, for letting him touch me and not stopping it. I hated him for touching me. I wanted to jump up and gouge out his eyes, chew his face off like a lion would. I wanted to get Gio and go home to the bungalow that wasn't even home anymore; but I only knew we were in Dryden, not how to get to my dad, not how to get away to anywhere. I wasn't in my safe, happy town. I was stuck and I was terrified and I got molested.

I was desperate to make it stop and make him quit touching me. All I could think to do and not get myself into a worse situation was to pretend to turn in my "sleep" and push his hand away. I have no idea how long he fondled me that night. I don't know if he'd done it before and that is what precipitated my compulsion to masturbate. I don't even know if maybe he was the one in the closet, without glasses, and I imagined it being my mom's old boyfriend as some sort of self-preservation mechanism. I certainly don't know why he did it at all. It felt like I lay there forever and grew up all over again in that bed.

Brad had threatened my brother's life. I did what I had to do to keep Gio alive. Lester was being bad too, so I think I assumed it was the same deal: if I told or tried not to do it, he'd hurt Gio. I went away in my mind and formulated my plan. I tried to act like I was turning in my sleep, hoping he'd never guess I was awake. That was enough to stop him and that was enough for me to be ruined. I was frozen turned away from him. I didn't know what to do. I was confused and was sure that I caused it to happen because of the nightie. I knew I certainly let it happen, if at least I didn't participate in it, like I had with Brad. I really started to hate myself then and there.

After that I could never be in a room with Lester without feeling some level of dread, anxiety or general discomfort. I didn't want to look at him or hear him or touch him, but I wanted to always know where he was and never be alone with him. I knew he was mean to my mom. I hoped, like with Brad, he would go away and never come back but he never left. Lester stayed around forever, and he wasn't the only unsavory character weaseling a way into my life.

CHAPTER 13

I'M STILL NOT sure how it all fits together but somewhere in those primary years, the bungalow, Meredith, and the other ladies disappeared, like Brad. They were in my life one day and banished to my memories the next. No one said where or why Meredith had gone, except to say she was crazy. Vickie-Jean and her photograph store and Dad's store, That's Amore, were almost all that existed. I'd never seen my dad look at anyone the way he looked at Vickie-Jean while they painted and flirted and fixed up his store for opening day. I knew she was more than a girlfriend and I wondered if I should call her mom.

I remember hearing my dad after church one night telling some friends he was done with women. He said something to the effect of needing to focus on Gio and me and getting the shop up and running. They all laughed and knew that wasn't going to happen with Vickie-Jean next door. Then Vickie-Jean started coming to Saturday dinners with our family. Saturday dinners were a big thing. Everyone came, Aunt Maria, Uncle Joe and my cousins, lonely people from the church or new guests we wanted to feel like family. Meredith came to some but not to many that I remember. Even my mom came to a few, but never Lester, or if he did I tried to blank him out of it. Probably he didn't because it was more than likely on a pick-up night she came and took us to the red house after dinner.

Vickie-Jean started to stay overnight… in my dad's room. I was a kid but I grew up in hell-fire church and I knew that was grounds for condemnation. Despite that, no one, not even Nonna across the street, who saw Vickie-Jean's car was parked behind my dad's said anything about it. And then the next thing I know, Dad told us they were married! Marriage happened in my Gramps' church. He was the one who married people. I'd seen dozens of weddings by then, but I hadn't seen theirs. I did notice Vickie-Jean's belly growing. I thought it was odd. She had always been such a skinny thing and then this belly. The belly, of course was the reason for the quick wedding. They happily announced to everyone they were expecting.

I don't know how I missed all the signs; in my head it seemed like it all happened during one short winter right after Christmas Lighting. By the first spring festival of the year, they were official. But I really don't know, and the Gianelli's don't tell their secrets, so I probably never will. I suspect she got pregnant and they had to rush the marriage but who knows.

The baby changed everything. I had to start sharing a room with Gio! It seemed unfair that Baby Martin got his own room, and Gio had to move into mine because we were twins. It was stupid! The boys should have shared. Not only did Gio and I have to share my room, we had to share my bed! I don't know what happened to his bed, but mine was a full bed and they made us share. I absolutely hated it because it got in the way of my self-stimulation activities, which occupied much of my alone time by then. I lost all my personal privacy and had this desperate feeling inside that I was compelled to gratify when it presented itself.

I worked out a deal with Gio and made him think that his habit was the reason for it. He rocked himself to sleep every night and got in trouble if the parents caught him. I let him rock, without telling, if he let me do my thing. It worked out for both of us for the most part. Sometimes, if I went on too long, he got mad at me and said I had to be done. I apologized every time but had to finish. I started to feel bad about how much I did it, and started to make deals with myself. I only wanted to do it at night, or when I was alone, or only "x" number of times but always seemed to break my own deals. It was a horrible, all-consuming, irresistible impulse; but never did I hurt the way I had as a younger child. No chafing, no burning, just compulsion and pleasure.

I wore nighties to bed at home too, not just at the red house; long silky ones, made especially for me by Nonna. I didn't really like to wear underwear and I'm not sure why to this day. It seems to me with all the issues I had with the area I'd want to keep it as covered as possible, but undies felt so bunchy. I hated them at bed time. My no wearing underwear behavior creeped Vickie-Jean out. I know because I don't remember her giving many spankings to me, but she did for not wearing underwear to bed. How she knew, I have no idea, maybe her gut told her something wasn't right with me, but she didn't know what it was or how do address it. I started to dislike Vickie-Jean very much.

Vickie-Jean was a rival for my dad's limited attention, and the new baby was a rival too. I did like Martin. He was cute and fun to play with, quick to smile and so incredibly small! He begged to be held and loved. Vickie-Jean was different than the date ladies too. Less interested in me, maybe because my dad was already hers, maybe because I was a weird little kid, but she seemed, like my dad, more into other things. Her shop, her photos, her friends at church and her son were more interesting than cultivating a relationship with me. Dad had had other girlfriends that would flirt with him, I think, by doting on Gio and I, but not Vickie-Jean. She had rules, and while she wasn't exactly like Nonna with her shaming, she was exacting in how things should be cleaned and placed and would always remind me to do this or that or redo-it until it was "just right," like what Goldilocks looked for. But, hard as I tried, nothing I did was ever "just right" the first time. I think that's why she reminded me of the Goldilocks story when I didn't do it right. I think it was her way of reassuring me, nothing is ever right the first time. Looking back, she never was as bad as my broken child's mind made her. I was a tough kid and besides that, my ability to follow-through with any task with any amount detail was limited. Living with Vickie-Jean felt like prison at the time to have to do and re-do every task.

Soon after Martin was born and Dad and Vickie-Jean were married and living together, I had to deal with my first bout of lice and my parent's first bout that I remember over us. Oh, how I hated those fights of theirs. Dad would yell at Mom on the phone about us getting lice at her house. Mom would insist it was a childhood thing. Dad would demand she come and "take care of it" and not want us back until it was gone. My mom would come over yelling at him about how convenient it must be for him to be the fun guy while she had to be the mean one. She took us to the red house and scrubbed my head raw with that smelly soap and pulled it back fiercely with those fine combs. I hoped that would be their last fight over us but, like with so many things in life I was wrong.

CHAPTER 14

I DID ONE of the worst things I would ever do not long after the lice fight. I have no explanation as to why. Nonna was our babysitter and watched, Gio, Martin and my cousins Billy and Andy and I after school until late at night because Dad and Vickie-Jean and Aunt Maria and Uncle Joe all worked late. It's wasn't a big deal when she began to watch a little girl from Gramps' church too. I was supposed to be excited that there was finally a little girl to play with but she liked dolls and I liked to play war with the boys. Her name was Melody, she was in first grade and she was afraid of the "Boogeyman." I found out I could make her afraid and it made me feel good. I don't know why, but it did. Nonna would tell me to be nice and play with Melody. I didn't want to but since I had to, I'd start out playing innocently with her and the dumb dolls but would find a way to make up a story about the Boogeyman until the poor girl was actually shaking with fear. Sometimes it was worse than that for her.

One of the many toys Gramps had at the house for us to play with was a race car set with flexible, blue, connectable, plastic tracks. Not only did the tracks make Hot Wheels go super-fast, they made the most beautiful "swooshing" sound as they cut through the air. I'd spin a foot long section of track in each hand like they were ninja swords and revel in the noise. It was perfect and predictable, and I could make it sound more or less "swooshy" depending on how fast I moved them. They slapped things with the most satisfying "whump" sound too; the pitch of which also adjusted depending on how hard or fast I swung them. I honestly had more fun playing with the straight pieces of the tracks, making sounds and noises, than I ever did racing cars on them. I wish I could say my motivation to hit Melody was simply to hear the "swoosh" and "whumping" noises—not that that would make it any better—but it was not. I wanted to hit Melody with the tracks because I knew it would scare her and hurt her.

I'd take her into Nonna's sewing room to "play," and sooner than later I'd make a game up about avoiding the Boogeyman. I would tell her, if she let me hit her, and kept it a secret, I could keep the Boogeyman from coming to get her. The poor girl trusted me because I was a big kid and let me hit her to keep the Boogeyman away. I remember I loved to hear the sound of the track hitting her covered backside and how differently it sounded on jeans as opposed to a thin cotton dress or ruffly skirt. I felt neither bad nor guilty about hitting her either, which unsettles me to this day.

I wasn't in another place, like when I floated away in a day dream while Nonna was lecturing or Lester was raving. I was fully aware of what I was doing and even made up scenarios to get her to allow me hit her. Maybe it was my child-like way of trying to make sense of what Brad did, or what I allowed Brad to do to me. Maybe it was a way for me to control something when everything in my life had turned upside down. Maybe it was a strange way to learn about pitch and tone. Maybe it was me proving to myself that I was the bad kid I felt like I was. I don't fully know or understand why but I truly wish I hadn't done it.

Third grade came and I switched to the Christian school. I don't remember much about it except we learned what an amphibian was, and that my favorite bus driver was named, "Rick." I know he was my favorite because he made me say so. Rick, the driver, was a curious man, but not like the bad guys in my life. He was strict and ran a tight ship, or bus rather. Even though he was militant and demanded our silence, he was safe. We weren't allowed to talk, only answer him, and if we did any other talking the whole bus would have to sing "The wheels on the bus." While it was a fun song, I can say from experience, it got old the 100th time around, so I think we were pretty quiet unless it was our turn to answer one of his questions. On the trip to school at a church in Wenatchee, he yelled out questions that we answered as a group: "What's your favorite color?" We'd have to answer. "Yellow." Everyone always said, "yellow," because it was the expected answer, but I didn't like yellow, even though the church bus was yellow. I knew it was a game, but I didn't like him making me say yellow, so I'd quietly whisper, "pink," and felt very proud of myself for defying him. He asked, "Who's your favorite bus driver?" We had to answer, "Rick" but I'd whisper, "Not you." (even though I'd never had another bus driver). I guess, maybe, he really was my favorite because Rick the bus driver lives on in my memory so does January 28th, 1986.

On that day, my stuffy, wrinkled, old sour puss of a teacher wheeled a TV on a cart into our classroom. She was unusually giddy and excited for us to watch TV. I think we'd already learned about the space program, NASA, astronauts and that this trip was special. On this shuttle, the Challenger, was a teacher and she was going into space! We worked on art projects all morning with the TV droning in the background. Then it started to get exciting. I don't remember the count down, but I do recall the lift off. I imagined riding in that shuttle being free of the ground and going up into outer-space. I was inside the shuttle, shooting off into the stars with the astronauts and teacher and then, quite unexpectedly… death happened.

CHAPTER 15

A HORRIFIC EXPLOSION instantly ejected me from my fantasy. I knew nothing of O-rings or liquid oxygen, but I knew there were people on that space shuttle. *I* had just been on that shuttle! Ms. McAuliffe, which sounded so much like Ms. McCutchen to me, that it could have been my favorite teacher, was on that shuttle! Her students were somewhere watching, like we were.

I met the permanence of death in that third grade classroom. I'd seen those astronauts, I knew their names for a while, I learned about them all and in one second of explosive tragedy... they were gone. The teacher, the astronauts, imaginary me. I tried to imagine them living through the fiery explosion, their parachutes too, even though at only eight years old I knew it was too big, too hot and too much of an explosion for there to be any hope. Still, I imagined that maybe they could make it down safely. But they didn't; they couldn't. They were dead. They had been alive a moment before. Alive like me, feeling, living, breathing but then they were gone. *Dead. Over. Dead. Dead.*

Like stifling heat on the hottest of summer days, death overwhelmed me. I'd seen funerals plenty of times, even seen... and, if I'm honest, touched the hands of the dead in their caskets during viewings at Gramps' church. They weren't real; I hadn't watched them die. The astronaut named Scooby (only he was really Scobee), Mike the one with my dad's name, Jarvis, like Iron Man's computer; they were all dead, dead, dead! They didn't get another chance to re-do the launch, like I could re-do a bad Pac-Man game. I couldn't close my eyes and wish I had only imagined the take off and they hadn't left yet. I prayed and it didn't change anything. They were dead; in seconds dead. I wondered if they knew. Could they have known in those moments before? I wondered why. I wondered what their dads and moms were thinking, I wondered about the teacher's students. I didn't know her and I felt shocked that she was gone. How did they feel? I felt bad that I didn't feel sad they were dead. People were dead and I didn't really care and that bothered me. I was frozen, not feeling anything but wonder. Did they even know they didn't exist anymore?

My teacher started making whiny guttural noises that slowly morphed into something like, "Oh my, oh my, kids, oh NO, oh no!" over and over again. They were dead. I watched them die and I couldn't do anything to take it away.

Nothing else in third grade mattered after that.

But life went on.

Our new family said good-bye to "fifteen minutes" pomodoro-style, to Monday night dinners of noodles and tomatoes, to late-night dates with tag-along kiddos and hello to a crying baby that was supposedly my new brother, dinners with two or three different sides along with the main at a new thick, solid oak table while Pavarotti or some well-winded woman covered Madame Butterfly. The new marriage took us away from everything I'd ever known and forced me into a world of culture and civility that was completely foreign to my alpine sensibilities.

That summer my dad and Vickie-Jean took the first of many "photography vacations." This one took us all down the coast of the Pacific into the deep heart of the racist South so Vickie-Jean could capture the essence of summer in the American South. I'm not sure why they vacationed in the summers when fires were raging and tourists flocked in droves to Leavenworth. They were young and in love and trusted Mark, my dad's best friend, to manage both stores and did what they wanted.

We took that particular trip as a family, photographer-style, and drove in our beautiful brown, brand new-to-us, eight-seat station wagon (of which two seats looked out the back window, and those were Gio and my favorite seats). The vinyl seats scorched my legs in the southern sun and our thighs stuck to them and made audible searing, sucking, sounds of pure pain when we pulled them off. I clearly remember camping in the Redwood Forrest under the huge trees. A biker stroked Babe the Blue Ox's balls at one of the tourist attractions along the Highway 101. That was strange to me because I thought an ox named Babe would be a girl and yet it had balls, and why was that? But when I asked, I was told we don't talk about things like that.

I vaguely remember Disneyland, hundreds of desert photo ops, tarantulas and holding flashlights in horror as Vickie-Jean tried to capture the movement and tiny hairs on the freaky, creepy crawly things that haunted my nightmares for years afterward. I remember that Gio spoiled a photo by a cactus when he pretended to rattle like a snake. Vickie-Jean booked-it back to the car like I wanted to do when they made me hold the flashlight for the tarantulas. Dad tried to be stern with Gio for scaring Vickie-Jean, but he couldn't help but laugh during the lecture, much to Vickie-Jean's chagrin.

Vickie-Jean seemed to always be sneering or stressed out the whole vacation. I've taken trips with my children now and understand the look better. Back then I felt like we were all trying to have fun and she was a sour-stick-in-the-mud, making Dad not want to play with us like he used to when he'd have free time. It was a work trip for her, not vacation. She had plans and we ruined them. Not just Gio and me, but Martin and my dad too.

Vickie-Jean could look at the horizon and know that in thirty minutes the most beautiful desert sunset would descend for exactly two minutes. That was all she had. Two minutes. Two. Two to get the perfect shot of the most unique Saguaro Cactus silhouetted in an umber sun... and we made ticking sounds like snakes, or Martin blew out his diaper and she "was on duty." I feel bad now. I wish I would have helped instead of hindered her plans. She wanted to be known for her talent, the beauty she captured, the things she saw through her lens. Instead I laughed and made rattle sounds myself.

We settled in the heart of the Deep South in a little no-name, hot, stuffy city outside of New Orleans, Louisiana. For the first time in my life I was introduced to prejudice. I think my dad and Vickie-Jean must have had an inkling of what to expect but I had no clue. Our skin was white and because of it, we were different. My parents made comments about "the blacks" and I heard whispers in stores about our color. I was taught in school and in church that color didn't matter. In rural, middle-of-nowhere, tourist destinations like Leavenworth, color truly didn't matter, but it most definitely did matter to the people of Louisiana... at least when it wasn't Mardi Gras and the tourists filled their coffers. It began to matter to me too. I was a sickly, olive face in a sea of lovely, rich darkness. There were pockets of white people and I noticed that Dad and Vickie-Jean clustered with them, except for when her passion for the perfect shot overrode her fear of racism. I was sad about it. I really, *really* wanted to touch a black face, hair, hands that were white on the inside but dark on the outside, but that was not allowed. I wished Vickie-Jean was more into shooting people than natural landscapes and sunsets. She could have been my reason to touch them. I could have helped her put them in position the way she had me sometimes get Martin in position for a shoot. I didn't get to touch them, but the smell of the oily, musky hair stayed with me.

In Louisiana, whites, for the first time in my life, were the minority, and the deep, dark black girls in the parks made me feel bad for being the color I was. Other girls in school in Leavenworth made me feel bad for being me but that was because of who I was; what I liked, what I did, how I talked—or usually didn't talk because I was too busy coloring in the sample pictures. But my color was the way God made me. All of a sudden, I hated my skin. I wanted it black so they wouldn't call me, "honkey" with dark hands on hips. I couldn't help it, I was white and they didn't even find out who I was to decide if they liked me or not. They hated me because I was white and I had the nerve to be in their place. So, naturally, like my parents, I flocked to the other whites. I stayed close to my family and the awkwardness that I already felt about who I was only intensified. I wasn't only wrong because I was a sinner and touched myself. I was wrong because I was white.

CHAPTER 16

I DIDN'T HATE the black girls. They just wouldn't let me play. I played with Gio at the parks and by the bayous while Vickie-Jean took pictures of Bald Cypress trees standing like ethereal sentinels half in, half out of the swampy waters people still swam in. I tried a few times to approach lovely black girls but I got the same cold shoulder and names, or once even worse.

"Get out of here nigger lover, we don't love you! Best be stepping away. Go on now! Best get on out!" A tall, light-skinned, black girl with straightened hair, pink press-on nails and hazel eyes so beautiful they made me catch my breath, stood boldly in front of the swings at one Mississippi riverfront park barring admission. I spent the rest of that day in Vickie-Jean's shadow, watching girls play, wishing I was dark like them.

I imagine that is how most minorities feel. Now I get overly concerned when I see someone of a different color in a room full of whites. I want them to feel included, especially by me, but not like I'm singling them out either. I want them to feel normal but know color is such an identifier, even though it shouldn't be.

But back to the story. Our next extended stay was in a beautiful, old Civil War era plantation house in Louisiana, away from New Orleans. I loved the house, the super smooth and shiny banisters, the creaky floors and cicadas that echoed all night long. I had my own room and it was all mine for a whole week. Maybe because I was away from Lester but for whatever the reason, the impulse and compulsion to masturbate significantly decreased the whole length of the vacation. I still had moments and spells where I'd want to stimulate myself, but I didn't have to make deals with myself or Gio on when to stop or how often to do it. Sometimes because I overthink things, I wonder, because Lester was usually the dinner maker, if maybe he spiked my milk with Benadryl before dinner to make me sleep hard and maybe he touched me a lot more than I remember. Sometimes I wonder if his hand slipped under the covers and mom's purple nightie more than that one time. There was definitely a decrease in my personal need to self-stimulate with time and space between me and him. Then again, it could have been an outlet to relieve stress and without Nonna's constant barrage of dos and don'ts and rights and wrongs, the decrease of anxiety in my life in general helped to ally the compulsion. I don't know but I was glad it wasn't as bad as that season in my life ever again.

Vickie-Jean started to make me take pictures on the trip too. I think she was trying to bond but I never appreciated it the way I think I should have. She was trying to do something with me, but other than enjoying the fast paced clicky-noise the camera made, I found photography boring. We spent a lot of time waiting and repositioning to find the right lighting. And of course, like I did with Nonna in the kitchen, I messed up with Vickie-Jean and the camera. I was too impatient. I didn't wait for the right moment or waited too long and missed the shot. I used too much film and over-exposed two whole rolls. I tried to do it right, but I wasn't good enough.

It wasn't all bad. My favorite part was when she took my rolls to the one-hour photo shops to develop for us to look at. Dad and Gio would go do their own thing. Sometimes Martin went with them, sometimes he stayed with us. We'd sit together in the house or hotel or at a park bench in the humid air and flip through my photos. Always we looked at what I could have done better. Seldom was a photo "just right," but oh, when it was! It was worth all the bad pictures for the one or, if I was really lucky, two in the envelope that were good. On the good ones, she would point out all the things I did right to capture the essence of the moment. Somehow those moments sounded like my mom playing Vaudeville, ragtime tunes on the piano. Especially *Oh You Beautiful Doll*, the one she liked to play for me most. Yeah, she tried to be a good mom. Both of them did in their own ways. Too bad they weren't my ways.

After we looked over the photos, before the boys would come back to meet us, we sometimes took more pictures or did more sight-seeing. She entered our photos into a big street art fair after we left the plantation house. It must have been one of the things we planned to do on the vacation because she had specially matted photos of her landscapes and buildings from her gallery back home packed carefully into an overhead storage container on the top of the station wagon. Her photos always won something, always. She was a true artist. When she talked about the fairs and shows she'd say things like, "I took first at the state fair this year, again!" and laugh her proud, *I'm humble but know I'm good too* laugh. She wouldn't say anything about me, or if she did it was something like, "Gia only placed third in the youth division," or "Poor Gia didn't place at all, she lacks a clear sense of contrast and symmetry; she didn't have a chance." I don't think the words were intended to hurt, but when I overheard them, they sure did, and I knew she said them more often than the times I heard too. She was one more person saying I wasn't good enough, and other kids were better. All I heard is that I didn't matter.

I only won one contest ever and, I must admit, it did feel good! It was at a state fair in Louisiana I think, although it may have been Alabama or Mississippi. Vickie-Jean had chosen the photo I entered. The photo was taken a fuzz before dusk and I'd caught one of several bald Cypress trees standing guard in bayou waters at sunset in the perfect light. On the other side of the murky river a bunch of young, black girls played next to a dilapidated shanty shack. The tree, lit on the right from the setting sun, was in full focus. The girls and shack across the water were slightly blurred and barely out of focus. I felt like a princess, and a fraud, when they called my name. No one needed to know I was trying to watch the girls and accidentally pushed the button at a perfect point in time.

I knew in that moment why Vickie-Jean loved the contests so much. I was a winner and I mattered! I never won anything or did good at anything but school but at that moment I was good at something else! Dad took me out for celebratory ice cream and got a picture of me by my photo and first place ribbon. Vickie-Jean was her usual quiet self, but there was an uneasy feeling in the car as we drove to get the ice cream, a tension only hinted at before that moment was uncomfortably tangible even through my ecstatic feeling of winning. I think it was jealousy. I thought it was because I'd won and she hadn't and it was a big fair. Any time Dad would say something about me, she'd say something about her next show.

Other than the brooding tension and thick, syrupy heat in the air, being a winner was grand. For the first time outside of a classroom I knew what it felt like to be a success. I even got to be the fair's "Parade of Ribbons" the next day and throw candy from a truck trailer with the other juvenile winners. I wasn't truly a success. It was simply an exceptional moment I got lucky enough to capture.

With all the fuss and stress that came with the different shows, and my being mostly unmentionable after that one blue ribbon, I started to dislike them as much as being shunned at the parks. Vickie-Jean was always winning and we always heard about how great she was when she would talk to others. Gio and I were practically invisible. Maybe the jealousy came from me. I don't know why the shows ended for me, but I stopped doing them and taking pictures even before that first vacation was over. I never really missed. I was fine without them. I realize now that Vickie-Jean tried to get close to me in a way she knew. I was such a messed up kid, so filled with misinformation that I didn't get it. I wish I had been able to bond with her. It would have made the next few years and maybe even my whole life completely different.

Despite the blue ribbon, the last leg of our vacation was the worst. The eastern Southern states were vastly different from the arid desert expanses of the west. The air was so thick with moisture I could almost drink it. The sticky, humid heat clung to me. Louisiana, Mississippi and Alabama were not my favorites and that's probably why it felt like we stayed there the longest. In real time we stayed three weeks in each of those last three states but to me it felt like three years. The good thing was that I had my own room again! Gio and Martin shared a connecting room in the bed and breakfast we rented rooms in.

It too was old and historical like the plantation house, but different. The bed and breakfast had once been an old, brick school house. Many of the rooms displayed remains of bygone educational trinkets; sliding chalk boards, wooden desks, tiny chairs. The whole thing wreaked of oldness. It's a smell I can't describe any other way. It was an old, musty, lemon polished wood smell. The stench told my nose and brain that the building had seen more people and heard more stories than I could hope to hear if I lived five hundred years. I thought at the time it must have been the memories of what had happened inside the walls for all those years that made it smell so. I imagined the stories of those before me, like words on the pages my mom or dad would read. Somehow in my imagination they turned into real teachers and students learning arithmetic and English. Then as quickly as I imagined them, I pretended their bodies morphed into nothing but colorful essence and their souls floated up into the air and seeped into the walls and lingered forever and always.

CHAPTER 17

EVERYTHING IN NATCHEZ Mississippi was old. That was why we were there: it was the oldest city in the state. The refurbished school, the civil war mindset, the dock we fished off of... everything was creaky and old. Gio and I spent lots of time at the old dock on the lake because we fished for catfish with strings and worms on hooks. Once we actually caught a big catfish! He was twelve or maybe even eighteen inches long. We caught him at the beginning of the day, and kept him on a stringer. Gio and I would watch him swim on the string and we'd pull him up to look at him squirm on the dock. We didn't talk about eating him, but we knew that was why we wanted to catch a fish in the first place. If either one of us knew how to skin and gut a fish we'd have done that sooner and the fish wouldn't even be a memory. But we didn't kill him or gut him. We played with Catfishy all day. We loved him and at the end of the day, carried him back to the schoolhouse in a bucket of muddy water. When Dad got ready to kill him, he told us what he'd have to do and wanted us to be there to help since we caught Catfishy. We followed along, but then when the moment came and Catfishy was to be beaten on the head, I don't know who stopped him, me or Gio, but we stopped Dad from killing him. We hopped in the car, just the three of us again, like before Vickie-Jean and Martin, and we went down to the dock to let Catfishy go free. I wonder how long he lived after dealing with us all day? I hope it was a long time.

The climate in the South was the worst. It was hot and sticky and buggy and beastie. The rain wasn't at all like Central Washington rain that came every now and then and refreshed me like a cool drink on a hot day. No, Mississippi rain was hot, heavy rain. People showered in it; I know because I saw them. Gio and I lay in the deep cement flood ditches that bordered most of the new roads with sidewalks and let the water wash over us in waves. There was so much of it when it would come. The rain waited to come, pooling in the air; a hot, sticky humid promise of the drenching to come.

Mississippi clouds were greedy. We watched them gathering and darkening for hours to the clicking of Vickie-Jean's camera shutter. Then, finally, the thunder rolled, low, deep, pounding like a heartbeat from the inside out, warning that the rain was coming at long last. Rain on asphalt miles away would blow in and hit my nose about the time the lightning would start up. The clicking of Vickie-Jean's camera always got lost inside the rumbles and rolls and storm stirrings. Then the rain, like an advancing army, rushed in and poured down in buckets so wet, so heavy it seemed impossible to believe. The storms would go on and on and on until the purged clouds thinned and dwindled. Then the whole cycle started again; clear skies, sweltering, southern, summer air, a greedy hoarding of excess water into billowy thunderclouds, a torrential rinse and repeat again and again and again. I don't ever remember fresh air down there; it was always thick, warm, and watery, ripe with rain.

Creepy living things infected the land too. Spiders and scorpions crawled around like the ground was cursed and they were put there to remind me it wasn't a good place. The ants bit, caterpillars could sting, and locusts left their eerie exoskeletons, like little evil watchers, on tree trunks. Snakes and crocodiles roamed the swamps and bayous we visited. The places Dad found to play with me and the boys while Vickie-Jean chased the perfect picture were full of critter danger. Dad found a big rope tied up in a tree and we played "Damsel in distress" the three of us, while Martin watched from an umbrella stroller. I got to swing on the rope and Dad and Gio tried to rescue me (only I usually pushed Gio away because I wanted Dad to rescue me. Gio was likely always there first because Dad let him win). We took turns swinging on the rope and climbing it too. Once during a tough climb, dad got stung on the hand by something. Who knows what kind of evil little bug got him, but his hand swelled up like the Michelin Man's hand. Needless to say going to the rope was over after that.

The bugs and beasties weren't what made me hate it most, though; it was the humanity and mentality of the people that was worst of all. I could actually put on the racism that hung in the air, like a straight-jacket. It was a coat I didn't want to wear but was restrained from taking off. I don't know if others wanted to wear it or felt forced to do so, like I did, but I was stifled in that overcoat of hate. Whites didn't talk to blacks, blacks didn't talk to whites and in their own monochromatic groups they never said nice things about the other color either. There was no reason for it. We are all people; it made no sense. It was stupid, pointless, hateful and unnecessary. I probably missed out meeting tons of girls because our colors were wrong. I hated the racism. I heard blacks make comments about us being "white-bread tourists" that best get on out of their county if we knew what was good for us when Vickie-Jean would walk up to unkempt porches in front of their tin shacks to ask if she could take some photos.

We couldn't get away from the racism. The people held on to their hate like the clouds held the rain, and racial violence erupted as often as the thunder storms did. The tension-snap, like the roll of the thunder always threatened in the distance. I didn't know who to be mad at or who to feel sorry for. There was a dark-as-night and older-than-history black woman who looked unexplainably beautiful to me, even in her dingy dress, wrinkled tube socks and slip on shoes. Her disheveled gray-with-black hair was combed straight back and rigid like duck wings on the sides of her head. I loved her unique beauty but then, with hands on hips she yelled in a screechy voice for us "pale demons" to all "get on to hell where we belonged." She was old so I wanted to feel sorry for her but her words were vicious. I wanted to feel sorry for us because we were ordinary people, not demons. Vickie-Jean was trying to capture her essence because that old lady was the Deep South. I don't know if any of Vickie-Jean's pictures quite reflected the hate that simmered, but the snapshots vibrant and sharp as ever in my mind.

Once, we inadvertently drove up on an all-black BBQ and almost made a racist rain storm of our own. We'd packed up in the station wagon and headed out to shoot like so many days, weeks and literally months before. I don't remember the drive to the beach, but I do remember when the tension-snap, that I always waited for, happened. Suddenly Vickie-Jean said, "Um, I don't think we're supposed to be here." Dad told us to roll up the windows and lock the doors. I didn't want to leave my favorite back seat and hop into the middle to roll them up. But my dad's tone wasn't one to argue with. He made it clear we were not safe and to do it now. I looked around and realized that ours was the only white skin in a sea of black people. Gio reacted at the same time. We both hopped into the middle seat, on either side of Martin, and rolled up our respective windows.

CHAPTER 18

DARK, ANGRY-FACED black men, all different shades of beautiful brown, started to follow the car. I think I remember one having a bat he was tapping in his hand. Dad and Vickie-Jean muttered to each other in worried hushed tones. The car got hot fast, or I did, and only thought it was the outside heat beating the AC like sometimes happened on especially sunny days. I could feel my parent's fear but wanted to look at the people. I didn't know why they were mad. I couldn't figure it out, and when it dawned on me it was only because we were white, I felt ashamed of my color. I looked at their different shades and loved them. They hid their blue veins in a colorful collage of brown, chocolate, black and coffee tones. All of us in the car were the same pasty color; pale, sallow... white, and our color did not belong in their place. I wanted to tell them I was sorry I was white, but that I was a good white person anyway. I knew their look said they didn't want me to talk to them. We drove out of the beach area and the angry faces stopped staring at us.

I don't know if Dad took a wrong turn, or if that was the right beach at the wrong time. I don't remember any shoots that day, only shame and confusion at the color of my skin. To this day, I am sorry I'm white. The privileges I enjoy because I am isn't fair to people of color. I wish every white person in the world could feel the way I did that day and the way I imagine people of color feel every day. It's a stupid reason to treat people differently. It's such a shame to judge based on color alone. There are plenty of valid reasons to question a person's integrity, character and humanity, but the color of their skin is not one of them.

Safety in Mississippi smelled like old, musty memories stashed inside that brick house. After the BBQ incident I think I begged to stay at the schoolhouse while Vickie-Jean went out on shoots. Apparently they let me because I don't remember any more shoots after that. I honestly don't remember anything of the South after that, we just packed up and headed home to my safe, happy village.

We came back in time for everything to change. My school changed back to public school for fourth grade. My house changed. And I changed inside. I'm not sure why it kicked in then and not before or after, but in fourth grade I started my personal love affair with music. We moved from the little house across from Nonna to an upstairs apartment, right in the heart of Leavenworth. It was nestled above one of the Bavarian buildings on the corner of Front and Ninth Streets. Dad and Vickie-Jean said they wanted to be closer to the shops and one day would move their stores into the spaces below our apartment when it became available. I personally think the move had more to do with Vickie-Jean wanting space between her and Nonna, who came over all the time; can't say I blamed her.

I loved living right in the heart of my perfect town! Tourists, with their different languages, dialects and tastes always made things in the old town feel new and fun and fresh. The only slow time came in the winter, after Christmas Lighting, when there was nothing but snow. After the rush of the Lighting, no local in their right mind cared too much about the deserted brick sidewalks in January. Quiet, snowy days felt like a sigh of relief after the influx of gloved and hatted humanity, which had crammed shoulder-to-shoulder in the streets for weeks on end, finally dwindled to a trickle.

Our town was a rare jewel, even though we didn't appreciate it as much as we could have, Gio and I both knew life in Leavenworth was special. Gio and I spent any free time we had visiting the Taffy Store because Mr. Beezly was a church member and gave us a little bag of candy a week... if we helped clean out the open wrappers and exposed candies. We were only too happy to help. We rode our bikes down the steep hill on Commercial Street, out of the Bavarian business district, right into Enchantment Park, probably about a mile down the road. We owned Black Bird Island, and ran, walked, or rode over the bridges spanning the Icicle River whenever we were allowed. We spent many happy hours fishing under their bellies or foraging for tourist coins tossed in the water after wistful wishes were made.

I don't remember the move out of the house across from Nonna's at all. What I do remember were the boxes in the new apartment. Vickie-Jean wasn't there when we moved in. Dad wasn't there either, except I do remember him telling me, with a big old smile on his face, "You get to unpack the boxes Gia! Pretend like this is your very own house and you can put things where you want them to go so you can find them." I don't know where he was or Vickie-Jean was while I unpacked—probably at their shops or maybe she was traveling on a photo shoot—but I remember having the hardest time trying to decide where to put kitchen supplies. I didn't want to do it wrong, although growing up with Nonna, I already knew I would. I tried to imagine where the best place for a cup, a plate and so on would be and put things in those places. I don't know how Vickie-Jean felt about a fourth grader unpacking her housewares, but I did a good enough job for her to leave all but the Tupperware (which she had an abundance of) and pans in the places I chose.

Our new loft-like apartment was open and spacious, with beautiful, wooden vaulted ceilings but it only had two bedrooms. I got the extra room, but my occupancy there was conditional; if I was naughty then Gio would get it. In the meantime, while he hoped I'd misbehave, Gio put his things in a little storage closet that was next to, but didn't open to, my dad and Vickie-Jean's room. He had a mattress on the floor but it was too small to fit a real bed or dresser. We nestled Martin's crib into a corner of the living area, and we were a happy, store-owning family of five in an upstairs apartment in down-town Leavenworth.

We were allowed to remodel it, which we did, a little at a time, for forever and a day. Dad and some of his firefighter buddies, who were into construction, fixed it up when free time and money would allow. They closed off some of the openness in order to add a room, which would become the master bedroom, connected to the main bathroom. They made Gio's storage closet into a guest bathroom, but it was so small it only had a toilet and sink so we all had to shower in the main bathroom.

The only thing I really remember about the remodel was the time during construction when I "lost" my room. The deal with "my" room was that, during the remodel, it was mine only if I was good. Well once, apparently, I wasn't good and lost the privilege of the room. Upon notice of eviction, I moved all my belongings in sorrowful sobs of childhood grief from the bedroom that was no longer mine out to the living-room couch. In my head I'd actually made it a nice, reasonable place to call my own until Vickie-Jean changed my plans. She told me I couldn't bring all my stuff out to the living space. I thought it was totally ridiculous for Gio to have my room *and* my stuff. In my opinion, it was wrong and unfair to make me lose my room, and one more reason to dislike Vickie-Jean and brothers and life in general.

CHAPTER 19

I SAY I started to dislike my life but in some ways, I feel like I lost my life when we got that apartment. I was no longer Gia, I was the built-in babysitter for working parents. It seemed to me like Dad and Vickie-Jean were always gone or busy. Vickie-Jean was forever visiting a studio or working with customers in her shop. Dad was a workaholic; of course, all the shop owners had to be to keep their businesses alive. With firefighting on top of it, he was hardly there. I don't remember him ever hanging around the apartment after the remodel, except for one Super Bowl, which was really weird because he didn't even watch football. He was usually busy doing something at the shop or church or the fire department. If he was home he was in his new master bedroom sleeping.

When he was there, we had a great time. We walked down to Black Bird Island or wrestled or listened to him read us stories. He was fun when he was around, so much fun. I know there's lots of debate about quality versus quantity and I can say quantity time with my dad was sparse, but the quality was golden. I wouldn't trade all the fun of our short pomodoro minutes for endless amounts of boring, do-nothing time. The moments he was there were fun and full and worth every single second. But he was gone most of the time.

I don't remember much of Vickie-Jean either. She was always at her shop, or out of town peddling her pictures to fancy galleries in bigger cities. Maybe, just maybe, she was there a lot more than I give her credit for and I blanked her out. Whatever the truth really was, with or without parental units present, I felt utterly alone in my new world.

There was so much loneliness in that apartment, especially when Gio would go out and play without me and leave me to watch

Martin by myself; and yet there were plenty of bits filled with my parents' drama. I remember, Vickie-Jean crying a lot. Once, it was over Martin's birthday cake she painstakingly decorated then forgot to photograph before cutting. I remember her walking toward the door with a suitcase in one hand, Martin in the other and anger plastered all over her face. I remember the times she told me to tell my mom lies on the phone and seething at my dad in hushed, angry whispers behind the master bedroom door.

The apartment time is different than any other time in my life in a way I can't explain. Maybe it's because my mind was transitioning from child to adolescent. Maybe it's because I was trying to sort out all of the trauma. Maybe it's because that's when I was learning how to play and make music and the way I processed things changed. Whatever it was, the memories from those years taste different than any other time...it's weird, and I cannot express it completely. And maybe that's why this part of the story is tough to tell or doesn't flow like other parts do...

Whatever the reason, my role in life became that of babysitter. Gio and I had to be available to watch Martin at all times after school. Gio wouldn't have it. He knew I wouldn't leave the baby alone, so he left me alone to go play. I even stayed home from school for sure on one occasion, maybe more, to watch Martin while Gio went to school and Dad and Vickie-Jean and Nonna were all too busy. I remember when Gio was out on the town that I'd be so jealous of his time away. Martin couldn't be left alone though because he was too little. I suspect he couldn't stay with Nonna the way me, Gio the cousins and kids from church did because of how long he was already with her every day.

Before the loft apartment, Gio, the cousins and I, would walk to Nonna's after school and stay there until the parents came to pick us up late in the evening or from Wednesday night church service. After the move, though, Vickie-Jean dropped Gio and I off at school then took Martin to Nonna's for the day. Nonna picked us up after school, with Martin in her car, took the cousins home to their place and then dropped the three of us off at our apartment home. I suppose everyone figured Gio and I were old enough to mind the baby for the evenings because we were only a block away from the store. But it never worked out that way; Gio never stayed home. I, alone, stayed with Martin most evenings after school.

Martin was a sweet baby. I often rocked him to sleep in the old wooden chair on the balcony as he lay in my arms in his diaper because it was too arid and hot in the summer time for clothes. In winter I wrapped him tight in a thick, fuzzy blanket because the weather was impossibly cold, but the outside beckoned me. I liked to sing to him, and I liked to watch him when he slept. I did like to take care of him when there was nothing else to do in the summertime because he always needed me. He didn't tell me what was wrong with me like grown-ups did and didn't try to start fights with me like Gio did. He enjoyed my company and soothing words, and I enjoyed his, so maybe most parts weren't as bad as I made them out to be.

Because I was oldest, by two minutes, and the grown-ups were always gone, I felt like I had to watch Gio too, but he didn't allow himself to be watched very well. He was like Dad, always busy and moving and on the go. What I hated most about Gio, was that he was always trying to start a fight. I imagine it results from having all of that energy and wanting to do something with it. I didn't have the energy he did. I liked to sit and read or watch the river flow by or play slowly and calmly with Martin and a toy. Gio liked to move all over all the time, like he couldn't wind down. If there was nothing for him to do and no one wanted to do anything with him, he started a fight so he had something to do. My twin sense usually picked up on when he was going to be especially ornery, but I was powerless to stop him. He'd go to my room and take a toy and play keep away from me with it. If I didn't care, he'd wave the toy at me or pull my hair or something to get me to engage. He always knocked Martin over to have someone yell at him. He liked to find bugs and push them at me or get into things he knew he wasn't supposed to. I tried to stop him, but he was unstoppable. Keeping him in line was like trying to attract a bee to a flower; if I could get him to hover over something, Martin and I would be safe from a sting, so mostly I tried to find him things to do.

Gio, like Dad, was fun to play with when he was not being mean. Once, after the remodel was completed, he and I decided we were going to break the world's swinging record. We didn't know how long we'd have to swing but we rode our bikes down to Enchantment Park, on the west end of town where the Cascade mountains stood like sentinels blocking the way to Seattle. The park was over-large for the town, made so to specifically accommodate the influx of summer time tourists. The swing set, a marvelous set of six in a row, was perfect for world-record breaking. We set up a milk crate between two swings and put a gallon of water and some snacks on it to eat while we swung. I'm not sure how long we stayed on those swings, hogging playtime from the tourists. I'm sure it couldn't have been more than an hour knowing our attention spans, but we tried our best. We talked and swung and swung and talked, and it was fun.

We'd ride our bikes to Dan's, the town grocery store, with carpeted aisles and overpriced marshmallows waiting for camping tourists that had to have s'mores. We bought candy or simply walked the aisles to see what they had in the store, to stave off boredom. Sometimes we shopped for the family. I remember once, on a bike ride back from the store, Gio had a gallon of milk in his hand and was trying to hold his bike handle too. He dropped the milk and it splashed and shattered all over the pavement. It surprised me how far the milk droplets spread. I got lost momentarily in the liquid droplets, they sounded like my mother playing the piano as they fell on the asphalt. I can't remember if he got in trouble for dropping it, but I still remember the sound of the milk to this day.

CHAPTER 20

IT WAS A Charlie Brown time in my life. Like the teacher in the cartoon, the adults in my life droned on in the background but their words were never clear. Yeah, that's how it was. The grown-ups didn't exist much in my reality. The real characters were my brothers and friends and my cousins, Billy and Andy, who were something between brothers and friends to me. All my close playmates were white-skinned, and after that trip down South I was more aware of their color than ever before. We lived in a town where half the population was Hispanic because of the orchard work, but all my friends were pastey white. Sam, red-headed and freckled, Priscilla, blue-veined and pale and Ellie, who was plain vanilla white. Sam lived in an upstairs apartment too, only hers was right on Front Street, the heart of town. She was a shop owner's daughter too. I thought her family was weird because she was named Sam and her brother was Pat. Either could have switched gender and their name still would have fit. She was probably the closest thing I had to a true friend back then. We often found each other alone in the city center and danced to the polka music or played our tourist version of 'I Spy.' We had to spy each other's tourists before they disappeared into the shops. Sadly, Sam's shop closed down and their family moved away before we even made it to middle school.

I think I only remember Priscilla because of her name and, well, because she was the fourth grade Miss Priss. She had the best of everything and everyone knew it, including her, and she reminded everyone of it every day. It was a small town and we locals only had each other so we put up with each other easily enough until middle school when socio-economic differences bloomed into friendship divisions and sometimes full-blown bullying. Both Priscilla and I would be bullies in middle school, on opposite sides of the divide, but as children we tolerated one another.

Ellie was the one I spent the most time with after Sam moved. I'd ride to her house, past Gramps' church, on my pink, Schwinn bike and remember staying the night with her at least once. Her bedroom was sort of an annex to the house, barely enough room for her bed off the living room. Things seemed weird at her house, but then again everything was weird to me back then. I assumed her dad was a creep like Lester. I don't know why, but I never felt comfortable around him. Ellie and I took a bath in her big, old ceramic tub once and maybe she said something or I just thought it, but I had the eeriest feeling we were being watched. I don't actually remember her dad or mom, but how she spoke of her dad reminded me of how I felt about Lester. Something he was doing was wrong, but what exactly it was, she never said… or I never asked, and now I'll never know. The only one in her family I truly remember was her little brother Jack, probably the reason we bonded… He was annoying like Gio.

Jack and Ellie didn't call each other by their names though, but only "Brother" and "Sister." Jack would say, "Sister, can I play with you guys?" and she'd say "No." He'd carry on like Gio would, trying to start a fight to have something to do and Ellie would yell, "Mom! Brother keeps on bugging me and Gia!" They too moved away. I imagine her dad got a better job in a different place. Leavenworth was a beautiful city to live in but work was limited and more people moved out than in.

Like the adults, school was mostly a blur. I guess when space shuttles don't explode in class, I didn't have cause to remember much. My teacher, Mrs. Farley, was wrinkly and old, with black curly hair and glasses that constantly slipped down her nose. She had a big, huge rump of wrinkled skin, the likes of which have inspired singers like Queen and Sir-Mix-A-Lot for decades. I cannot listen to "Fat-bottomed Girls" and not flash back to Mrs. Farley at the chalkboard in fourth grade.

She was more than a rump of wrinkled skin, Mrs. Farley made me write my first full page report, and could have been responsible for the unfolding of my love affair with the piano. I did my report on Frederic Francois Chopin, a classic Polish composer whom my mother was a huge fan of. I liked hearing her play his work very much and took the opportunity to learn a little more about a man I admired. Once again, like in every other grade, I aced the project. I was a great student but unlike any project before Chopin stayed with me. I played and replayed the cassette tapes of his nocturnes (compositions inspired by the night) and started dinking out Clair de Lune as best as I could anytime I found a set of ivories. Music started to fill my blood. I heard it everywhere and sometimes only the tinking and clinking of the keys could cool the terrible rage that was beginning to percolate inside me.

After spring break, Mrs. Farley made us bring deodorant to school and keep it in our lockers. She made us all take deodorant breaks after recess. I can only imagine how stinky it smelled in there with a bunch of pre-pubescent children all hot, sticky and sweaty as the snow melted into spring-time warmth. Ahhhh those bodily functions and how they humiliated me that year. Not only did my pits start stinking, but once I sneezed and this huge string of green snot hurled out of my nostrils. I quickly covered my nose, praying to God, who never answered me, that none of the kids saw what happened. I pretended to have a bloody nose and grabbed a tissue from Mrs. Farley's desk to cover my nose and asked to go to the bathroom.

Another time I was horribly sick and knew I was going to throw up. I tried my hardest to make it to the bathroom in time. I made it through the doors, but the first stall wasn't clean, so I tried to switch to the second and missed the toilet by inches. My vomit splattered on cracked, gray concrete but I felt so much better. It didn't occur to me to clean my own mess. My dilemma was between telling the grown-ups what had happened or quietly going back to class like nothing had happened at all. Conscience won out and I went to the office. I was going to tell on myself, but before I could, the male P.E. coach came in and was laughing about it to the secretary. Only years later did I wonder why it was that the *male* P.E. teacher was the one to alert them to puke in the girls bathroom, and how he could have known so quickly…weird but whatever.

CHAPTER 21

MY NIGHTMARES WERE relentless after the remodel. I don't know why I had so many, but I hated them. They always involved a silhouetted devil-man coming to get me. Sometimes he was on Black Bird island, sometimes in my room, once in a closet – like *that* closet, but always a fiery devil-man. With the dreams came a searing, white-hot heat that ran up my back from the base of my spine to my neck. I felt like I was on fire and the dream-fire would ignite my sleeping body. Thankfully, the heat and sweating would wake me. Once awake, I would know it was a dream, but I'd still be too afraid to move or even breathe for fear he was actually in the room. It felt like he was in there with me, waiting for me to somehow confess my lucidity so he could attack in real life.

The dreams terrified me. Sometimes I stayed as stiff and still as I could until the dawn broke through the Rainbow Bright curtains Nonna made me. Then, in the light, when I could see and be sure Devil-man wasn't there, I could also sleep, until Nonna or Vickie-Jean came to wake me for the day ahead.

Usually it was Nonna who woke us up, with Andy and Billy in toe. She came over to do the morning wake up most school days. She liked to wake us early and take us all over to her house to make us breakfast before school. Vickie-Jean hated Nonna's morning breakfast routine as much as Nonna insisted on doing it. I know this because I heard Vickie-Jean complain about it to my dad on more than one occasion. I think if Nonna wasn't watching Martin, the breakfast routine wouldn't have happened but Vickie-Jean needed Nonna to keep the baby while I was in school and Nonna would only do it if she could take all three of us to her house for breakfast.

It was so hard on nightmare days to get up and leave the apartment. I would fight the command until Nonna started bellowing in Italian for me to wake up... 'or else,' because 'or else' meant she was gonna throw cold water on my face to get me up and moving.

In those days, Gio and I went back and forth between Dad and Mom like two softballs in an awkward game of catch. Christmases rotated but summers were always with Mom because Dad and Vickie-Jean were so busy at the shops or gone fighting fires or on photography vacations. Apparently Vickie-Jean had no interest in taking two bratty step-children with her on anymore shoots... or maybe they had a parenting plan to abide by and summers belonged to my mother. I'm not sure exactly why it all worked out the way it did, but I know I spent the most time with my mom when school was out and the sun what hot and high in the sky.

What I remember best about the visits weren't the visits at all but rather the opportunity to be a kid again, which mostly meant getting pummeled by Gio more than usual. Gio and I would stay home at Mom's place, away from the hustle and bustle of the city, away from the rest of our friends, away from the streets of Leavenworth and be all alone. Our parents worked in town and Lester was in the orchards and we had free reign. Unlike Martin who was always with me and Gio or Nonna, Trent went to daycare so I never had to watch him. Instead me and Gio had hours on end of nothing but free time. Of course, we always had Nonna checking in on us, even at my mom's, but I felt so free most of the day without the burden of watching a younger sibling.

I especially liked to walk from Mom's red house in the orchard to Dryden's little river front boat launch and watch the fishermen put their little boats, kayaks or inner tubes into the Wenatchee River. They got lost in the moment, with their trailers and wenches, even on vacation, life was serious for most of them. Men in action, men of action, like my dad. They didn't sit around in blue clouds of smoke and pompous arrogance complaining about the establishment, like Lester; they did stuff. I liked to watch them.

About that time, we made another move with Mom, Trent and Lester. This one wasn't nearly as traumatic; but change nonetheless. Honestly, I was glad to get away from the secrets locked up in that house. Mom moved from Dryden to Wenatchee to be closer to her new jobs, because she got two in the big city. Compared to really big cities like Seattle and San Francisco, Wenatchee is small beans; but after growing up in little old Leavenworth, with exactly two main streets that were only bumper-to-bumper during festivals and summer time, Wenatchee, with its car exhaust and flurry of people, was a bustle of business I wasn't used to. Twenty-five miles is as good as trans-continental in childhood and the drive from Dad's to Mom's new place seemed like an eternity after the move.

After they moved, we stayed almost every day of the summer with Mom, Trent… and *him*… except for when we went over to his mom's in Arlington, a small farm-town ages west, over the mountains. We went almost every Tuesday. It was an all-day event. We got up before the sun, packed ourselves into his stale, smokey extended cab pick-up, and drove away from the morning as fast as we could. The sun always caught us, though, and before we got to Mamaw's it was daylight, but not necessarily sunny and bright like our side of the mountains. The Coast, as we called it, was usually overcast. Now and then we could find a Tuesday with a friendly, mild sun, like what I was used to in late spring; but for the most part it was balmy and temperate and smelled like wet dirt.

As much as I hated Lester, I loved his mom, my Mamaw. She was Southern and talked with a drawl like the people in the Deep South had. She loved animals and they were everywhere at her place. Bunnies especially, but also dairy goats, llamas, chickens and turkeys, cats, kittens and pigs maybe too. She had a large garden and roadside produce stand that employed two or three people. Lester worked it on the days we were there. I could play outside if I wanted or go into the house and play piano or watch nothing special on the big TV in the corner of her bright, spacious rambling ranch house with moldy sun-lights in the roof.

I learned to play the piano there, on a chipped, old turquoise-painted upright that Mamaw had tuned every year. Mom had nothing better to do, so she spent the afternoons teaching me or Gio chords or simple songs and then put us to practice while she peeled potatoes in the kitchen with Mamaw. I had nothing but time to do nothing but whatever I wanted. And in no time I wanted nothing more than to play the piano on those Tuesdays even more than going outside. I learned lots of songs quickly and became rather good at it.

At least I was good at something somewhere...

I was never good at Nonna and Gramps. Their house always felt safe to me. Walking in their door was like climbing inside a warm, fuzzy pile of blankets on a soft bed in the middle of winter. Even though I always wondered what I was going to do wrong next, because of Nonna's persnicketiness, I loved her house even more than Mamaw's. It wasn't the house's fault Nonna couldn't cheer me on instead of criticize me so much. I hated never getting anything right with her. I was always too loud, too messy, too restless, too naughty, to wiggly, too, too, *too* much of me.

The older I got, the more my wrongness focused on what made me *me*, like how I spoke, how I did or didn't look at people, what I said, how I stood or sat in church. It became not only what I did, but *who* I was that was wrong. There were so many rules with Nonna... and Jesus was so much a part of her life I began to associate Christ with rules and assumed that without God maybe she wouldn't be so picky about everything. Gramps wasn't like that, though, and he was the pastor, so I couldn't entirely make the connection between rules and religion but I started to suspect that to be religious meant to be all stuffy and picky like Nonna.

CHAPTER 22

THE REMAINDER OF my childhood summer days were spent in Wenatchee up a canyon road. The house was beige and white and set in the center of a small orchard. Lester went to work in it the second summer we lived there. Mom always worked late night shifts in the bars playing piano and slept until late in the morning so it felt like we spent a lot of time alone there, like we did in Leavenworth. Alone was different at Mom's. I knew if need be, I could wake her. I wasn't in charge of anyone either. Me and Gio were on our own until Mom woke up and she made a point to tell me she'd never use me as a babysitter but would hire me to help if ever the need arose. And I don't remember being a built-in-babysitter for her in the summers. I was only a babysitter once, and that time she asked first and paid me. My mom did lots of things wrong, but giving me those breaks from being the one in charge of other kids was good and I really appreciated knowing I could be free to go and play with Gio or alone.

By then Trent wasn't the only sibling. Hannah, my baby sister, was old enough to be toddling around. I was used to babies so I played with her a lot. Trent was a sensitive, caring little kid, and finally old enough to play with me and Gio outside some too. He wasn't big enough to do everything Gio and I did, but he wanted so badly to fit in. He'd come outside and play in the yard or in the orchard trees, but not too often. Mom liked for us to play outside, sometimes even locking the door to get us to stay out there. There was always something to do out there so it wasn't hard to get lost in the freedom of being a kid allowed to play unsupervised for hours on end.

It was the complete opposite of the never-ending nagging, responsibility and rules and duties at Dad's and Nonna's houses. At Mom's we could really play. We picked cherries, explored the old, dilapidated barns in the area pretending they were haunted, or we were archaeologists finding yet undiscovered treasure. We climbed knotty cherry trees when Lester and the *pescadores* (pickers) weren't around. We investigated long forgotten secret hiding places like old chicken coops and pilfered rusted tools, trinkets and sometimes even shoes left in the useless outbuildings scattered around the orchard property. Mom and Lester had a couple bunnies from Mamaw's and also dogs and cats, so there were animals all over to play with as well, which was nice since Dad and Vickie-Jean hadn't had a dog since they'd been together. Our husky stayed with Nonna and Gramps after we moved to the apartment.

I idealized time at Mom's even with the bad parts because I wasn't constantly condemned for being bad or loud or messy or sinful. I imagine too that I made it out to be so heavenly in my mind because it never lost its novelty. We were there for summer stretches that always seemed like a respite and relief, a vacation away from my real life.

It wasn't all good, though. I was constantly wary of Lester and the sinister things he did in the dark to my mom and to me. When he was around I needed to know where he was to be sure he wasn't near me or mad at my mom. Thankfully he worked a lot in the summer and was seldom home, only in the evenings when Mom was out working. He was off on Tuesday and Wednesdays but Tuesdays we spent at Mamaw's so there was really only one day a week I had to anxiously watch out for him.

I still liked to play dress up, but I made sure to do it privately. I didn't want him to see me in a nightgown ever again, so I stayed in my room when I was being a princess or model in the nighties. I never came out in them again, and hid them under my mattress, pushed back by the wall. I remember him barging into my room sometimes, once when I was goofing off pretending my giant baby doll was a boyfriend. I was kissing "him" the way I saw on TV and I felt dirty inside. I don't know if I felt that way because I was caught playing kissy face with a doll or because I didn't want Lester to see me doing anything like that because he might think I liked it and try to do it to me. I tried to ignore Lester as much as possible unless it was expected I speak to him like saying, "thank you," after he made dinner or drove us places. I didn't want him to think I wanted him to touch me again. Someone else touching me *there* felt wrong, and at Dad's we didn't touch each other at all, neither in good or bad ways.

The only place I really touched people was at Gramps' church. The people there were always patting me on the head, pinching my cheeks sweetly, giving me hugs or swinging me up in the air. Touch was safe and good and public there. I never felt afraid for anyone there to lift me or hug me or hold me on their lap. In fact, I liked it. Francine, one of the old, fat ladies was my favorite to sit with. She always hugged me into her soft side, under an armpit that smelled a little like baby powder, during service. Uncle Jim was cool too. He was a big giant of a man, with the deepest baritone voice I'd ever heard. He was famous for stretching his big strong arms out whenever he saw me and pulling me in for a good, safe, musky hug that somehow always turned into a noogie on my head. Yes, church touches were good! I'm glad for them or I may never have liked to be touched by anyone after Brad and Lester's perversions.

When Lester was home and Mom worked, we watched the most hideous movies. Some were straight horror films that festered the devil-man dreams. Others were borderline pornographic, with fully nude women and sexual acts playing out before our eyes. Mom was oblivious. We weren't allowed to tell her. I hated it and was fascinated by it all at the same time. Watching people having sex together made me feel something inside that I couldn't explain and I liked to watch it. It aroused me. The urge to masturbate was compulsive while I watched them. I knew it wasn't okay, but it felt impossible not to when those shows were on. I'd find places in the living room where I thought what I was doing could go unseen. Although, I'd become an expert in the ability to stimulate with little or no movement by tensing the right abdominal muscles, often not even having to touch my clitoris. I thought I was hiding but I imagine Lester the molester knew good and well what I was doing and somehow got himself off on that as much as the movies.

The soft-porn was bad enough in the movies but the worst part was how the sex and sexual acts were always semi-violent and the plot lines dark. We didn't watch romance movies where a husband and wife were filmed making love sweetly or playfully to bring the other pleasure. I guess we didn't even watch "normal" porn, whatever that is. No, his regular stack of movies were mostly based on violence and domination. The main plots of the two that are still stuck in my head were about horrible bullying and torture, witchcraft and demonology, purposeful killing, brutal rape and promiscuous sex. In each of the regular movies there was one lone good guy trying to muddle his way through the badness. In both movies the "hero" triumphed, with plenty raunchy sex of his own along the way, but the damage was already done. I saw evil. It didn't matter that good ultimately prevailed. The bad guy in my real house let evil play out before my once innocent eyes, and I didn't always hate it.

CHAPTER 23

I LIKED TO watch the sex parts of the movies over and over again and would get an anxious thrill when Lester went for his secret movie stash, or came home with other rented videos. His movies were bad in so many different ways, and I knew it, but my mind and body wanted to watch them. It was another reason for me to start to hate who I was. If I liked to watch it, and Gramps said all whores and whoremongers (and I knew what whores and whoremongers were) had their part in the lake of fire, well then I was on the highway to hell, like the song we sometimes listened to on the way to Mamaw's house. I knew that I was filth, because who, other than perverts and sickos, would like to watch that stuff? I hated that doing the wrong thing felt good to my body compared to the oppression, shamefulness and guilt I felt at Dad's. I knew watching the movies was not okay because Lester didn't want us to tell Mom. They were secrets. More secrets to keep, more compartments to create in my mind. I was good at keeping secrets, so I never told anyone about the movies, but it was probably more because I didn't want anyone to know I liked them. I figured it must be the bad in me. Nonna was always saying I was bad so it must have been true and that was why I liked to watch them.

The bad in me grew but the shame about it was never so small as when I was at Mom's. There, in the orchard house, we all shared the badness. I wasn't the only one, and no one made anyone feel wrong about it. We were in it together and didn't talk about it. We also didn't talk about Lester inviting me up on his lap while the movies played. We didn't talk about the panic that shot through me. Sure he knew what I was doing hiding in my corner of the living room that must have made him want to call me over. We didn't talk about me pretending like I didn't hear him and staying still right where I was. We didn't talk about how his hands stroked himself or how Gio sometimes left the room quickly. We didn't talk about the little kids being in the living room with us, like this was typical family TV viewing. Then, when Mom came home super late, we all pretended like life was normal, even when she wasn't.

There were two distinct versions of my mom, almost like she too had a very different twin. Either she was fully engrossed in life, playing around the house and having fun, taking us to parks or her friend's performances in summer theaters or farmer's markets, or she was a zombie, numb to the world around her, alive only to the music that pooled in her soul. Lester called them her, 'music moods.' When she was in one of her moods, no one else existed. She was alone in a house full of children, oblivious to us. She would sit on her bench, as her fingers made love to the piano. We learned to dance to the music and wait for her to come back to us or leave for another night of work mumbling, "I am a concert pianist, not a vaudeville sideshow," or something like it.

No matter how much noise or commotion we caused, she wouldn't plug into life until the music was out of her. I suspect now part of the time her moods were drug-induced but I know she was also exhausted. She slept so little after being up half the night. Caring for our needs was tough, but the music flowed from her so she went to it, as I was learning to do, for solace. I couldn't blame her, I felt the music in me too. It screamed to come out once I knew how to play. I know I spent as much time at the piano as she did each time we visited.

It had to be hard to be that good, to have that much talent and promise in your bones, and then come home to a tiny house in the middle of nowhere Washington. She truly could have been world class but her dreams, like my dad's, died when she birthed twins so young. She never came out and said it; I put that on myself but I always felt responsible. The paper clippings of her in performances, of talent shows and competitions won, of places she was invited to play, ended when Gio and I began. She gave us life and we killed her dreams. I would have felt more sorry for her if I didn't watch Vickie-

Jean fight so hard to keep hers alive, even when she had a kid… and took on me and Gio.

Sometimes it felt like my mom could go for days without talking to anyone. Even Vickie-Jean and her preoccupation with planning trips for new photo shoots and keeping her precious cameras in top shape acknowledged my existence. Even Nonna and her preoccupation with all we did wrong acknowledged our existence. Gio and I were in the way or in the wrong at Dad's but at least the women who cared for us were mentally and physically present. When Mom was in one of her moods she wasn't with us at all, not Lester, Trent, Gio or me. She was gone. I accepted it as part of who she was because it was so common.

Her emotional absence sucked as much as when Dad was too busy to be physically present in my life. But when she was normal, she was a fine mother, at times even great, like at Mamaw's every Tuesday. Her times of clarity and attention to us were second only to Dad's pomodoro minutes. Dad never lost his temper and when he took the time to be with us, he was all about fun; same with mom. When they were with us, in the moment, being parents, playing, loving, reading, teaching, I felt no shame and I felt complete. It was the way it was supposed to be all the time. It was the way I wanted it to be forever, but it never lasted.

Mom's temperament was certainly more volatile than Dad's. We never really knew from one minute to the next if she'd notice us or pretend like we weren't there. When she did notice, sometimes she would yell or get upset; or she'd talk but it seemed like only her body was in the conversation. Her eyes and mind and soul were vacant and unfocused. But then sometimes she would hyper-focus on the frustration of having to direct so many unruly kids to do what she wanted us to do. I think Trent was the mildest mannered of us all. I know Hannah, Gio and I kind of wiggled, squiggled and giggled all over the place, frustrating her plans.

I don't mean to say my mom was altogether bad. There were plenty of times she was a good mom. She often took us older three to the city pool during the day, while Hannah hung out in daycare two days a week. Mom, tight, toned and tanned laid out on a beach chair all day to sleep while we played in and out of the pool, jumping, splashing, calling her to watch us cannonball. I thought she was beautiful to behold in her bikini. I was proud she was my mom when she looked so normal, sunning herself like the other moms. No one there would ever guess a mom like that could have moods like hers.

CHAPTER 24

MOODS OR NOT, Mom's fingers found the ivories every day. I grew up listening and learning some of the finest pieces of classical music ever to be written. It was so common in my world that I took the beauty and wonder of it for granted. Unstable, yes, but, oh what talent she possessed in those long, slender fingers of hers! All things considered, it really would have been a much worse childhood without her music-making that comforted me both with her and away from her. The melodies she played were anchors that stabilized me when I was most afraid and they would become rocks I could crash into when storms, and moods would start to rage inside my own mind.

Her favorites, of course, were the dead guys: mostly Mozart and Chopin, but also Beethoven, Rachmaninoff and Bach. Then there were her rock-and-roll contemporaries: Billy Joel, Elton John and Ray Charles. Their's were the songs she played in the clubs, that she hated to admit she loved; she was, after all, supposed to be a classic performer. She would record modern concerts and performances and play them on the TV the way Lester played the bad movies. She had dozens of VCR tapes of recorded MTV rock videos and she'd sing to them while she played along or lazed around the house.

On good days, she danced around and sang to us while she cleaned, or would have us all wet our socked feet in a bucket of suds and "mop" the floor while we sang those pop rock songs together at full volume. *"There's always something there to remind me..."* She encouraged us to dance while she played and give her requests for our favorite songs. Piano lessons were almost exclusive to the visits to Mamaw's on Tuesdays, but sometimes in the orchard house, she'd watch over me, or sit beside me while I played too. Music was an ever present part of our existence.

On bad days, though the music was still there, it wasn't as lighthearted. She would sit and practice hour after hour at her vintage Baldwin upright, sometimes repeating the same piece over and over again, until it was almost maddening... almost but not quite. On those days when the piece would end the silence hung, anticipation grew and we all collectively held our breath, hoping, and if I'm honest, sometime praying, that she wouldn't start the same piece yet again. Then the first note, like the reset button on the Atari game, told us all we were in for another fresh round of whatever was torturing her that day, whether it be a nocturne or waltz or some elegant composition of her own. I preferred it when her own work struck her because at least then there were variations as she figured out how she wanted the piece to flow. I'm not sure if the playing helped her moods or prolonged them but eventually she'd pull out of it. Her ears would hear us, her eyes would see us and we existed again. It was almost like coming to life, it was wonderful to be real to her.

I still wonder what her moods were all about. Was it from drugs, exhaustion, depression or did she have some other mental illness that a pill could've treated? Sometimes I think it was simply the greatness of the music itself, trapped inside her pathetic life, trying to escape.

I started to get in the habit of escaping too, and I'd take Hannah with me. I didn't want her to be around when Lester brought the movies out. Whether I was fascinated with them or not, I knew it wasn't right. I didn't want Hannah to grow up the way I was. And I especially didn't like thinking about Lester doing something to her. She wasn't as old as I had been in the red house but I knew what bad men could do to little girls. I didn't want him to touch her or tell her to come sit on his lap while they were playing. I wanted her to stay innocent.

I guess the worry for Hannah and the weight of the secret got to me and I wanted to tell someone what had happened. Gio was the one person in the world I was closest to so I told him my secret about Lester's fingers in the bedroom that one night in the red house in

Dryden. We were both outside, climbing the already picked cherry trees beside the house, and the words came out before I could think about it, or the implications of telling him.

I figured my secret was safe with him. I didn't say it to be vindictive or mean or even to get Lester in trouble. I just needed someone to know and maybe secretly I wished if someone knew then the anxiety about him doing it again or doing it to Hannah would stop.

Gio misunderstood and thought that I meant it happened that summer. He went ballistic on Lester. I was afraid, so afraid, but something inside me loved Gio more than I ever had before because he was so mad about it. The accusations and confrontation started a huge fight... over me. Lester called me a liar up ways, down ways, in ways and out ways in his sneering, push-his-glasses-up-his-nose way. He was red, even on the top of his balding head. Red and sweating and pacing all over the living room talking about how messed up I was. Mom got in on the accusations and name calling too. She didn't defend me. She was as mad as he was.

"Why would he do that, Gia? Why? And why do you get along with him if he did? And why wouldn't you tell me instead of Gio?" She asked, hands on hips and waited for my answer.

I didn't have one. "I don't know. I thought you'd be mad..."

"Oh I'm mad! This is serious Gia! That kind of stuff can ruin a person. This is not the first time you've done this! You can't go around saying things like this! What would possess you?"

On and on she went, like she did with Lester. In my head, I started to sing the familiar song, *'Shut up Mommy, shut up Mommy, shut up Mommy...'* to drown out her accusations which were somehow worse than Lester's sneering tyraid. It felt like they spent hours verbally beating me because I told Gio what Lester did. Then, to my horror, my one defender, Gio, even started to question me since both the big people were denying it.

I was alone with what I knew he'd done. No one believed me. There was so much confusion about when the incident actually occurred when I tried to explain it. I couldn't articulate it clearly and they wouldn't listen anyway. Eventually, I retracted it to make everyone shut up; but I know what he did that night all those years before. I know I didn't dream it and I didn't mix him and Brad up in my head. I just wanted the shame and name calling to stop. I didn't speak of it anymore, to a family who wouldn't believe me. Like the Marriage of Figaro, we ended the composition in a grand finale and then silence. There was no applause at the end, only silence and a big, fat, nasty secret we all shoved into our closets, and like the rest of our whispers and secrets, we never spoke of it again to anyone.

CHAPTER 25

IF IT HADN'T been for Nonna and Gramps, I think we might have forgotten all about church in those later elementary school years because my mom and Lester didn't have anything to do with God and Dad and Vickie-Jean were too busy at their shops to go. Nonna picked Gio and I up most summer Saturday nights at Mom's, or bright and early Sunday mornings from the loft. Even if I didn't understand or pay attention to them, I was as used to Gramps' sermons as I was anything else in my life.

He gave his sermons, from a modestly raised platform at the front of the room that Nonna insisted on calling a sanctuary. It was more like a camp lodge than a hoity-toity place that should have such a fancy name as sanctuary, but we all humored her. Often his lessons were emotionally charged but always they were all talk. All I heard was, "...*blah... blah... blah...*" My Gramps would drone on and on about forgiveness, and blood, brimstone and redemption and whatever other big words I didn't understand. He did series on how to be happy, or how to be blessed and talked about what it meant to be a Christian or know God. I internalized a lot more than I realized, but at the time, it was just what we did on Sunday.

I did like it when he had fun guest speakers or preachers. Missionaries had fabulous stories from wonderful places. When they spoke I could pretend I was there with them, fighting the devil and feeding the hungry. He had one guest pastor that came with a choir in silken maroon robes. Guess where they were from? That's right: the Deep South. A petite, chocolate colored lady with a mint-green pill hat and veil sat at the organ and made music in the background of his whole sermon and I fancied myself doing something like that someday. I wouldn't have to play in bars like my mom, I could play for a dark black traveling pastor man! The choir hummed the whole time the preacher was singing and dancing, and dabbing the sweat from his forehead during his sermon. The congregation was encouraged to participate with enthusiastic claps and shouting 'amen' or 'hallelujah' when the Spirit moved us. But I did not, because the pastor's punctuated points at the end of pivotal proclamations reminded me too much of Lester's lectures.

The whole affair was more of a performance than a sermon. I'm not sure if it impressed God or not, but it sure impressed me! That pastor man would squat down with an "ummmmm hummmmm!" and shoot back up, grab a hankie and wipe his beaded forehead, bobbing like a chicken, or puffed-up rooster. He'd come to a crescendo of a point, with the Bible held high in the air, and then declare, "I got ta, got ta, got ta make you see people! Do you see it? Praise the Lawd if you see it! Do you see His kingdom comin'?! Shout to the Lawd if ya do!" The congregation was full of "Yes Lords!" "Preach its!" and "Amens." There was a dramatic increase in participation from our humble little group, like we too were performing. I have no idea what he was trying to get us to see, but the delivery was remarkable and for quite a while after that, I imagined myself traveling with him, serenading his sermons at the organ with my own pill hat and veil.

Despite my weekly church visits, there was a distinct absence of God in my homes at that time. Where God should have been, nightmares and scares were in abundance. The devil-man dreams were so real. Once I dreamed that he was going to take Martin to hell. I tried to save him, but the devil was so hot. I reached for Martin and my hand bubbled and sizzled like bacon in a cast iron skillet the closer I got. I had to retract it. The harder I tried to get Martin, the hotter the devil-man made him. Then the searing heat invaded me. It crept up my spine to settle like white-hot fire at the nape of my neck. I woke, sweaty, scared and alone in my bed. The heat has only happened twice outside of dreaming for me. Once when I was caught red-handed stealing, the other time was when I smoked crack (the only time I smoked it by the way, but that's for later in my story). The point is, the sensation was terribly remarkable. I could feel it start and avoid most nightmares by waking up before the devil-man made things too hot. Sometimes I was lucky and could catch myself dreaming, and change the whole thing. I would disappear from the devil-man and make believe I was in a cotton-candy cloud or inside the smell of good perfume, but sometimes it wouldn't work and that was worse than the heat. I would know I was only dreaming, and it wasn't real, but I couldn't wake up or make the devil-man leave me alone until the heat burned in my neck.

The devil-man was always Brad, or Lester, or a combination of the two, or all the bad guys I could imagine but the nightmares were exacerbated thanks to Steven King and The Shining. I think it's peculiar how at my mom's, horror and porn was normal to watch with Lester and didn't really seem to bother me; but the TV movie of The Shining in the loft apartment did me in. Maybe it was the fact that Gio and I totally rebelled to watch it that made it so bad. It happened when the parental units worked late…again…and I was alone with the boys…again…

A commercial came on our tiny thirteen inch, thirteen channel, two knobbed TV, to advertise The Shining later that night. Before leaving Dad said, "Don't watch that movie, it's scary." I felt the way Eve must have felt in the Garden of Eden when God told her not to eat of the Tree of the Knowledge of Good and Evil. Maybe the reason it was so bad was because it was my first real contemplated act of deliberate defiance (except for the bus chants with Rick). Who was Dad to tell me I couldn't watch it? I was a big girl, I was used to being home alone and I had certainly watched scary movies before.

Gio and I decided to watch it. Maybe, like Eve, I talked him into watching it with me when he wouldn't have ordinarily done it, but I think not. I think Gio was easily as interested in defying Dad and watching it as I was and I didn't have to coerce him at all. However it happened, Martin was asleep by then, tucked snugly into bed after a healthy and nutritious microwavable meal. It was healthy; Vickie-Jean always pre-made meals and put them in the freezer or fridge for us and all I had to do was thaw and heat. Sometimes Nonna would bring us food and with it a reminder that all sinners would have their part in the lake of fire, and usually a reprimand for me on having too many tangles in my hair or wrinkles in my bedspread. Unfortunately for my sleep-life Nonna didn't come that night. Gio and I, in full rebel glory, plopped ourselves in front of the tiny box and watched The Shining. I didn't get too much of the grown up stuff, but I paid attention to the good parts with Danny, the boy. I did not care about crazy man Jack or skinny-Minnie Shelly but I was fully engrossed in Danny's story line.

The movie didn't seem too scary. I was used to a mad man. Danny rode around on a Hot Wheels bike in a big house, whoop-de-do! I didn't get what the hype was all about. Then the girls showed up and the movie consumed me. Weird words on walls, a crazy cook, and those terrific zombie girls. The movie was one of my nightmares come to life and I couldn't wake up because there was no heat in my neck, because it was real! It felt too wrong in my little soul to watch it. The movies Lester played felt too wrong to watch too, but Lester was with us. The sexual excitement or arousal or whatever that inward feeling was that I liked to feel, kept me there to see what erotic acts would pop up amid the violence, scariness and witchcraft on the screen. The TV movie had nothing I wanted to stay for. I kept waiting for Jack, or the black man to do something to Shelly or the girls but there was no superfluous sex built into the plot. It was all psychological and it messed with my head! The whole movie felt bad and to make it worse, there were no grown-ups in the house to protect me from the terror. The grown-ups that were in charge in that house, made it clear we weren't supposed to watch it and there we were, alone, watching evil on TV.

The scary girls appeared in the hall and beckoned eerily, "Come and play with us Danny." That was it. I couldn't watch another minute. I had to leave! But where?

CHAPTER 26

THE ONLY THING I could come up with to escape the fear was running to Dad and Vickie-Jean's bedroom and hugging the big white Bible with fancy, old-fashioned pictures and gold, gilded edges. It was base, and I was safe! Safety came from Jesus, and Jesus and the Bible always went together. I thought if I stayed far away from the TV and prayed, "In the name of Jesus," while I held onto the Bible and looked at white-man Jesus pictures, maybe the bad, yucky, scary, evil feeling would leave. Gio laughed at me, called me a "chicken" or whatever kind of name a little boy can come up with to call his sister, but I wasn't coming out to finish the movie. I was staying in the closest-to-safe-place I could find, with a shield in front of me to push away the bad thoughts.

Before too long, Gio was sitting in the room with me, on a dark night, on their bed, with the Bible. I don't remember reading it but do remember there was something about *His* name and something about holding the Bible that really did comfort me. I didn't want to let go of the Bible for fear the evil would come back if I disconnected physically, so I kept my hand on it. Who knows how long we stayed there, grounded, sequestered to the top of a bed? It seemed like forever. I had deliberately defied my dad, and was punished for it even though he wasn't there. My only saving grace was that Bible.

When I was afraid and there was nothing else to do or nowhere else to go, I went to the Bible and called out the name of a Savior I didn't know. If only I could have made the connection then that I ran to the Bible because it's the word of God and His perfect love casts out all fear. If only I'd have known Him then, really known, Him not just His name, maybe things would have been different. But I did not know Him, only knew that when I held the Bible something about it felt safe, and when I was around people that really did seem to know Him, things felt steady somehow and I could crawl on their laps and look into their eyes and feel sure things would be OK.

It seems like that movie was a turning point in my life. My mind fragmented into crumpled, compartmentalized boxes of religion, reasoning, repetition and obsession. I was torn up about what was right, what looked right but was wrong, and what was clearly wrong and how to handle it all especially when the grown-ups all had their own ideas about right and wrong, good and evil. The rules of right and wrong, good and evil, truth and lies started to fuzz together depending on who I talked to and where I was. Up to that point I don't know that I ever doubted God's existence and that He existed in Trinity: one God; Father, Son and Spirit. Three but in One. I accepted this but God was always far off, away from me, away from the closet, away from evil. God hated evil and I'd done and seen so much already. I assumed that God was disgusted with my badness. So I never got close. God was someone I heard about like President Reagan, or Madonna, but didn't really know.

It took a long time until I honestly admitted out loud that I doubted God's existence or who God actually was. I learned to fit the part of good, Christian girl quite well at church and probably sounded and looked like I was totally sure of religion. I directed my prayers to God like a spectator directs cheers to a football team, or a child wishes to Santa. I even fooled myself sometimes; but I did not know God. All I knew was that something about the Bible made me feel safe even with the murder, rape, violence, and scary imagery inside the pages that I could not comprehend.

I started to obsess over strange things and my teacher, Mrs. Watford, was a focus of many of them because I watched her so much. She was a young, tiny thing and she wore very cute and fashionable clothes. Her bright yellow, Latin-looking top with puffy-elastic-cinched sleeves was a special fixation one day. In my opinion, the elastic part of the sleeve rested too far up her left arm. It drove me crazy. All morning I couldn't hear her lesson because her left sleeve was higher than the right. I cringed when she moved her arm up and down, and I wished I could telepathically make that sleeve fall down to be even with the other. I imagined it moving into place, imagined what it would look like put back where my brain needed it to be, but it wouldn't go. At recess I found her on the playground and grabbed that sleeve and pulled it down to relieve my worrying over it. "Ouch!" she said. "It's been there a long time and hurts to move," she said. It hurt her? Did she even know how hurt I was that her sleeves weren't even all morning? I guess it went to an acceptable evenness then because I don't remember the sleeve bothering me the rest of the day.

The other thing that really got to me in her classroom were marks on the chalk board. She wrote white chalky words and numbers on the green background, then would erase most of them and carry on to something else when the particular lesson was done. Often, tiny chalk marks stayed on green to taunt me. Little top parts of a capital "H" left un-erased or lower hooks of a "j" or "g" would scream at me. I couldn't hear her lesson, only the left over lines. They would remain and I had to look at them, stare at them, to try to make them go away. I never could make those ticks, on the board go away with wishes or all my thinking might. I tried to endure them during lectures, but sometimes I had to go to the chalkboard and erase especially obnoxious marks. I didn't get permission to rise and erase, but I didn't care. The white had to go. I don't know how many times I wiped off her board mid-lesson, but I couldn't focus on what she was saying if it wasn't clean.

I started to cut grass and snow plow too. On regular intervals we drove all over the Pacific Northwest to drop off Vickie-Jean's pictures in different galleries. On those trips, and the drives that took me and Gio to Mom in Wenatchee, or that family to Mamaw and the piano in Arlington, I imagined that I cut the grass or plowed the roads. On summer-time rides, I visualized the grass, and whatever else was in the way on the side of the road, cut down to within six inches of the ground. With winter snow storms came the plowing day-dreams. I plowed the snow a whole car length further to the right, leaving no trace of ice behind. Hour after hour, ride after ride, I lost myself in imaginary cutting and plowing. Something about making everything even and low and clear soothed me and I liked to imagine it.

Another odd fifth grade obsession crept in and infected my brain. It was not soothing and certainly didn't bring comfort. It made me go a little nuts because I couldn't control it. There were no triggers. I could be sitting in class, reading a Highlights magazine, or watching Alf on TV and my brain would suddenly fixate on squeezing ketchup out of a bottle. I imagined drizzling ketchup, from one of those generic red cylindrical ketchup bottles, down the inside of a hot dog bun filled with a nice juicy Bavarian Bratwurst. The problem was, at the end of the bun, I couldn't stop the ketchup from squirting. It always continued past the end of the bun.

Every time, over and over again, I squirted the ketchup but I couldn't stop it. It was my daydream but I couldn't end the flow. I'd get anxious about it and get upset with anyone who interrupted the thought. Many real-live brats, buns and cups of ketchup were devoted to making sure I could stop real ketchup even if I couldn't stop the imaginary ketchup. No matter how hard I concentrated I couldn't stop the dang ketchup! I told Nonna once and she laughed her head off, so my ketchup obsession became the quirkiest of all the secrets I kept.

CHAPTER 27

MY OBSESSIVENESS DIDN'T carry over into my cleanliness habits. My room was always messy, at least messy according to others' standards. When Dad married Vickie-Jean, he switched from one neat freak in his mom to another in his wife. Maybe I was a normal kid but had women in my life who had fastidious standards of cleanliness, or maybe I was a pig; either way, I hated how much I had to clean, clean, clean for them. It was boring, it was dumb, and it was stupid. My mom was no slob, she kept a good house and made cleaning kind of fun with the songs and suds on socks, but Vickie-Jean and Nonna showed me how to really clean. Maybe their obsessions with dust and dander were where my obsession with grass, snow and ketchup came from.

I felt like I had millions of chores to do for Vickie-Jean around the apartment and the shops, and for Nonna at the church. I couldn't play until my chores were done, and they were never done, or never done good enough so I had to redo everything all the time. My most dreaded chore were the dishes. I *hated* doing the dishes and there were always dishes to do because Vickie-Jean made elaborate meals every morning that I got to reheat and clean up every night. I washed them by hand because Vickie-Jean didn't think a dishwasher was a necessary kitchen appliance. I hated dishes and I hated Vickie-Jean because she got all the glory for perfect dinners and left the mess, the grime, and the dirty part for me. By the time Dad got home, after we were all in bed, and it was just the two of them, with clean dishes in the dish-rack and re-heated food on two plates, I'd hear him tell her how wonderful dinner was. I don't think he ever told me how wonderful the shiny plates were. The venomous hatred sprouting inside me undoubtably grew from seeds of jealousy because Nonna made me clean as much as, if not more, and I never felt toward her the ugliness I started to feel toward Vickie-Jean. Once my hatred for Vickie-Jean took root, there was no stopping its growth. Like black buds of bitterness it bloomed. She made me watch Martin. She made me clean her house and took all the credit. She always talked bad about me. She made me break down boxes at the shops and dust the shelves without any kind of payment. She always corrected the way I talked and walked and cleaned, and she talked bad about my mom.

I don't honestly know if there was anything she could have done to rectify the situation by then, but I think the contempt was mutual between us. I saw it in her eyes when she looked at me and Gio. Or, rather, I saw the difference in the way she looked at us and the way she looked at anyone else, except Nonna, who also got 'the look.' Her eyes, normally big and bright and full of life, dulled. Her forehead creased and eyebrows scrunched together. Her nostrils flared, ever so slightly, and her full upper lip would subtly, unconsciously, curl upward. She reminded me of a surly dog ready to bite in seething anger, frustration, hatred or maybe some kind of jealousy of her own.

Our relationship would never be amiable and yet courts and circumstances deemed, this woman a safer, better mother figure for me than my own biological one. I didn't yet realize... didn't realize for a long time, that my mom had serious addiction and mental health problems. She was not a safe person for kids to be around for extended periods of time. As time aged me I came to understand that music moods, silent treatments and much of what my mom did and allowed in her life, wasn't safe behavior. I never associated the men and the abuse and the moods with my mom's mental health. They were simply part of life where she was concerned. Regardless of her moods and choice of men, I loved her.

I wanted to be with my mom and I missed seeing her once she moved to Wenatchee. Because the drive to Wenatchee was longer, our school-year mid-week visits became bothersome and in short order were dropped from our regular routine. We only visited mom occasionally during the school year... and endlessly during those wonderful and dreadful summer vacation weeks. Because she was once again absent from my life, I wanted her when I was feeling bad as much as I wanted to touch the Bible. I did not want Lester though so I guess, in some ways, I liked it best when I got to miss her from afar, but I couldn't admit that to myself.

I felt like the freakiest freak of a girl because my parents were divorced and I lived with my dad and wicked step-mother instead of my mom. Again, I didn't get it was because her poor choices made her an unstable place for me to safely live. I just thought life was unfair. Even if I had realized my mom was part of the reason I had been molested, because she was the woman who brought men like that into my life, because she made poor choices and we had to deal with them too, I still wouldn't have appreciated Vickie-Jean talking smack about her. No buddy better mess with a girl's mom! That's all there is to it.

Vickie-Jean and I never grew a mother-child-bond that could have counteracted the bad she talked about my mom. Not that it would have helped if we did. I don't remember doing anything fun with her. Well, maybe the photo competitions were slightly fun, but other than that, we didn't do anything together. She didn't help me learn to play the piano, or with school work, or read me books. She didn't play games or set a tomato timer for even the fewest minutes of fun. Nothing with her was fun, only work. We didn't talk except about how bad I did a chore or how long she would be at the shop or gone traveling or shooting or how stupid my mom was. We didn't go places together, or cook together or shop together. We didn't even clean together like Nonna would do with me to show me how to do it right after I got it wrong. The only relationship Vickie-Jean and I had was that of slave and overseer.

I was never good enough for Vickie-Jean to appreciate, but was, apparently, good enough to be left in charge of the house and the boys when she and Dad were gone. Maybe if we had some sort of emotional connection I wouldn't have resented the cuts about my mom so much, but we didn't, so every bad thing she said about my mom was one more bud of bitterness on the tree.

Like me, there was nothing my mom did right in Vickie-Jean or my dad's eyes; and Vickie-Jean, especially, made sure to let me and

Gio know that. If they would have kept their mouths shut and cultivated our relationships with them instead of smacking down my mom it might have been different. According to Vickie-Jean, Mom couldn't even put the right kind of rubber bands in my hair. Mom would do my hair up in the coolest braids and hair-do's when I visited her. I loved having her play with my hair and style it, probably because it was positive attention. It never failed, though, when I came back to Dad and Vickie-Jean, the first thing Vickie-Jean would do is let me know those bands weren't coated and would split the ends on my hair. All I thought was, *"At least my mom fixed my hair!"* At least my mom gave enough of a thought about me to sit down for a few minutes and plunk out songs on the piano for me to learn, or show me finger spacing, or talk to me while she braided my hair. At least my mom wanted to spend time with me. At least I mattered to my mom.

CHAPTER 28

DESPITE HER PUFFY, uneven sleeves, and left-over chalk marks, Mrs. Watford was my saving grace that year, I don't know what I would have done without her sweet, sing-songy voice, stickers and red lettered 100% marks on papers. She was lovely, the first since Mrs. McCutchen to really capture my heart… And I mattered to her! She was an exceptional teacher. She had us line up on the way out to lunch and someone got to say grace if she didn't say it. It was as much an honor, to be chosen to say grace as it was to be first in line. I don't remember anyone saying silly prayers; I don't remember ever saying the prayer either. All I remember is that she felt like a lot of the people at Gramps church: soft and good.

Mrs. Watford would find nice things to say about all of us and seemed genuinely proud of the work we produced. Her kindness alone made me want to do well in school, but her recognition of good work inspired me to do even better. I craved being noticed for doing something good. It was the exact opposite of what I was used to. I liked hearing her say nice things about what I did. I fantasized about her becoming my step-mom. "If only Ms. Watford could be my mom," I'd think, "then people would like me."

At lunch Ms. Watford sat with us at our table. Nonna made breakfast and Vickie-Jean made dinner but I made my own lunches and my favorite thing back then was a good, fatty butter and sugar sandwich. It was a great lunch for a kid. I don't know if I ever packed anything else in my lunches, though. Maybe that, mixed with missing school on multiple occasions to watch Martin when Nonna couldn't, and the parents' needed a sitter, and my affinity for school and budding quirkiness made her take special interest in me. Or maybe Ms. Watford took notice of all her students but I only paid attention to her time with me. At lunch she always seemed to find a reason to talk to me about my life and family and asked me pointed questions. I answered honestly, never telling secrets, simply answering her questions: *"Gia, do you get to see your mother much?"*, *"Do you like your step-mom and step-dad?"*, *"How many of your brother's diapers do you think you've changed this week?"*, *"Were you home alone again with Martin last night?"* I wasn't trying to get anyone in trouble, genuinely not realizing some of the answers I provided might be cause for concern. Compared to the bad stuff that happened to me with Mom's men or the shaming I felt with Nonna, being left alone a day or two to watch Martin wasn't so bad, and making my own lunches certainly wasn't bad. The Latino kids I went to school with had to stay home to help a lot more than I did. I don't know what it must have sounded like coming from my lips, so matter-of-factly, so innocently. But it did get someone in trouble.

Vickie-Jean flipped out about me telling 'our business' to other people. She gave me the nastiest lecture for talking bad about her at school. How could I, how *dare* I make myself a butter and sugar sandwich and take it to school? I really didn't get it; I was probably standing there with a dumbfounded look on my face that she took to be sinister but I really couldn't understand what the deal was. They were good sandwiches, and I wasn't wasting food which was another big issue for Dad and Vickie-Jean. She was yelling and so upset she was almost in tears because I made myself food, like I was supposed to, and ate it all, like I was supposed to. She made me feel like Nonna for doing something wrong, something I was expected to do and did my best and still screwed up. I didn't even know making myself lunch was wrong. I was supposed to make my own lunch and lunches had sandwiches...what was the big deal?

There has got to be more to the story than I remember because that was really a lot of drama over what I made myself for lunch. Maybe the parents were confronted about me staying home to watch Martin. Maybe they were embarrassed by school officials because it made the Gianelli's look bad. I'm not sure, but I think I had school lunches from that time on. Who knew a yummy sandwich could cause such drama? I still made them for a snack when no one was around but that lecture sucked, and Vickie-Jean held it against me for a long time, so butter-and-sugar sandwiches became the sweetest little secret I ever kept all to myself!

Then that Christmas, the final nail in the coffin of Vickie-Jean and my relationship was pounded in with a colossal lie she forced me to tell my mom. I can't explain why, since my dislike for Lester was so strong, and Mom's moods were so uncomfortably awkward, but I loved going to my mom's. At her place I didn't have to do any unreasonable chores, I didn't have to babysit every evening, I didn't screw everything up, and I could be a kid. I could keep Lester's movie secrets, and the garden in the closet secrets, and the touching secrets to myself. Mom was a decent grown-up to visit with, she played the piano with us and read to us and I felt like she mostly liked me. I thought she even loved me back then. And visiting with her wasn't getting to see her alone, but Trent and Hannah and Mamaw too. When I went to Mom's, I got away from Nonna and Vickie-Jean's oppression. Leaving was freedom. There was the rush of the preparation and packing and the hustle and bustle of the visiting itself and the junk-food farewell feast mom let Gio and I have the last night of every long visit in the summer or at extended breaks. Going to Mom's was one of the only things in my pathetic little life I looked forward to.

If Mom would have still been with Brad and I had to deal with his kind of evil, I'm sure I wouldn't have liked visiting at all, but it was just Lester the night stalker I had to avoid. I loved everything about visits except that Lester was there. Lester was a necessary evil of visiting Mom, but if I was cautious of where he was and dodged him, the rest of the visits were fun. All of the good parts of going for visits outweighed his badness. Wanting to see her didn't mean I was OK with him. I always had to be smart and be on guard. I should have been safe at both my houses. I didn't put myself in that position and I didn't ask for it and it doesn't imply anything about me for wanting to go to my mom's. I was a child and I wanted to see my mom and brother and sister. If all I had to do was avoid contact with Lester, I knew I was smart enough to do it. What he did, and the secrets we kept, ate away at me but it always had, so I didn't know any different. The fear and anxiety of him doing it again was ever present and got progressively worse with every visit, but it was a price I was willing to pay to get away.

Christmas was my favorite time at Mom's. She went all out. Decorations galore, Christmas carols replaced Bach, sprinkly cookies baked in the oven, fudge bubbled on the stove, and fake snow stuck on her windows. Any Christmas carol I could imagine was at her finger's beck-and-call. She was usually in a sociable mood at Christmastime too. I loved Christmas and I loved planning the visits with her. That Christmas, Mom and I were talking on the lone phone in the loft apartment, planning our Christmas cookies. We were going to start with sugar cookies and I desperately wanted her to get the shiny silver ball-shaped sprinkles and she promised to fetch them from the store before Gio and I got there. The flesh-colored buttoned phone was mounted in the kitchen connected to the hand piece by a respectable six-foot coil of cord. I could move around the kitchen easily but the cord wouldn't reach far enough to go anywhere private.

All of a sudden the woman who was always at her down-town photo gallery was up in my business...

CHAPTER 29

VICKIE-JEAN SCRIBBLED notes then shoved the yellow pad across the counter toward me. I slid down the cabinets, scrunched up in a ball, and put my head down, to pretend like I was alone with my mother. But I was hen-pecked! Vickie-Jean set the pad on the floor and pushed it at my feet. Pushed it, and pushed it, and pushed it. She was worse than Gio. She was relentless and wouldn't leave me alone. Finally, resigned to her intrusion, I looked. Gray, cursive lies filled the sheet.

She wanted me to tell my mom I couldn't go to visit. She sat next to me and wrote things on the pad then pushed the dumb excuses at me, tapping and circling words on the paper until I said them. Stupid lies, like I didn't want to miss seeing Martin that Christmas. Yes I did, I saw him all the time, babysat him so much that I knew what he was saying before his own mother did. I didn't care about seeing Martin at Christmas, I wanted to see the wall of white while driving over the wintry pass to Mamaw's. I wanted to see Trent and Hannah. Vickie-Jean penciled and pushed me to say that I didn't want to miss having Christmas with my dad on Christmas day. I suspected Dad wouldn't even be there because the Russians, who didn't celebrate Christmas, invaded Leavenworth in full force and were great for the coffers since most other stores were closed. I didn't care about him anyway, I wanted to spend Christmas with my mom making cookies.

The lies came out of my mouth but I felt like Vickie-Jean was making me say them. Maybe we'd talked previously and somehow, trying to please her or agree with her I might have said I didn't want to go to my mom's. Maybe she suspected the abuse from Lester and the drug use going on and was the one person trying to keep us safe the only way she knew how. Maybe it was well-intentioned, but I wanted to visit my mom and she made me lie. I heard my mom's heart breaking on the phone. Mine did too, I didn't want to say those things to her. I didn't want to miss out on going and I don't know why I said it except that I didn't know what kind of trouble I'd get into if I didn't do what Vickie-Jean wanted me to. I hated her, I feared her and wanted nothing more than to get away from her but the lies she wanted me to say came out of my mouth in obedience to her pencil-tapping demands. I felt horrible about lying. Gramps and Nonna always said, "*All liars will have their part in the lake of fire,*" and I was lying to the woman who gave me life. I was hell bound for certain.

For the two weeks of Christmas break that we should have been with my mom, Gio and I got to dress up like happy little elves and help bag and wrap customer trinkets in green and red tissue paper at That's Amore. We were free labor. The Russians kept us busy on Christmas day too. We were at the shop bright and early after a special breakfast at Nonna and Gramps. Martin was the lucky one. He got to stay with them for the day, and when Gramps was home, it was all fun and games, jokes and magic tricks. I wish I could have stayed and played. I wish I wouldn't have lied to my mom and could have been with her and Trent and Hannah. I would rather have been anywhere but in a shop for Christmas.

Our gifts came later that evening, after closing time, after picking up Martin, after Leavenworth was calm and quiet, after Gio and I could hardly wait any longer. Dad and Vickie-Jean called the busy day good quality family time and a financial success. I called it work, but at least there were presents to be had, so I admit, I was excited to see what was under our sparkling tree.

Two gifts; one for me, one for Gio. Martin, too young to remember the day, had nothing to fill his little pre-school hands. They told us there were no individual gifts that year, we were a family and the presents were ours to share. It sounded stupid until Gio opened the large golden package Dad handed to him. Inside was a brand new Nintendo! It was a glorious gift and I'm sure I heard the angels singing hallelujah. I can't begin to guess how many hours of my life I devoted to making super Mario jump and Link run through mazes; but even better than the time I spent playing, was the relief it provided me. Cold winter evenings in the loft were far more tolerable with Gio hunting ducks instead of pestering me. The silver foil shoe box I opened contained postcards of lighthouses, beach houses, lobsters, crabs and alligators. I didn't understand at first, but in the mix of postcards were five airplane tickets.

The present was another family vacation, this one to the Atlantic Coast the following summer, weren't we lucky? They said it was going to be an amazing trip that would last the whole summer. All I heard was that they were going to take me away from my mother for summertime too. I wondered if Vickie-Jean would make me lie to her again. I was mad before I'd even explored all the places the postcards promised we'd visit. I didn't know if it would be a fun vacation. All I knew was hate.

The hatred bubbled up and blocked my view of any love they had for us. Dad, and especially Vickie-Jean, were keeping me from my mom. I was powerless to stop their control over my life and I blamed Vickie-Jean most. I wanted to rip her face off, but instead I slapped tears off my own face when they fell out of my eyes that night in bed.

As it turned out, all my angst was for nothing, the trip got postponed. At the end of my fifth grade year, retail space finally opened up under our loft apartment and we moved That's Amore and the Gallery of Light and Landscape. The remodel and move was chaos I'm sure, but to my anxious delight, Gio and I got to stay at Mom's for most of the summer like usual. The space was beautiful; an old musty storefront where no shops could quite stick and no restaurants could quite fit. The space had been a boutique, a candy store, a snack shop, a stuffed animal store, but nothing stayed for long. Dad hoped, because of the years and established patronage of the Gallery and his store, that people would still come and it would keep both the Gallery and That's Amore afloat. If he was anything, he was good in business and his hope was proved true.

The new space was so magnificently big after those tiny places in the Obertal Mall. The creaky, thick-planked wood floor added character; the cracks and peeling paint on plaster boasted well-seasoned charm. I might not have participated in much of the remodel and move but I was there enough to get caught up in the excitement of the new, old place. Dad's firefighter friends helped bring over the merchandise but unlike the move into the apartment, I didn't get to unpack the store's goods. I helped pack things oh so carefully into boxes with our roll of tissue paper that I'd wrapped customer gifts and trinkets in for years. It never occurred to me that my parents trusted me to pack; it felt like slave labor every time I visited them.

That year, visits seemed to be coordinated with Mom and Lester's family trips over to Mamaw's. We spent one week with Mom, then on Tuesday evenings, as they headed home from Snohomish county, they left us with Dad and Vickie-Jean. The following Tuesday morning, on their way over, they picked us up. I loved visits to Mom's because I got to see Mamaw, and get my treasured piano lessons, and only had to deal with Lester's creepiness every-other Wednesday night after Mom went to work. I hated visits to Dad's. Gio and I worked that whole summer packing and moving. Once things were up and running we had to keep That's Amore's shelves stocked for tourists. I thought it was rude how they expected us to wrap and pack and stock Pisa after Pisa and penne and ziti into boxes while they got to stand at the register and chat. I wanted to talk about art and life in a Bavarian town and count back money, or at least get paid for what I did, but it was better than babysitting, so there was that.

They sort of combined the shops but kept both names so tourists weren't confused. The Gallery of Light and Landscape, because of Vickie-Jean's fame and following, was nestled smartly toward the back with four foot tall dividing walls flanking a wide opening to separate it from That's Amore in the front. Much to Nonna's chagrin, Dad and Vickie-Jean opened a wine tasting bar within That's Amore. Dad partnered with a local winery and exclusively sold their wine. They were church members that got whispered about a lot because they owned a winery and according to Nonna, alcohol was the devil's brew and no drunk would have a part in heaven. I remember a long, heated argument, that included some angry Italian words, between Dad and Mr. Virgil, the winery owner, and Nonna and

Gramps. I felt like they shouldn't be fighting about what Dad sold in the shop or how Mr. Virgil made his living. It seemed strange that two men who went to church and paid their tithes could be in so much trouble for working. I didn't get it, but in the end Dad and Mr. Virgil won because the Virgil's still went to church and Dad sold their wine in his shop.

Everything was different because the shop was right downstairs and the parents were so close. No more having to call if I had a problem with Martin or Gio. All I had to do was thump down sixteen indoor corridor stairs (I should have walked like a lady but I thumped and Vickie-Jean always made me redo my steps) and I could tattle. Usually I got in trouble for making a problem where there wouldn't have been one if I could "behave like the big one in the situation" but it was nice to have them close. It didn't feel like I was always alone with the boys.

Except for the tasting bar, the new shops had the same old routine; same ambient Italian folk music, same trinkets, canvases and reproductions. The wine drinkers were a new thing for me. They reminded me of the Bible verse in Proverbs that made fun of drunks. Their faces turned red, their voices got loud… but they bought more Pisas than sober tourists so it worked for our bottom line. Despite the move, that summer was both Dad and Vickie-Jean's most profitable ever and they promised the postponed vacation would come next summer.

CHAPTER 30

HORMONES RAGED AND secrets swam inside me, my families confused and frustrated me; middle school was not something else I wanted to add into my life. But I had no choice. Before the leaves even changed colors, school was in session, and for some reason I turned into a Gio sized bully. It was paradoxical because on one hand, I was an academic all-star compelled to please my teachers and submit the "best" work; but on the other, I liked to pick on kids who were more socially awkward than me. It was hard to find kids more awkward than me considering the fact that I always had my nose in a book and looked like a stereotypical geek. I felt sorry for "special" kids so I didn't pick on them, but I really projected the disgust I felt about myself onto other girls who made easy targets.

It was and wasn't completely intentional, but like I did with Melody years before, I found my target and let her take the brunt of the hate I felt toward myself and become the focus of others' negative attention. Gail Morton had a slightly younger brother and seemed, in a lot of ways like me, a little awkward and a little on the geeky side of school. Her family life was mixed up too. We could have been good friends considering she lived up the street from the red house Mom used to live in, but we went to different primary schools and never quite connected back then. What I put her through in middle school never allowed for friendship after that. I probably missed out on a great friend.

Because of the whispers and secrets I navigated, I had become a master at manipulating conversations. I learned how to imply things and turn focus subtly. I could drive conversations and steer people away from, or toward, a subject I wanted. Like a composer, I created the mood and provided the ambiance and let others think and feel their way through it so they thought it was their idea all along. That's how I ninja-bullied Gail. When I'd get teased for being a brainiac, I'd mention on the play-ground that I saw Gail's dad walking out of a bar drunk. When Tommy Smith called me a cry-baby because I had a temper tantrum in class, I told someone I heard Gail went to the nurses and the nurse was checking her hair for lice.

The ironic thing about the lice story was that I actually ended up with lice for like the millionth time right after I started the rumor about her. Or maybe I started the rumor about her being a dirty-lice-baby so no one would think it was me? I can't remember how it flowed sequentially but nonetheless, I accused her of being bug-infested. I swear those stinking bugs could see my hair a mile away and leap for it! But to avoid being suspect at school I let the whispers fly that Gail was the bug head.

I was so mean to her. Sometimes I pushed it past whispering. At a group assembly, I adamantly and loudly refused to sit next to the girl with lice, full well knowing I was the one who'd had it. She was red-faced and horrified, I loved to see her cry and know that I did that to her. Somewhere inside it felt bad and mean, but on the surface it felt powerful and gratifying to know I could humiliate her and there was nothing she could do to stop it.

To Gail I may have been a nightmare but to my teachers I was an overachiever, and to the other kids, brown-nosing made me one of the low hanging fruits that was easy to pick on. I remember once I tried out for a play. I wanted a little part, just to be on stage and see how it felt up there, maybe then I could understand why my mom wanted so badly to perform. When the clique of pretty, popular girls found out, they made sure I knew I wasn't good enough to be in it at all, no matter how small the part was. There were enough of them to fill the cast, if no one else tried out, so they wanted me to drop out. Their bantering was relentless, but I had to know, and I thought it might be my only chance. I was the only outsider to try out, I felt like a sheep in a wolves den, but I gave it my all.

To my surprise, the teachers cast me as the lead actress! The geek, brainiac freak was going to be the star. I panicked. I told the director-teachers that I couldn't be the lead because that part was supposed to go to, Priscilla, Miss Popularity herself. Everyone knew the part was hers, but I crossed the queen of Alps Middle School to please the teachers. They told me I was good enough to do it. They were impressed that I could remember all the lines for try-outs. They wanted me and I liked being noticed by grown-ups.

After I took the part, the meaner-than-me girls made my life a living hell at the one place that used to give me the most joy. They started a rumor that my mom slept with the principal in order for me to get the part and my dad slept with the lunch ladies for me to get free lunch. I started memorizing my lines and cry myself to sleep because of the girls bullying. But when I stood on that stage performing, with only Nonna, Gio, Martin, and my cousins, Billy and Andy there to watch me, I knew why my mom loved performing so much. I disappeared from real life. I was someone else. I could handle the bully girls lies and absence of my parents because all eyes were on me, and I was the star.

I hated being picked on at school but I didn't realize, until much later, that I was as guilty as they were. I made Gail feel that bad when I said things about her. Empathy finally found me later in life, but it was too late to shield her from the mean in me. The damage was done. I was a messed up little kid and couldn't see what I was doing even as it was being done to me.

Then, while I was still finding my way to manage life in middle school, I was told that a new sibling was coming. I prayed for a sister, asking a magical fairy god, I didn't personally know, but hoped granted wishes like a genie—even though I'd never had my wishes granted before—that if there had to be a baby could it please, at least be a girl? God did not heed my request. Alex was not another little sister. Instead, I got another brother to babysit. With the exception of Hannah, boys surrounded me, no matter where I went. Gio, Martin and Alex with Dad, Trent with Mom, boy cousins, boys, boys, boys!

Vickie-Jean and new baby Alex had to stay in the hospital a few days so Dad came home the night the baby was born alone. They hadn't told us, if they even knew, what the baby's sex would be. I knew as soon as Dad walked in the door. I looked at him; he looked at me and shook his head negatively with down cast eyes. It was impossible for me to have another brother, but I did. Dad bent down on one knee and held his arms open. I fell into them and cried and cried. I wanted a little sister so badly, but it wasn't to be. He tried to soothe me, but I cried all night. As soon as I saw Alex, though, I was in love. Brothers are annoying, but when they're babies they sure are cute! I didn't think of the extra responsibility and babysitting and poopy diapers when I saw him for the first time. I just wanted to cuddle him.

CHAPTER 31

I STARTED TO compartmentalize my life and, to an extent, myself in middle school. At Dad's I was maid and baby sitter. In the shop I did the things a responsible shop-keeper's daughter would do (only I never did it good enough). If I was at Mom's I had no rules, I did what I wanted, when I wanted, where I wanted (as long as my bike tires were inflated). Church was separate and distinct from either home or school, they didn't mix, and they didn't mingle. Maybe church and Nonna's house were the same. If I was at church or with my grandparents I was churchy. I was smart me, quiet me, cruel me, kind me, saintly me, lake-of-fire me, depending on the setting. At school, I was the picked-upon "A" student that picked on other less fortunates. There were only a few exceptions that come to the top of my mind where things weren't so separate.

I'm having a hard time trying to decide how to tell my middle school story because of how differently I behaved depending on where I was. A few things that colored those early puberty years no matter where I was stick out. I met a friend who I loved and hated all at the same time. My friend lived with me for many years. He had a name and he felt so real to me, like a dad who was always there, or a friend who never left me alone. I could go to him whenever I felt an emotion I couldn't name or deal with and he gave me release. No, not Jesus, I didn't know Him, and not a boyfriend either. My friend's name was Pain and he probably became my first real addiction. I experienced compulsions to masturbate, and I obsessed over things, like the ketchup and snow plowing, but Pain was more of a high, a release, a fix than what had come before. Pain was a way to avoid my life and deal with it all at the same time.

Pain was an awesome way to not get in trouble for smarting off or being disrespectful. He helped me handle jeers and jabs at school and Dad and Vickie-Jean not being there, and Nonna telling me that people like me went to hell, and Mom's moods and Lester's creepiness. I loved feeling Pain and knowing it was my own little secret. I'd already learned not to tell others what I did to my body so no one knew about Pain. I didn't whisper my secret to anyone. Thus began the silent rages and the mutilations and my journey into self-harm, before it was a trendy thing for teenaged girls to do. It was my first coping mechanism before I met any drugs or Jesus. Pain was a way to deal with the emotional landfill piled inside me: a mix of trying not to piss Vickie-Jean off, trying not to get in trouble or be called a liar, and dealing with getting picked on in school.

What I'd come to realize was that if I went along with what people wanted, no matter what I really thought, people were pleased, and they didn't get angry or upset. It was only when I expressed my own opinions or ideas that bad things happened. Even with Melody and Gail, if I would have not expressed myself, they would not have been hurt. Brad reinforced the idea of going along for me too. As long as I went along with what he said, Gio could stay alive. As long as I didn't say what Lester did, the family didn't freak out.

Pain gave me a way to not agree with what I was pretending to agree with. I could rage against humanity and the universe would rage against me. I could hurt myself, give me pain and let go of wanting to be heard or understood. The weird thing about it was, when I was in a rage, I really didn't feel the pain, only something like a "fix." The closest high I can think of that's like it is a runner's high, so it must have given my body some sort of adrenaline or endorphin rush.

The rages and mutilations started out simple. I'd go to my room when I was overwhelmed either at school or from Vickie-Jean's mile-long to-do lists, turn my music up enough to drown out what came next, and kneel over my bed and scream as loud as I could into a pillow. The scream was guttural, not from where my voice usually came from, but from down low inside me. It was deep and evil-sounding and it burned and stung my throat coming up. The louder I screamed into a pillow the more fire burned in my throat, but the pain felt good, not bad. It might be only me, but finally someone knew, someone felt what I was feeling. Sometimes I had to get my body in on the rage too so I'd shake and gyrate and flip around on my bed. I had so much energy and anger that I couldn't deal with. The flipping didn't help me calm down but it was a release of pent-up frustration and energy.

Once, I grabbed a handful of my hair and yanked. I was trying to see if I could get a chunk out as big as the chunk Lester pulled from Mom's head that one night in the red house. I yanked and pulled and it hurt so *good*. I don't remember getting a big wad of hair, but I do remember having a secret welt that I could feel. After that fit, while the pain was still there, if I got frustrated, I didn't have to run to my room to rage, I could scratch my head or tap my fingers on the welt and remember the pain. It would soothe me to remember the release when I felt the injury. My hair hid the welt, and I liked the pain so I needed to find other ways to make pain without drawing attention. I knew if anyone found out, something bad would happen. I wasn't particularly keen on pulling my hair and hitting my head because, well, I knew I was smart and I didn't want to cause permanent brain damage. Admittedly, I came to that conclusion after having knocked myself out with a hard hit into a harder-than-my-head wall. I graduated to pinching, and it worked for a while. As Vickie-Jean or Nonna or Lester would lecture or make me do and re-do something, or tell me how bad I was, I'd pinch my thighs as small (for maximum pain) and hard as I could. I tuned out their words and the hurt they caused and concentrated all my focus on the pain, sucking it in, soaking in it like a dip in an oasis spring in the desert. The longer they took to tell me how life really was, the harder and longer I could rage right there with a pretty little smile on my face. They never knew how badly they hurt me, but I did, and that made it better.

The rages evolved into scratching. My favorite places to scratch were the tops of my legs because even in the middle of fire season, no one could see the lines and scabs hiding above my shorts. Thanks to the family's conservative views on dressing, my shorts were always longer than mid-thigh so I had plenty of room to scratch my flesh raw... and did I ever! The first time I scratched was after a visit from Vickie-Jean's hoity-toity buyer from some place back east.

Vickie-Jean was overly stressed from it and naturally took it out on us. Clean this, stop that, do this, she wouldn't let up. If she saw me, she had something in the shop for me to dust or straighten or photos in the back stock to categorize in case the buyer wanted multiple lithographs. I was so tired of her going on and on and never being done with the work. I still had math homework to do and Nonna was going to be bringing the little boys home shortly and I couldn't take anymore chores. I ran out of the shop, up to my room and cried quietly on the floor until eventually the rage flooded into me. I didn't have music on or a pillow handy to scream into so I pinched my legs until they were both red and welted. I liked it but it wasn't enough hurt to soothe the angst. I started to dig into my flesh in long searing strokes, from my knee up to the top of my thigh. Not a light, little scrape, but deep, hard scratching. The first pass alone removed a layer of skin, and I didn't stop. I kept on and on like she did, until I had four nice, neat straight red lines on the top of each leg. Then when it looked as bad as I felt I closed my eyes and felt the release the self-induced pain gave me. I didn't need to rage the rest of the time the buyer was there because I had my pain to feel. The scratches stuck to my pants in an oozy, pus layer. Alone in my room for days afterward, as the wounds grew crusty and knit my flesh back together, I picked fibers out of my beautiful scabs. No one knew—at least I don't think anyone knew—how I raged. It was my secret and I wouldn't tell. I kept the pain private all through middle school. It was my escape, no matter what compartment of life I was functioning in.

CHAPTER 32

THINGS WERE PROBABLY never as bad as I thought they were being a shop-keeper's only daughter. Compared to my mother's house and what happened in her care, it was by far the better alternative. Granted, nothing I did was ever good enough but I wasn't sexually exploited or physically abused. I was just overworked and under-rug-swept when the chores were done. The real problem was that I couldn't handle the emotional symptoms of the abuse I suffered or the names I'd been called, nor could I help or control the way Vickie-Jean seemed to feel about me. I was a child and I only saw things my way; she never accepted Gio and I like she did Martin and Alex, and I neglected to see all the attempts she made to connect, instead I attempted to escape her clutches.

Work, like I imagine it was for my dad, became a great escape for me. It was bound to happen, being a Gianelli and all, but the serendipitous way it did still brings back so many fond memories of my first real work outside my home and shop.

The apartment was special to me, especially during Christmas Lighting, when our Bavarian world welcomed the Savior of the world for the tourists who came to see us from all over the world. The town prepared well in advance, and by the middle of October, the metamorphosis was in full swing. Leavenworth turned into a winter wonderland. I loved hanging the clear, bright Christmas lights outside and was allowed to do it every year from sixth grade on, after I proved my worth as an expert Christmas light hanger.

It was as simple as that. Other shopkeepers around town asked if I wanted to hang theirs… and offered to pay me! It was fulfilling enough to pull them taut and see them glowing in their bright, even lines up and down the brick columns and eves, but the money made it even better. The straight lines of the shop and apartment's facade were always my favorite to decorate. The long brick columns that held up stout shop roofs, the symmetrical rectangle windows done up so neat and nice; no one could guess what a messy, tangled, emotional wreck the girl who had strung them was. Straight, neat, bright, beautiful, everything I was not. I don't remember anyone saying I hung them badly either, which was huge to me considering nothing I did was ever good enough.

It was while hanging lights for my family that I found yet another escape hatch. The third floor of our building had an attic! Up there I felt like Roger's and Hammerstein's Cinderella in their 1964 musical version of the story. I was Lesley Ann Warren and I sang "In my own little corner," and that was my life. I met the music and the movie at my mom's one summer. She was playing it for some summer theater and we listened to the songs and watched the movie a million times every day while she played each piece to exquisite perfection. My mom knew I felt like Cinderella so we sang the songs together at the piano bench. Why couldn't she have made better choices? Why couldn't she have been safe? Why couldn't she save me from all the people who tortured me? But she made bad choices, and wasn't safe, and she couldn't save me, but she gave me that movie, she gave me that song, and passed on a love of music. And Dad… Why couldn't he make time for me? Why couldn't he see how overworked I was? Why couldn't he let me be a kid? But he bought that building and in so doing, gave me that attic and together my parents gave me my own "little corner" where I could be whatever I wanted to be. I still smell the musty attic air and hear Mom playing when I sing it:

> *I'm as mild and as meek as a mouse*
> *When I hear a command I obey.*
> *But I know of a spot in my house*
> *where no one can stand in my way.*
> *In my own little corner in my own little chair*
> *I can be whatever I want to be.*
> *On the wings of my fancy I can fly anywhere*
> *and the world will open its arms to me.*

I'm a young Norwegian princess or a milkmaid
I'm the greatest prima donna in Milan
I'm an heiress who has always had her silk made
By her own flock of silkworms in Japan
I'm a girl men go mad for love's a game I can play with
cool and confident kind of air.
Just as long as I stay in my own little corner
All alone in my own little chair.
I can be whatever I want to be.
I'm a slave from Calcutta. I'm a queen in Peru.
I'm a mermaid dancing upon the sea
I'm a huntress on an African safari… it's a dangerous type of sport and yet
it's fun
In the night I sally forth to seek my quarry
And I find I forgot to bring my gun.
I am lost in the jungle all alone and unarmed when I meet a lioness in her
lair
Then I'm glad to be back in my own little corner,
All alone in my own little chair.

After Dad found out that I loved it up there… and that there was a ton of open space he promised the attic would someday be my room, far away from the boy's mayhem. I waited and waited and watched as three-quarters of it turned into a storage space that I got to run and retrieve merchandise from quickly on the busiest of summer festival and Christmas Lighting days. I can't remember which year the last quarter of it finally became my room, but I was so happy to have a floor to myself. Dad designed a little nook for the bed, and hung huge, mirrored closet doors at the storage end of the room. I spent hours hiding away up there, pretending to be a runway model, or reading, or doing homework, or anything to avoid being where anyone could find me to have me do something. It was sweet solace from a hard life.

CHAPTER 33

GIO AND I gradually grew into unpaid store hands as we grew into early adolescence. I'd like to think it was because my parents realized it wasn't good to leave me alone and in charge of the boys with nothing more than a hand-written to-do list from Vickie-Jean of all the other chores she wanted us to do too; but realistically, I think they had a lot to do at the store and we were free labor and it was cheaper to pay Nonna to watch the boys than hire help. My dad and Vickie-Jean were always at work; always, always, always at work. It felt like they were never home but when Dad was running the shop, he didn't make me feel like a failure at everything, didn't make me work so much, or re-do work I'd already done. He was actually kind of fun. One of my favorite things to do with him was play board games at a little green card table behind the shop counter. I remember Dad, Gio and I taking turns at Risk, Yahtzee, Life, and Monopoly, between customers of course, on days when Vickie-Jean was out of town showing pictures at some museum or far away gallery.

What I loved most about shop time alone with Dad was that, though he expected us to work, and was a fan of Vickie-Jean's to-do lists, he seemed to appreciate us being there. He never let us be totally free to do whatever we wanted like Mom did when we visited her, but he participated in the work to be done and made me feel like a person and not slave labor. He didn't correct, and over correct, and make me re-do like Vickie-Jean. He didn't shame me and fuss at me and worry over how messily I'd done something like Nonna either. He really made me feel like my help was valuable. I didn't feel like a burden when she was away. I felt like he wanted me, but had to help keep the shops up and running. I loved times like that, but they were few and far between. Summers were punctuated with dad's firefighting absences, and time alone with Vickie-Jean was punctuated with "deep cleaning" lists, probably so she didn't have to see our faces around the store so much. She had us dust and stock the back room, and only called us up if it got too busy at the counter for her to wrap trinkets and ring up customers alone. When they were both there, we never existed quite the same as when it was only Dad. I don't know why I didn't think to resent him for the difference I just wished for her to be gone.

I loved Martin and Alex, and still watched them plenty when Nonna dropped them off at night and the parental units were still working. I don't remember ever missing school to watch them after fifth grade but I did have plenty of time alone with the little boys. I fed them Vickie-Jean's dinners, and wiped their faces. I sang favorite songs, played favorite games, kissed boo-boos. I bathed them and dressed them for bed. In a lot of ways, I felt like a sort of second mother to them and loved it when they'd run to me instead of Vickie-Jean for comfort.

Thankfully, I don't remember ever treating them mean like I did Melody; the closest I came to mean, was to experiment with them. I was really getting into science and they were fun subjects. I'd feed them something sweet then something sour and watch their faces change. I'd tell them "sweet," and "sour," and see if they could say it too. I made funny faces and told them the "feelings" my face was showing. I poured really hot water on their left shoulder and really cold water on their right while I bathed them and watched to see what reaction I'd get from them. I wanted to see what they did, and like on Sesame Street educate them too. There again, were no devious intentions, simply a curiosity over how I could affect them depending on the different variables I added.

Like with Trent, the older Martin got, the more he was included in our games even if we never had the bond with him, or any of the other siblings like we had with each other. Alex had taken Martin's place as baby and he was the typical baby in the family, spoiled and used to getting his own way.

I avoided Vickie-Jean, when she was home, the way I avoided Lester when I was at Mom's. It wasn't because she did bad things but because she always had something for me to do. She had those lists, page-long lists of to-dos ready for me every day at home and at the shop. Before I could play or do homework, I had to finish my list. Maybe she was trying to help Gio and I organize our day, but she never said that. She said she expected me to complete my list before anything else. I was afraid that if I argued, something bad would happen so I did my list like a champ, but never from top to bottom. Sometimes I started in the middle, sometimes I did the odd numbered tasks first, or started at the bottom and worked my way up. It was my silent act of rebellion, she never had to know so nothing bad ever had to happen.

When Dad was gone, Gio didn't do his lists. He would go play. When she found out she would yell and scream at him and lecture, lecture, lecture. Her lectures to Gio weren't like Nonna's lectures. With Nonna, we knew it was "all in love" even though they went on and on and made us feel like garbage. Still, somehow we knew Nonna loved us. Not Vickie-Jean. At the time I was pretty sure she hated Gio or at least very strongly disliked him. I didn't think she liked me much either, but her dislike for Gio was no secret. She was brutal to that boy, especially when Dad wasn't around. He could seriously do nothing good in her eyes. Her lectures broke down his essence and since we were twins, I internalized what she said about him. She shot below the waist and went for the key words that tore down anyone young or old, tearing up his character, his skills, his behavior. She called him mean things: "devil spawn," "evil little boy," whatever she wanted, because he wouldn't do a chore or talked back. He should have done his list. I told him to do his lists. He refused. Maybe in a way he was the things she said, maybe her saying it made him it.

Gio was no easy kid to deal with, and the woman should get a medal for not actually drowning the both of us in the tub when we were smaller and she had the chance. Gio wasn't the evil creature she made him out to be all the time but he was combative, willful, kinesthetic and hyperactive. All my rebellion was focused on self-harm, bullying at school or in passive actions, purposely hidden from others; his was literally bouncing off walls sometimes! Gio and I had our own fights and issues. Some of our fights were knockdown, drag-out brawls. I'd get mad at him during them, but we always reconciled and came out buddies. Not so with Vickie-Jean.

I remember a beating Gio got once. He forgot to take the trash out—well, he forgot or chose not to, whatever the reason, I heard her raging on him the way I raged on myself. I came down from my safe place to see what was going on. I knew she sometimes got rough with him physically, took him down, man handled him when Dad was gone and he was extra bad, so I was trying to watch over him... without having her negative attention directed on me. They were in the kitchen fighting. Only it wasn't really a fight, at least not a fair one when she was still so much bigger and he was trying to do what he was supposed to. Gio wasn't a frightful boy but I saw sheer terror on his face. My twin brother, my other half, was deathly afraid and like a scary time before, with a different creepy grown-up, I froze.

The trash was full and messiness was not tolerated in Vickie-Jean's house and the trash was Gio's job and it wasn't done. She gave us our lists, and I tried to always do my lists, I'd rage during or after, but I did mine. For whatever reason, Gio didn't do the trash that day and he was scrambling to get it out while she punished him. It was not a long monotonous driveling lecture like Lester would do, in fact, it was almost quiet but metered with rage, hate and vindictiveness. It was like all the anger inside her was because of him and him alone and she was going to make him pay. She was hovering above him, leaning over his back as he pulled the trash bag out of the trash can. Seething, she she hissed, "You worthless, no good, evil little devil, you *will* do what I say and you *will* do it fast, do you hear me?" She wouldn't give him space to move, she enveloped him, spewing her venom into his ear. Maybe she was trying to be militant, hoping that would work with an unruly kid, but it seemed horribly mean to me. He scurried to the door and down the stairs to the dumpster and she was right there on top of him.

He looked back at me desperately, terror drawn tight across his face. We both knew he was in for it.

CHAPTER 34

I THOUGHT SHE was going to push him down the steps and he was going to die in front of my eyes. There was nothing I could do to save him this time. No sexual act, no hideaway plan, and worse than that, I was frozen in place, powerless to stop her or help him. I didn't want her to push me down the stairs too. I didn't want to leave him alone. So, I watched and did nothing. I didn't leave, I didn't call 911, I didn't plug my ears like I sometimes did when Mom and Lester fought. I didn't try to stop her or distract her from hitting him. I stood silently by and watched her beat my brother, the one I tried so hard to protect, and couldn't ever save from bad stuff. She wailed on his back while he stumbled down the steps. Full-on, all out pounding on him, I'm sure I remember the hand print bruises on his back, but all covered by shirts, no one else ever knew. She beat his back all the way down. Thankfully, she didn't push him; that would have been worse. I guess it made her feel better because she calmed down after that.

I figured I knew how she felt. I had hit a kid and it made me feel good in some disgusting way, but I never considered it being wrong until I saw Vickie-Jean hit Gio. I was playing when I'd done it. It was a bad game, it was a mean game and I knew it wasn't nice to hit, but for me, it was a game that I could control the rules to. When I saw Vickie-Jean going off on Gio, that's when I realized how wrong I was. I knew I was guilty of hurting her and causing her terror. I knew that look of fear in Gio's eyes because that's how Melody looked when she knew I was going to hit her with the race track. I had all the power over her, and she was too little to fight me. I could hurt her or play nicely and I chose to terrorize her. I was sorry then, for hurting her, sorry for Vickie-Jean hurting Gio, sorry for any kid anywhere that got hurt like that. I hurt myself to pay back the pain and terror I realized I put Melody through. I didn't want Vickie-Jean to get me. I wanted to take back what I did to Melody, I wanted to help anyone who was getting hit. I wanted to help Gio, but I was powerless to stop her even if I could have moved from my frozen position. There was nothing Gio could have done, except maybe taken out the trash like he was supposed to, to avoid the beating. I'm pretty sure though, with how angry she was, she would have found something to hit him for.

I don't remember any other beatings; maybe she did beat him and I didn't see it, or maybe she totally lost it that evening and never physically abused him again. I do remember that look on Gio's face and it still haunts me. Knowing that was what Melody felt too shamed me and changed me. They were both terrified. Vickie-Jean did it to Gio, but I put that same look on someone else. Maybe because we were twins I was able to feel what he was feeling and that's why I felt the terror so intimately. It was primal fear. Guilt and shame exploded inside me. I was evil. I belonged in hell for what I did to Melody. She belonged in hell for what she did to Gio.

I was wrong to hurt Melody. I knew I ought not to hit and scare her. I hadn't lost my cool like Vickie- Jean but I still did what I did and knew it was wrong. I was wrong, it was wrong, I deserved to be punished for it, Melody didn't deserve it and should have been protected from me but I was a child. I didn't fully understand or grasp what I was doing to her or how it would damage her.

Vickie-Jean was wrong to hurt Gio, but she was an adult. Even if she was beyond angry or maliciously wanted to rip Gio's head off, she shouldn't have done what she did! Children should have some grace to account for their need to learn and gain experience but adults should be expected to behave correctly. If she was too mad to deal with the situation, she should have walked away. She should have, but she didn't. She's not the only one; sometimes anger or the need to control others gets the best of people, but the emotional bruises never quite disappear.

If there had ever been hope for us to build a relationship, it died that day and another secret was born in its place. We never spoke of it to Dad or anyone or even each other; we were twins, a look was all we needed. He laid on his stomach in his bed and said without words that he hated her too.

After that, Gio got mad at everything and everyone, and I got the brunt of a lot of his anger. He started fights all the time. A few of them were really bad, and not surprisingly all of them took place when the parents were out of the apartment. Once, Gio, Martin, Alex and I were home alone. Gio reared up and the fighting got physical pretty quickly. Even though we were the same age, he was developing into a young man and was much stronger than me by then.

I was no match for him. He came after me ready to hit me and I didn't want to fight. I didn't want to be like my mom and keep going for more, which I admit to doing plenty of times, but that time, I was done. I tried to lock myself in the old bathroom but couldn't get the door shut in time. He got to me and I got it good. I'm lucky I crouched into a fetal position on top of the toilet seat because the pencil he stabbed me with, only punctured the meat of my leg just below my knee cap and didn't get me anywhere else.

I think it scared him when the pencil stuck into me; but it enraged me. I went into the kitchen and grabbed a wooden spoon. Vengeance would be mine. What I didn't know, that Gio realized, was that the parents were coming up the steps and almost to the front door. I came around the corner from the kitchen, with a spoon raised in my hand ready to attack. Gio had Alex in his arms and was holding him saying, "Please Gia, don't hurt me or the baby!" The parents opened the door to what looked like me going after the boys. No one cared that Gio had antagonized me and stabbed me. I was busted, sent to my room and stayed there for a long time. When my dad finally came up, he tossed a bag with a training bra in it at me.

"Vickie-Jean bought it because you're getting perky." Silence... breathing... eye-contact avoidance. Then, "I'm so disappointed in you Gia." That was the extent of Dad's lecture or explanation of 'perky.' He walked out of my room a moment later. I was mortified because my dad gave me a bra and because he caught me being bad, but, like usual Gio didn't get busted for the part no one saw, even though there was blood on my leg.

I had my rages and I think Gio plotted ways to watch me get in trouble to help him cope with things. One time, I was hidden away up in my attic room, oblivious to the world below, when all of a sudden, Vickie-Jean started yelling for me to come downstairs right now. I went down and she was freaking out about me locking Gio in his bedroom, which had a lock on the outside. I didn't lock him in there. I had no idea who did, but I didn't. I told her it wasn't me. She insisted it was me. Then I got in trouble. Gio told me later that he snuck out his window and into Dad and Vickie-Jean's room. He was the one who locked his own bedroom door. His whole point was to get me in trouble and he did.

Sometimes when the rages came, I didn't scream into pillows but onto paper as well, and Gio used this against me too. I had one of Vickie-Jean's stupid to-do pads and wrote in it. I wrote everything I felt like she wanted to say to me, but never did. It was full of hate and disgust and probably not a good thing at all to write, but it was much better than hurting myself, I knew that even then. I was trying to be a little self-controlled, like the Bible said God's people were. But Gio found it and turned it in. I got in trouble, again. Dad told me it was not okay to write that stuff. I tried to explain it was a way to get out how I felt. He didn't accept it; he didn't want me writing mean stuff like that. So I got in my trouble, Gio was happy, actually got kudos for telling on me that time, and I learned all over again, that it's wrong to express myself.

CHAPTER 35

SOMETHING IN ME distanced myself from Gio after that. Until then we were almost like one person: thinking, doing, going to the same places. But we were different. He wasn't me. He wasn't even really my friend anymore. I couldn't trust him. I had to do life alone, keep my mouth shut, and my secrets to myself and pretend all was well. The writing stopped but the rages went on.

The differences in how we were treated compared to Martin and Alex became more apparent to me as we got older. Gio and I had our fights, but we were a package deal. He never left, I never left, we were a "we." Up to then I figured Vickie-Jean treated us different because Martin was a baby. He got more photo shoots, more clothes, more time with the parents, and more patience when he did something wrong, but as he grew it remained the same. When Alex came along, they both got special treatment that I couldn't justify simply because they were much younger. Nonna treated us the same but Dad and Vickie-Jean did not.

It was painfully clear that Gio and I were by-products of Dad's past. We were afterthoughts in every decision and we weren't necessary to their family—we were unwanted burdens to it. The little boys were part of the family, they were included, wanted, but Gio and I were throw-away kids, that got thrown with Dad. I felt like the only reason they wanted us was for slave labor and so my mom couldn't have us. Gio and I had to go to bed when they came up from the shop, even in the summertime when it was still light outside. Martin and Alex got to stay up and visit with them.

There was a vent in the attic and through it, I could hear what was happening in the living room. There was plenty they said that meant nothing to me but when they talked about us, I listened. Vickie-Jean spoke often of how terrible Gio and I were, how troublesome we were, what problems Gio caused, what dish or shop trinket I broke...because I was the most awkward and gangly kid she'd ever seen. They discussed dance lessons and for a short time enrolled me in some. When I proved hopeless because I was too uncoordinated, they had a conversation and decided to stop the lessons. After that, in her nightly reports on my failures to my dad, she started to call me Grace if the story involved stumbling or accidentally breaking something. Then her talk would switch to their precious boys, their perfect creations, the ones she wanted and loved and were worth coming home to after they shooed us off to bed. I can't say I ever resented Martin or Alex for the love they received. I just wished I could be loved too. Like an evil sinner, I simply coveted it. I was such a bad person, I wanted my parents to love me like them. I coveted what I wasn't good enough to receive. I should have been happy to have a roof over my head and food in my stomach.

When she looked at me her eyes never shined the way they did when she looked at her boys. I didn't see the same unveiled hate that flamed in them for Gio, but neither was there love or acceptance. The look was the same she gave to long lingering tourists after store hours. I exhausted her. I couldn't do her lists right, couldn't stay on task, couldn't sweep the corners good enough, get behind the toilet far enough, scrub the tub white enough, brush my teeth long enough, walk down the steps quiet enough. Nothing, nothing, nothing I did was good enough. For a long time I tried to make her happy, I really tried, but I didn't measure up and burdened her life. She didn't shame like Nonna, she just had me do and re-do, over and over again until whatever work I was doing was good enough. She exhausted me! It seemed like anytime I came around her she had some piece of work for me to do: stocking trinkets, dusting oils and pasta boxes, washing wine glasses, scrubbing a faucet, a toilet, a counter or dish, so I tried to avoid contact with her if at all possible.

Like with Lester, I was on high alert and aware of her whereabouts at all times; the only difference was that I never worried about Vickie-Jean sneaking into my room at night. I was simply her Cinderella. I worked for everything she and my dad provided and if I didn't do it right, it was because I was "just like my mother." When I heard her coming, if I had enough time, I'd hide so she couldn't find me because the only time she sought me out, was to put me to work. Gio spent most of his time away from home, with local friends at Blackbird Island, Enchantment Park, in their houses or outside riding on his bike. I wasn't outdoorsy so I hid from her in my room until I got my own jobs that kept me busy and less dependent on her chores to get my daily bread.

Despite my frustrations with the delivery of their lessons, the Gianelli work ethic was benefiting me greatly. I started two lucrative businesses in middle-school. Admittedly, my mom gets credit for the idea for one of them, but they were still my operations. When I visited her, I always complained about the work I had to do for the shops.

"They should really pay you, you know? I bet there are a lot of shop owners that would pay a pretty penny to have a little worker bee like you."

I never thought I could get paid for the work I was doing. I set out to see if she was right. I offered services to several shopkeeper's, not for a penny, but for a fraction of minimum wage. Most of the shops I ran between were already familiar with me because of Christmas light stringing but the new, regular pay was a dream come true. I delivered coffee, lunch and dinner from one local vendor to another. I rode my bike to Dan's Market for emergency pick-ups of this or that. I did menial shop work like dusting, stocking, scrubbing walls and floorboards. For four dollars an hour I did anything they wanted. It was a good little side job but my real money came from my paper route.

I inherited the route by some stroke of great fortune from an older local boy who went to Gramps' church and headed off to college. His mom worked in Das Sweet Shop, one of the places I made regular deliveries from and knew I was a good worker. She recommended me for the route and I will be forever grateful for that simple act of kindness. I was the best paper carrier Leavenworth had ever seen. The route and prep for it was what my body, so hungry for rhythm, movement, routine and repetition needed. Wake, stuff, fold, and throw, fold and throw, follow the route, fold and throw.

Like my dad and Gramps before me, my job trumped everything, even visits with my mom. I had to stay in Leavenworth to deliver papers so I got in the habit of only going to her house on no-school Mondays and then only for the day so I could be home and up and ready for paper delivery the next morning.

My paper route was my best buddy. I didn't need real friends. I was up every day including Sundays…fold and throw, follow the route. I found out why Dad and Gramps loved work so much. Work was rewarding, and like school, I was good at it… as long as I wasn't working for Nonna or Vickie-Jean. I took that dinky little paper route of fifty local downtown patrons and more than tripled its size in the years I had it through door-to-door sales and other route acquisitions. I think I owned the route from sixth grade on, but I can't really remember because all the middle school grades blend.

The only thing I didn't like were the wake ups… especially in the dead of snowy winter. I wanted to stay in my warm attic space tucked away from reality, but I had to get up because papers didn't fold and throw themselves. I was always up before the crack of dawn, except for the late spring and summer months when the sun started to beat me. I liked the quiet and still of the town at rest and somehow the dark before dawn never seemed as scary as middle-of-the-night darkness. The streetlights and silence were my companions and together we watched the world ease into morning and brightness. The sun, on especially brilliant days, painted the snow-capped, tree-capped, or autumn-colored mountains pink or orange or my favorite… an eerie magenta that settled thick into the crevices of the Cascades.

I needed few supplies, so my expenses were minimal. I had to buy my papers, rubber bands, plastic sleeves for rainy or snowy days, and my paper bags (which only needed to be replaced once every year or so). I chose to add a little goodie to my deliveries once or twice a month. I'd tuck a mint or hard candy into the fold where it couldn't fall out upon tossing. In order to grow my route I also purchased and tossed extra papers to houses with the type of people that seemed to like the news; nice cars, nice yards, slightly more affluent than the average Joe. After throwing them a complimentary paper for a month, I'd go to their house on the next collection day to see if they wanted to continue to receive the daily paper and pay me for it. It worked for me, I added customers, I didn't lose them. I didn't miss a house, at least not often, I didn't throw at windows or screen doors. I put papers where they asked me to, and people liked how I did my job. When I collected their money the last weekend of every month, for the next month's deliveries, they told me "thank you" and that I did a good job. I was praised for what I did, not put down. I loved hearing people say good things to me.

CHAPTER 36

FOR THE FIRST time ever, ever, *ever* in my life outside of school, I was finally good at something and I got credit for it! Sure I was good in school, but there were hundreds of other good students. I wasn't exceptionally smart or gifted so I never stood out. To my customers though, I was the best. They even said it: "You're the best paper carrier we've ever had." Over and over again I heard how good I was at my job; I think I liked the praise as much as the money. And I liked the money that came with it a lot!

My boss was satisfied with my work too, at least he didn't say anything bad about my work, which in my book was as good as telling me I was doing great because I was so used to everything I did being criticized. Every month he asked me, how many more customers I added and how I did it, how long my route was and shook his head. I imagined it was pride, but I don't know because I didn't see that look at home to compare it to.

I budgeted my money in order to have enough to buy supplies but I always had extra. It was a good thing too because after Vickie-Jean realized I was making good money, she told my dad (in one of those living room conversations) that I should buy my own clothes and school supplies. That was fine with me because I bought myself name brand clothes instead of the generic ones she got me. The added clothing expense put a damper on my dream of buying a full-sized electronic keyboard, but I was diligent to save at least twenty dollars every month toward the purchase.

I can't remember what originally piqued my interest but I started to collect newspaper articles about serial killers. I loved scouring the paper for them and reading about them. I imagined the killer in the act of his violence. My favorite that I read and reread was about a Russian serial killer named Andrei Chikatilo. He was sick and sadistic I don't know why I wanted to read it. To think that someone could do that, and get away with it for so long scared me and impressed me all at the same time. Somehow in my head, though, Brad's abuse was never that bad, I imagined he was Brad, and I imagined it was Brad who was caught and that he wouldn't be a threat ever again. I guess it was a way to tell myself what happened to me wasn't that bad, and it could have been lots worse.

I bought a spiral notebook and taped the articles into it and kept my serial killers secret from everyone. It felt good clipping and saving them in my contemporary book of death. Part of me wanted to be like them and rage like that and take out my anger on the world. I knew, though, that if anyone knew I "admired" a killer in some way it might cause me a lot of problems. I don't know how long the obsession with the clippings lasted or where my book of killers ever went to, but by the time I moved to Mom's my compulsion to collect them and know them was gone. It was a collection of convenience; I had a job that allowed me access to the articles, so I amassed them.

There were so many great things about my jobs; work really was better than my family. Not only did I like what I did and feel successful at it, I got a thrill out of everyone telling me how great I was at it, I had money to spend and a new hobby to boot. There was nothing bad about working. Every payday was a treat, every compliment a boost to my ego but some times were better than others. Christmastime collection was my favorite because I got presents! That's right, I got gifts from people who already paid me! Trinkets from people who already told me how great I was. It was a misunderstood, under-rug-swept girl's dream come true. Until the Christmas I got more gifts from my customers than I did from Dad and Vickie-Jean.

That Christmas hurt bad.

The bad Christmas was Gio's last Christmas with Dad. Unlike that year's Christmas at Mom's where she planned gifts for everyone equally, at Dad and Vickie-Jean's, Martin and Alex's gifts far outnumbered what Gio and I got. I guess Vickie-Jean figured if I was old enough to make my own money and get Cracker Jacks and crocheted doilies from customers, I didn't need Christmas gifts from them.

The disparity between us and them was obvious. We didn't go to the shop right away like usual; instead, all four of us kids walked out of our rooms to find a corner of the living room sheeted off and hidden from view. Dad pulled me and Gio aside quickly and told us it might seem that the little boys got more, but it was because they believed in Santa and all. We passed out the presents under the tree, and we all had a nice little pile. My collection included three packages from my parents and the rest came from customers.

Then Dad took the sheet down; unlike the group family gifts of the year before, everything revealed was for the little boys. There was a mountain of toys. Das Kinder Shoppe, a tourist toy store, had gone out of business after the summer rush proved to be a bust for them. The parents bought a large portion of the inventory for Martin and Alex. When Nonna came to pick up the little boys an hour later she too was taken aback. They told her they were helping friends in need and got everything at a discounted price. She told them, she thought it was excessive.

It wasn't a surprise to Gio and I. We had known for a long time that we got the left overs. I got a cassette tape, a Sony walkman and an eight dollar gift box of perfume and lotion (I knew it was eight dollars because I'd seen it in a store the week before). My customer's gifts outnumbered my parents' if not in quality, at least in number. The boys' were worth a whole toy store and I was worth exactly eight dollars and a walkman. There was nothing else from them. I knew it was petty of me, but I was devastated. It might as well have been a slap in the face.

While I had wanted a walkman for quite sometime, and should have been grateful, I knew in an instant the amount spent on Gio and I was minuscule compared to the little boys. But, it wasn't all about the money, it was about the message that Christmas sent. They didn't have to spend any more money on us. They could have made me something special or taken me somewhere. Vickie-Jean could have snapped a picture of me throwing papers and put it in a cheap frame. Dad could have wrapped up one of our board games with coupons to play with him. But nope, I was an eight dollar after thought when they bought milk probably. My disappointment was evident, and evidently it annoyed Vickie-Jean.

When Gio asked, not so quietly, why I was crying as we gathered up the scattered Christmas paper, she reprimanded me from across the room where she was playing with Alex, "You had plenty of presents under the tree, Gia, don't ruin the day for everyone, OK?"

To an extent, she was right, I was reacting like a spoiled preteen; but it wasn't about one Christmas, it was about life as a less-than. I felt like a victim, of what I don't know, but a victim nonetheless. I memorized every word to every song on the tape and with it remembered the pain of that morning. It was my tribute to a lousy Christmas.

And then Vickie-Jean went and got me my own mountain of gifts.

CHAPTER 37

I WAS TURNING into a young lady, I had jobs, like a grown-up, and though the phase was passing, I still sort of liked Barbies. Vickie-Jean liked to bargain shop and sometimes took me with her. One consignment store we visited had every kind of Barbie house, car and toy fathomable. There was even a condo with an elevator, an airplane fuselage, a corvette and an RV. At Vickie-Jean's insistence that it would be fun, I invited several girls from church and school to my birthday party the next year. I think she even called ladies from church and town to be sure their daughters could make it too. I got every single Barbie toy that had been at the store, and clothes, beautiful Barbie clothes, and shoes and Barbies too.

I was excited and confused at the same time. They were Barbies, and I liked to play with them, but it was, like what Nonna had said about the boys' Christmas stash... excessive. Not only that, it was so out of character for what I was used to. Vickie-Jean was right there the whole time snapping pictures of our smiles and the toys. I remember thinking it must have been a show for the other girls and their mothers, it couldn't have been just for me. I was the girl that messed everything up, so why would she do that for me if there wasn't some hidden agenda behind it? I couldn't accept that she would do something nice for me for the sake of being nice, but I never discovered an ulterior motive if there was one.

We set up all of the Barbie toys in my attic room and I remember playing with them for hours upon hours. I was better at set-up than the actual play though. I escaped to places far away in my mind to imagine what Barbie did, where she went, which Barbies would be in the story of the moment and what they'd wear. By the time I had my dolls dressed, the scene in my head was played out and I was bored within a few minutes and moved on.

My Barbies acted out more than a few naughty scenes like in the movies I watched with Lester. I liked that feeling, the urges, the tension, whatever it was, playing erotically with them could conjure up inside. I especially liked that I could control the story line. My Barbies didn't get hurt and my Kens were kind; big, tough, strong but kind. Usually after the sex play with Ken and Barbie, I would bring myself to a climax... at least when I was alone. I don't know if I was once again acting out of the trauma I'd been through, or not, but I do know, I wasn't the only girl that made Ken and Barbie make out. Boys measured their penises and compared one to another, and girls, well, some girls I knew made Ken and Barbie do it. It was scandalous and hot and always good for a giggle when we were done.

The Barbie toys were a huge gift to receive. It was such a weird and rare showering of stuff, I'm not sure if it was to "make up" for the bad Christmas or what, I couldn't figure it out. I wasn't even used to getting extra school supplies or new clothes from Dad and Vickie-Jean. The Barbie birthday doesn't fit into a childhood where a child was hated as badly as I felt hated, but neither do dance lessons, or having a room of my own built for me, or long summer vacations. Vickie-Jean couldn't have hated me like I thought she did, and allow all of those things. She couldn't have been as bad as I remember she was, but I couldn't connect with her.

I can't understand why the nice things she did are muted in my memory banks but the unfair parts still scream through the years. Were there more bad than good times and that's why? Were my expectations of a step-mother unfair? Whatever the reason, the disparity sticks out. Once we all drove to the shoe store in Wenatchee and went shoe shopping. I had my heart set on the popular brand but most of the styles were far more expensive than the thirty dollar budget Dad and Vickie-Jean allotted us. I found one style of the cool brand that was within my budget. Gio didn't have it as easy. He pouted and complained that there weren't any kinds of shoes for him under thirty dollars. I'm sure there was some off-brand, that would have fit the bill, but Gio insisted there weren't any. Tension and temperatures rose until Gio eventually settled on a pair of football cleats that were under the allowed amount. He wasn't happy about it, Dad wasn't happy about it, Vickie-Jean probably thought it was more proof of how ungrateful we were compared to her beautiful boys.

We rung up the shoes separately. With tax mine totaled thirty-two dollars and sixty-five cents and I had to pay the two dollar and sixty-five cent overage myself. I was glad I decided to bring along a little money for that very reason or I would have been forced to choose a generic sneaker. Gio's were next, barely under the budget, he didn't get the difference. Then the little boys got their shoes. Alex got a baby pair but Martin scored. His shoes, before tax, were sixty-five bucks.

Every injustice, every verbal knock to who we were and who our mother was; it all hit me there in the shoe store, because Dad was watching it all play out. Vickie-Jean was hardest on us when Dad was gone, but here she was buying her little precious one shoes that cost more than Gio and I were allowed together and Dad said nothing while Gio and I struggled. Martin was barely in school, he didn't need brand-name shoes, and even if he did, I thought we all should have had the same standard. If they were willing to spend that on him, shouldn't they have given us at least that much, and anything beyond we would be responsible for? I must have looked mad because Dad and wicked-step mother explained the whole return trip how Martin was too young and incapable of coming up with the extra money for his shoes, but we were plenty old enough to save and come up with the money for our own. I thought it was a stupid argument. But, in their defense, they were young thirty-somethings dealing with difficult kids and a difficult situation; they probably didn't realize how unfair it looked to the two of us outsiders. But that shoe shopping trip changed my life forever.

CHAPTER 38

THE BOY WHOSE life I saved, who was my twin, an actual part of me, whom I had never lived without... left me. Gio laced up those shoes and walked out of dad and Vickie-Jean's life the day after school got out. He never came back to live in Leavenworth... over a stupid pair of football cleats. Of course there was also the beating, and the name calling and the obvious disdain from Vickie-Jean especially aimed at him. It wasn't about the shoes, I knew that, but they were the last straw.

Gio brought up his plans to Dad after talking to Mom and Lester about it a few weeks before school was out. I implied that I was thinking of moving into the city too, but had to figure out what I'd do with my route. As far as I know, Dad wasn't aware of Mom's moods, or Lester's porn habits, or what they grew in the closet but begged and pleaded for us not to move, nonetheless. I liked the attention the threat gave me. All of a sudden we mattered to Dad again. It didn't matter to Gio though, no amount of feigned attention would sway my brother. Gio was done, he made his decision, and he was never going back. He begged me to come with him. Dad begged me to stay. I was torn.

Dad promised to spend more time with us, to do more things with us, to be around more, work less, and even made the effort while Gio was still living there. I fell for it. I wanted bright, red pomodoro time back. I loved my dad, I wanted my dad. Like a drunk promising to quit, he promised to work less. Like a drunk too far gone, he was lost to me. But I believed him and, the truth was, I had work of my own I was chained to in Leavenworth. Gio saw Dad's addiction for what it was, and refused to stay.

My hope in Dad, obligations in Leavenworth, and reservations about Lester may have kept me from moving, but I didn't spend much of the summer at the loft either. The long-postponed and anticipated vacation to the East Coast was upon the Gianelli family, but the family no longer included me or Gio. I couldn't go, Gio wouldn't go and Vickie-Jean made hasty arrangements for me to stay at Nonna and Gramps before they set off on their next grand adventure.

My time was largely my own and I filled it as best as I could with work to forget he was gone. Days started early. I was up with the sun throwing my papers, then delivering shopkeepers wares one to another or doing other odd jobs for people in town. I was usually done in town by early afternoon and rode my bike to Aunt Maria's vet clinic to clean animal cages and stalls until she took me to Nonna's. When work was finished for the day, the loneliness got to me. Nothing had changed at Nonna and Gramp's house but it was somehow empty. He was gone. He picked on me, annoyed me, and frustrated me, but I didn't know life without him. We would sit down to dinner together, Gramps, Nonna and me and it should have been a lovely, special time, but it was too quiet. I missed Gio, so I found a way to see him but avoid Lester.

My bike had long been my main means of transportation, but it never occurred to me that I could use public transit until one especially smokey mid-summer morning. A city bus stopped to let a passenger out as I tossed a paper and the stubble-faced man that got off, unhooked his bike from the rack at the front of the bus and rode off to whatever business he had to take care of. I had a bike. I had plenty of money for bus fare. I had no idea how to use city transit. I watched and learned about a way of life I'd never even noticed before and found a way to get me to my brother when I was lonely.

A few days later, I detoured from my usual route to Das Sweet Shoppe to talk to a kind looking older lady waiting at a bus stop along the highway. Highway Two was barely a block uphill from the main part of town and for a long time I thought it was named that way because it divided Leavenworth in two. She explained to me how our simple city transit system worked. Buses were numbered based on their route and they followed the same route over and over all day long. Fare was one token anywhere in Leavenworth, all the way to the town of Cashmere; and two tokens would get me to Wenatchee. Tokens were fifty cents a piece and sold in gas stations and city halls. The bus numbers, stops and times were listed on the bus stop signs. I could sit anywhere I wanted on the bus and to stop it, all I had to do was pull the chord.

I figured I knew everything there was to know about riding the bus and was ready to try it out. When my chores in town were done, instead of biking to Aunt Maria's clinic, I bought some tokens and waited at a bus stop. Aunt Maria's clinic was east, but I boarded a west bound bus and was a little embarrassed when I had to wait alone with the driver at the end of the route until it was time for him to turn around and head back. We passed the stop where I boarded and continued another mile down the road to a stop on the highway a block before Aunt Maria's. I wanted to get off but forgot to pull the chord. I panicked inside but pulled the chord and disembarked at the next stop like that was my plan all along. I struggled to unfasten my bike from the rack and had to back track a few blocks but still got to Aunt Maria's quicker than I would have riding my bike. I was an independent woman, capable of traveling anywhere I wanted, without any adult help in coordinating.

It took a while to get the hang of how it all worked, but in short order I could use city transportation easily. I told Nonna and Gramps, Mom and Aunt Maria what I was doing and scheduled myself to have Mondays and Tuesdays off of town chores and vet cleaning. I'd take the bus to Wenatchee Monday morning after my route was delivered and stay the whole day until the last bus back to Leavenworth left. I be with Gio and visit Mom and Trent and Hannah and leave most days before Lester even got home from the orchard. On Tuesdays, I would catch a ride with them to Mamaw's, play with Gio and the little kids, get piano lessons from mom, run around on Mamaw's farm, then sleep safe and sound at Nonna and Gramps.

It was perfect! It was everything I wanted from Mom's house without the creepy parts I anguished over. I felt guilty for leaving Hannah to manage it all by herself but I imagined Lester only touched me because I looked like my mom and Hannah did not resemble her at all. I pretended she was safe and the fighting and moods and porn didn't exist because I found a way to avoid them in my world.

GIA'S SECRET   155

Gio and I were lazing in the dry, dusty heat, outside at Mom's one Monday, when he made it clear that he was never going back and equally clear I needed to move too. I think he felt as alone as I did. I told him I couldn't. It was too much Lester for me to handle. I was willing to put up with the anxiety of him for short, quaint visits, but every day for the rest of my life was impossible. No matter how hard Gio begged, I couldn't consider Mom's an option any more than he could consider going back to Dad's. Vickie-Jean to him was like Lester to me. We understood each other the way only twins could. Our green eyes locked in silent acceptance of what had to be. I could handle Vickie-Jean. I had my rages, my jobs, my paper route and clippings, my school work and Gramps' church to occupy most of my time. I couldn't handle Lester, but I couldn't protect Gio from Vickie-Jean, or expect him to endure anymore of her for me. I knew he needed the distance to stay safe.

CHAPTER 39

OUR RESPECTIVE RESOLVES waxed as summer waned until there were only two Mondays, then one Monday left until school started. Bus rides to Mom's stopped. Dad, Martin, Alex and Vickie-Jean returned. Life without Gio was as empty as Dad's promises had been. With but one slave left to oversee, Vickie-Jean's lists grew longer. They were impossible to finish before the parents came up for the night and shooed me off to bed, but I was sure to always at least get the trash out in time. I never realized how much of her Gio had shielded me from but finally understood why he begged so long for me to leave too.

That fall was a major adjustment. The teachers were more serious and less easy to please. I saw a few new faces and was painfully aware that one was missing. Gio should have started at Alps Middle School that year. His friends found me and asked where he was. To them Wenatchee was a world away, to me it was just a choice I questioned every day.

Alps organized their class structure based on an intelligence system. I don't see why in the world a school would make the smart versus dumb kids so pathetically obvious to their students, but they did. After my little play performance I was identified as one smart cookie. Each grade was split in half: the smart half and the idiot half. The really smart kids were assigned ".1" classes (6.1, 7.1, 8.1) and the "special" kids were .8s (6.8, 7.8, 9.8). The first day of each year no one knew who was smart and who was dumb until they labeled us. Somehow I ended up near the top that year with the smart-ish kids. I didn't know many of them and although I liked being bumped up to a smarter level, I hated having to learn new social rules.

It was a rush of changing classes, academic competition, pressure and preparation for high school that I hadn't known before. Though I liked the challenge and wealth of opportunity to learn, the bulk of the smarter kids seemed to be rich kids too. I don't know if it's the way I perceived it, or if it's that "those" kinds of people invest more time and energy into their kids and that accounts for their success. The rich kids dressed in the name brands that were fifty times more expensive just because they are name brand. They were always going to do this or that fancy thing with their fancy family and then complaining about it like it was a chore to go to a real live symphony in Seattle or a wedding or movie with their family. My family didn't do anything together and these kids were belly aching about cool stuff.

I was socially awkward, inept and uncultured. I belonged with the average kids not these elites. I felt out of place among preppy, whiny kids who talked about their doting parents like they were a burden. I had a mom with music moods and a step-mom that demanded work from me. I wore off-brand, unpopular clothes. I had a broken family, I had a weird way of relating to people. I was at the bottom in this mix of adolescents and knew from experience that sticking out was a way to make bad things happen. I hung back and didn't express myself a whole lot. I tried to always agree. I found that as long as I agreed, nodded my head, and didn't ruffle feathers I could get by under the radar.

I made some new, smart-ish friends, mostly because we were alphabetical neighbors. Marci Geliski sat in front of me in most classes and Kate Gilmore, behind. Familiarity didn't breed contempt, it bred camaraderie, companionship, cohesion. Marci was a big talker, especially for such a little girl. Stick thin and full of life and energy, she couldn't sit still and neither could her bouncy blonde curls always twisted and tangled up. She reminded me of a little mouse, scurrying here and there bringing back her morsels of gossip to share.

Marci had a happy Catholic family that was hard for me to relate to. I liked that she didn't make me feel lower than her like most of the other smart kids. She made me feel okay as I was. But I was always nervous I'd say or do something to make her talk about me, so I listened more than talked to her. Kate on the other hand, didn't have a happy family and wasn't rich. She was like me; we never talked much about what life at home was like. Other kids talked about the relationships they had with their family, how they hated it when their mom made them go out to lunch with them, or their dad forced them to go fishing, or the funny thing their brother said at the dinner table. Not Kate and I, we escaped our realities when we were together. We crushed on the same famous boys, we watched the same movies, we dreamed of life when we were grown up.

I don't remember spending much time at her house, probably a combination of her own secrets and my paper route kept that from happening but Kate stayed a lot of nights with me and I wasn't so alone. She accepted me as I was and together we created wonderful far away fantasy worlds. One of our favorite things to do was act out or write out movie screen plays. Neither one of us would admit we still played with Barbies, but it happened more than a time or two. The older we got the less the dolls came out and more we let our words come alive on paper. Of course I always had to pick a song that expressed the feelings we were trying to evoke and make a cassette sound-track to accompany us. Sometimes our stories were innocent and adventurous, but more often than not, there was an element of sexual fantasy involved.

We'd conjure up stories about dangerous or super strong men overpowering women and the heroes that would save them. We took turns writing lusty parts of our screenplays in a spiral notebook that traveled back and forth between us. In class, we spent as much time writing out our fantasies as we did working on school work. More than a few pages were x-rated story scenes that rivaled Lester's movies. We were both confused and damaged girls and it was a way for us to get out what we had to keep in. I wrote out scenes based on Lester's movies and the fear his adult rage instilled in me, I assumed she was doing the same. We wrote about how much we wanted to run away and escape our lives. We made plans to live in Wenatchee or Seattle and wondered how we'd survive on our own.

It was all fun and games until my dad found the book and talked to me about it. I'm sure my parents snooped in my stuff in order to find it because I don't remember leaving it out. I always kept my diaries, full of my fears and confessions, ditties and lyrics, hidden

GIA'S SECRET   159

from sight and frequently moved them; and when it was with me, the book stayed safe with them. I don't know if they read my diaries but Dad chewed me out about the naughty notebook. He wanted to know how I knew about sexual acts like the ones Kate and I wrote. I shrugged sheepishly, actually contemplated for the smallest fraction of a second if I should tell, then lied and said kids at school talked about eating people out and giving head. He shook his head in disgust. I'll never forget the way he looked at me. It wasn't like when I was a child asking about masturbating, it was something different, something that made my insides curdle. I realized one more time how bad I was for knowing what I knew and doing what I did. He made me throw the book in the dumpster behind the shop. I cried myself to sleep that night, and dreaded telling Kate of our notebook's fate.

CHAPTER 40

WE MAY HAVE lost our notebook but our fantasies lived on. We had crushes on famous boys and then one day realized there were some middle school boys that we liked too. DJ and Dwight were our imaginary middle school boyfriends. We had classes with both of them, which means they were smart boys and probably rich too. Dwight wasn't attractive in my opinion, but was crush worthy for one reason or another to Kate, and since it was her fantasy, I let her have it. DJ, on the other hand, was more than a little aesthetically pleasing to me. He was a boy growing into man with lines of definition taking shape in his body. It was hard for me not to get sweet on him. I tried in seventh grade to talk to him during a group project dissecting a frog. He clearly had no interest in knowing me, that or he was too engrossed in the dissection at hand to care about a girl.

DJ was the only real boy I ever imagined going out with and I don't know why because we didn't even talk save that one fleeting conversation. It was a short lived imaginary affair though. I had a dream that DJ, Dwight and two creepy brothers cornered me. I never really knew the brothers in real-life but they somehow reminded me of the twin girls in "The Shining." In my dream, I was changing in a bathroom stall in the girl's locker room when DJ opened the door. The other three boys were behind him and stared at me as I stood there naked.

I felt helpless and exposed, afraid and cornered, like with Lester as a little girl that one night. DJ reached his hand up to touch my face. His fingers were warm. They traced a trail from my ear down my jawline. My mind didn't like it, but my stupid body did, even though I was cornered and ganged up on. I couldn't figure out why my body felt that way when I was so afraid. I was aroused the same way I was during the bad movies. When DJ's hand moved across my mouth I bit as hard as I could onto the meat between his thumb and index finger. Fiery hot pain flashed in his eyes as I severed the chunk of flesh from his hand. A fiery hot trail up my back woke me, saved me. I never liked DJ again. I didn't want to like boys at all, because of that dream... and Lester. I didn't want to be afraid and aroused at the same time. I hated how the two were starting to go together. The fear wasn't worth it when I could get myself off with no fear.

Christmas vacation came and went with light stringing, tourist singing and Gio and I going back and forth together between both parents' places; then school politics pounced on me like a mountain lion in an alpine tree line. Just when I was settling into friendships, they started me back after the break in 7.1. I was sure I wasn't *that* smart but I tested well so they put me in at the top. Before then, I never struggled to get good grades. I read the directions, did the work and always got A's, but it was easy work to do. 7.1 was hard, it challenged me and I had to work and actually apply myself to keep my As. I could handle the work—if I'm honest, I liked having to work for my As, they felt a little more like trophies than participation ribbons that way. The rich kids, though, were brutal.

Marci and Kate were replaced by Priscilla and the other preppy kids I'd never mingled with. Priscilla with her long held grudge and penchant for noticing those without Esprit or Benneton brands was queen of 7.1 and was determined to make my life hell. I was alone and there was no doubt, among the elite, that I was the scummy kid. I was the bottom of the barrel, the awkward, off-brand wearing girl geek, only there because I was smart, not because I hung in their social circles or did the sports or after school activities their parents had them in. I was only there because I was smart. The problem was, I wasn't *that* smart. I still feel like that grade structuring system was sort of social experiment, to see what would happen. What happened to me was subtle, sneering bullying; enough to destroy me, even though the remarks flew under adult radar.

Day after day, hurt and humiliated, I went home and begged my unplugged parents to let me go to the Christian school. I promised I would pay with my own work money to do it, I just didn't have enough for all the tuition. They always said no and told me bullying was part of life and it would pass. I felt like it was punishment for what I'd done to other girls. I couldn't move to Mom's because of my jobs and Lester but I couldn't take the bullying.

With no hope of relief, all that was left to me was to let the hurt out. If I had a piano it would have come out on the keys, but I didn't have enough saved for my keyboard yet. All I could do was rage. I screamed all the names the girls and boys called me into a pillow in a scary guttural wallow. I slammed my hands and fists into anything hard that didn't cause a thud downstairs. I scratched, punched and slapped myself until I was scarred, welted and bruised. And I got up every morning to do it all over and over again. Lester was starting to look preferable to my absent family and horrid school days.

The only good thing about the whole ordeal was finding my school counselor. His name was Mr. Wilson. He was dark-haired with a thick, walrus mustache that covered his lip and bobbed up and down when he talked. He was the words and wisdom I needed in my life. I told him all about my new seventh grade woes with the "smart" kids. I tried to keep my concerns compartmentalized and focused on school. He never knew about Lester or how Gio leaving made me feel more alone and abandoned than I ever expected it to. Most problems I shared were about the bullying and hard schoolwork. I cried and complained about how mean the kids were and how I couldn't make it another year with them. I might have even said I'd rather die than be in 8.1 the next school year. I liked Mr. Wilson. It felt good to have a good man take time out for me. Never mind it was Mr. Wilson's job to listen to me, I liked having a father figure there for me and help me work through my emotions. It made me feel like I mattered.

Luckily for me, unlike a lot of ladies that have been sexually abused, I knew some really great guys. I wasn't afraid of all men, only bad guys. I had no reservations about talking to men or anything like that. Someone said once that since I had no fear of talking to men, I was probably an attention seeker and would sooner or later blame any man I talked to for some sort of indecent act. I wasn't looking for attention and I didn't accuse anyone else ever. The only two men I ever said molested or abused me are Brad and Lester. No one else has done anything so vile, so wrong, so disgusting. I was hyper vigilant and always on the look-out for men like that because of them, but there were no others. My male teachers kept relationships professional, doctors, and men at the church, in town, anywhere were safe and good. No one else did to me what those two did. Like so much of my life, I put them into their own evil box of badness in my psyche. It freed the rest of me up to accept that most men were good... But still, I kept my eyes open for the bad ones.

Mr. Wilson, like most men, was a good guy and he set me up to appreciate counseling for the rest of my life. I was safe in his room hung with pictures of Yosemite, Snoqualmie and Zion National parks in shiny black, plastic frames. Sometimes I got lost in the nature scenes and wondered if Vickie-Jean would agree with the lighting or angle. Sometimes we talked about stuff I was supposed to keep inside. It was a relief to purge bad feelings, and vomit them out, and away from inside me. I couldn't admit what the rages made me do to myself. I knew I was out of control and if Mr. Wilson knew about them he would have had to tell someone to keep me safe, it was in his disclosure statement. So I kept the rages a secret, lied about the scabs when he noticed them at the fringes of my shorts, and never spoke of Brad or Lester for fear I would get yelled at the way I had at the first disclosure.

I wish the counseling would have kept others safe from me, but alas, broken people break others and I, as I had done before, found a victim and destroyed her. I tried everything I could think to do first to avoid being a bully; but I couldn't move, I couldn't change schools, I couldn't leave my grade-level assignment. I remembered before how the deflection worked. It seemed like finding someone else for them to target was my only option. I needed someone equal to me, ripe for the 7.1 tribe's picking, close enough to catch attention within their peer group. Before the snow melted, I found my mark... Bianca the buxom beauty.

CHAPTER 41

WHAT TURNED THE girls' attention away from me was gossip, and I was skilled in the art of rumor-making. If a lot of church gossip could tear grown women down; I figured a little could make mean girls forget all about me. I didn't intended to ruin Bianca, only to deflect negative energy that had been aimed at me onto someone else. The Bible says, gossip is like a sweet morsel that goes into the inmost being, and it's the truth. Gossip is the bell that can't be unrung, the lightning strike that starts fire season, the bad apple in the bin... All I had to do was say one little thing.

Bianca Guerro was one of the most developed girls in middle school. She was also smart, flirty, bi-lingual and beautiful; she was a perfect mark. Socially speaking, Bianca was barely further up the hierarchy than me. Her family was well off, especially among the Hispanic population. She wore trendy clothes and she was graceful, not awkward. She was nice too, talked to everyone from 7.1 to 7.8, she even talked to me. I should have made friends with her. She could have been a friend but I made her a victim. She had a flaw I could easily exploit. Bianca told fantastic stories; stories that were too far-fetched to be true and everyone knew it. To her face everyone smiled and nodded and participated in the conversation, but behind her back I heard the other 7.1 girls question the veracity of her stories. Did her dad really know the president, or whoever else she was bragging about? Did her mom really travel to exotic places? Was she really in Cancun the two months she missed school the year before? She said she saw the most amazing things, went to the most glamorous places and it really seemed like she told lies about how great life was for her. And she also had the most amazing stories about other girls. She was a little rumor mill herself and "swore" she saw So-and-so kissing the skuzzy boy, or heard that Such-and-such's mom was on drugs. Who knows, maybe her dad really did know the president, or she really had seen some of what she made up. I was good at mimicking so I impersonated her in front of the other kids before she got to class or the lunch table. The other girls would giggle because we all knew how far-fetched some of her stories were. It was a simple ease in.

They listened to me and didn't make fun of me. Like I had done before with Gail, I used Bianca as my outlet. I didn't think about her feelings or her life in middle school. I was miserable every day and instead of appreciating one of the girls that was nice to me, at least to my face, I used her. Sensationalism got the best of me; I had to keep upping the ante to keep from losing their attention and falling down socially again. I planned huge monologues pretending to be her, I put cups under my shirt in the cafeteria and sauntered around pretending to be her. Whenever we saw her coming, everyone acted normal, but I'm sure she knew.

It seemed to me that Bianca' stories got more fantastic the more I made fun of her behind her back. Like raging was for me, telling stories must have been her coping technique, but the more sensational she got, the more fuel she added to the fire. All the while, to her face I played nice, even talked to her more than I had before to hear her stories so I could imitate and humiliate her socially. I was aware that what I was doing to Bianca was mean, hurtful and absolutely wrong; but I was an evil sinner so what else could I do but be evil and sin? Middle school was horrible for me because of the very things I was doing to her and yet I persisted. More than that, I pre-meditated the mean things I would do and say about her. Probably part of the reason I only had one close friend and was so picked-upon was because I was a mean girl too and no one wanted to get close to me.

The bullying went on through spring and into the warmer days that signaled the school year ending. I felt like I needed a finale to keep Bianca the target in the mean girls' minds through the summer. I decided we all ought to write her hate mail, pre-cyber bullying. I told the 7.1 girls my plan and recruited a few more outside our class to write letters too. There was no shortage of volunteers. We ganged up on her. Fifteen or more mean girls wrote mean letters and plotted the day to give Bianca her hate mail. I collected all the letters and after we laughed about them at lunch for a few days we put them in a giant yellow manila envelope. Another girl put the envelope on Bianca's math class desk during our passing period. I didn't see her face when she read the letters. I can only imagine how badly it hurt her.

The principal came around to each and every classroom later that week and told us all about a horrible act that had been perpetrated. He was careful not to go into detail, but worded the lecture in such a way that all of us involved knew what incident he referred to. We didn't have an all-school assembly scheduled so we could learn the horror of bullying, there was no simulation to experience how it felt. All we got was a group of disappointed adults, administrators and teachers lecturing us for the rest of the week about how wrong and mean bullying was and how anyone involved owed a sincere and repentant apology to the offended student.

No one called me out specifically, but I knew the adults disapproved of the behavior. Their disappointment gave me pause and made me think. I was the source of Bianca's pain. It was the first time I thought about Bianca's feelings. Up to that point, what I had done to her was all about diverting attention away from me. With every lecture, I felt a little more ashamed of what I'd done to Bianca until the shame overwhelmed me. I was guilty. I was wrong. I was sorry. I knew I needed to repent.

Without fanfare or consulting the other mean girls, I took the long, shiny waxed linoleum walk to the office alone and turned myself in. Teachers and office staff were talking about how terrible the incident it was and how mean girls could be to each other while I waited at the counter. The principal noticed me and asked who I needed. I broke down, I cried, and confessed my sins to the god of the school. I told him, right there at the reception counter that I was the mastermind behind the hate mail. His face looked like Mom's when I told her Lester had touched me. He didn't believe me. Then his face changed again, to utter disappointment, "It was you?" he asked and walked away shaking his head.

I don't remember any discipline, don't know why he asked that question to me the way he did and don't ever remember anything more about the incident. I tried to apologize to Bianca, but what could I say after hurting her so badly? It didn't seem enough to tell her I knew what I did was mean and horrible and that no matter how big and ridiculous her stories were, she didn't deserve to be treated like that and that I was sorry. Five letters strung together to make a bad situation better. She needed more than 'sorry', she needed it to never have happened. She needed me to pay for being mean. I needed me to pay. I wanted punishment for her sake. I wanted to be in trouble so she could know the wrong had been made right. I got nothing, and 'sorry' wouldn't fix her heart.

Turns out I was the mountain lion in the tree line and with that, seventh grade faded into a shameful memory.

CHAPTER 42

THAT HOT, DRY summer was much the same as the summer before it, except the family didn't have any amazing vacations to take without Gio and I. My days were busy and my pockets were usually always full, but I barely spent a dime. I was close, so close, to having enough money for the keyboard I wanted. I dreamed of the day it would be mine and started taking the bus to the music store once or twice a week to be sure the one I wanted was still there. I spent nights upstairs, alone in my own little corner of the loft, dreading another school year in Leavenworth. I didn't want to face the mean girls who haunted me and I simply couldn't face Bianca after what I'd done to her. I knew I had an easy solution. I could go to a brand new school and start fresh. I could move to Mom's. Gio, looking a little less boyish every time I saw him, still begged me to move with him. It should have been the answer I was looking for.

It was the first time I seriously considered the move. Vickie-Jean was horrible to live with and all the middle school drama made school an unsafe zone. It almost made Leavenworth worse than Lester. Almost. He was still too angry and sniveling and creepy. I couldn't do it, not for Gio, not to escape the mean girls, not even to avoid seeing Bianca. No matter what the next school year would bring me, Lester was worse. And so, summer turned like the leaves did and eighth grade changed everything.

Whether it was the hate mail or my begging Mr. Wilson to move me, I do not know but, they put me in 8.5; far, far away from my perceived tormentors and my victim. The move down made the rest of middle school bearable. I had a peaceful year with average kids, most of whom I knew: other shopkeeper's kids and church friends.

The school work was easier, but the boys and girls asked questions if they didn't understand the problems. They didn't just "know" the way to do things like the smart kids did; they learned to do things. They liked having the teacher teach them, and so did I. They were more relaxed too. They didn't worry so much about who was the best at each sport or which brand was most popular to wear.

They accepted me for me as long as I accepted them. I felt connected to them like I never had in 7.1. "We" were the 8.5 class. We had our classes and walked together in a sort of herd of average awkwards unlike the smarter kids who were mostly out for themselves, clustered into their cliques of three or five. It was easier to survive and stand up against them as a pack. And we never threw one of our own to them the way I'd done with Bianca. I stayed friends with Kate and hung with her at lunch and PE. The mean girls meant little to me that year.

Not surprisingly, music was my favorite class. We didn't compose anything but played the instruments we chose, or were assigned. I was assigned the piano because the music teacher, Ms. Bryant, knew my mom and knew I knew how to play. In class, I sometimes drifted into music moods like my mom. I didn't tune out the world completely, though, but I wanted to, and understood better than ever how she could fall into them. I'd get a melody in my head and get lost in the tones that danced like bouncing colors behind my closed eyes. I plunked along to the basic little songs we learned but when Ms. Bryant stopped us, I didn't want to. I was compelled to continue. It took all my self-control to stop, and even then she had to bark at me quite often, to reign me in.

A few weeks into the school year, she pulled me aside, "Gia, sweetie, I know you love to play the piano, and you're good at it, but you're not the only one in class. You have to stop when I call the class to attention. They don't know what you do and it's my job to teach them. If you want to play, come in early, the school doors open at seven o'clock, and the room will be all yours. You can play away then, and in class you can be a part of the class, OK?" I agreed and the music room soon became another little corner; the bench, my own little chair. Tucked inside alone, in the morning, before children filled the building and roamed the halls like ants, I could create happiness, sadness, anger and rage. Yes, even rage and it sounded like fingers on keys, not nails on skin. I barely raged at all on myself that year, although the piano took a grave beating, as did the Yamaha keyboard I bought brand new from the Strings and More Music Store in Wenatchee with my mom sometime in July.

I tried to write my own sonata and fancied myself to be like one of the greats. It was nothing like my favorite sonata in C major by Mozart, the most famous of all young composers. Mine was a dark and glorious thing more like Beethoven's Moonlight sonata, full of low tones and high runs. It reminded me of Ichabod Crane's midnight ride away from the headless horseman and other frightful things that happened in the night time in closets and on stairwells.

It was easy to remember how it all went together at first, as if the notes themselves told me how they should be arranged, but the more I added, the harder it was to keep it all straight. Once I was sure the first movement sounded on the piano the way it sounded in my head, I figured I had better put it down on paper before I forgot. The second movement, like the first, came to me without effort, but I wanted to record it for all time and humanity exactly as it appeared in my mind. Because I kept looking at the notes for what to play, instead of listening to the music in my head, I never fully memorized each movement, but rather read along with the music the way one would sing with a song on the radio.

Like everything that made me, me, I hid my sonata from the world. It was the grandest of all my secrets. I was terrified that people wouldn't believe in it the way I did. I wanted it to be a masterpiece, but knew I was a messed up kid and couldn't possibly compose anything great at such a young age. I was no Mozart. I played and wrote my music when I knew no one else would bother me. I couldn't risk anyone telling me this thing, this extension of who I was, this horrible, wonderful composition of sound and sentiment was anything but okay just the way it was. It should have been my secret forever, but someone found me out and refused to pretend that my sonata didn't exist.

CHAPTER 43

PAUL INGERSOLL SAT behind me in almost every class, and by default we came to know each other as the year progressed. As it had with Kate, familiarity bred comfort not contempt in our case. I can't say that I liked him, because I didn't. I didn't like any real boys after the scary dream about DJ and besides that, he wasn't attractive to me. I'm sure, though, if he'd have pursued me in his dark and mysterious way, I could have started to like him; but he never did, so neither did I. He had a gloomy, quiet, foreboding personality. He didn't talk much, wore lots of black and Heavy Metal band shirts, liked chains and heavy combat boots and drew gloriously grotesque pictures of skulls and zombies. His art and dress looked a lot like what I felt inside.

I had an obsessive habit of looking over my sonata sheet music before classes started to be sure it read the way it was supposed to sound. He looked over my shoulder in math class, got too uncomfortably close to my ear, and asked me what the notes meant. I told him I was writing a sonata and slammed my spiral shut, embarrassed to be caught.

"Nice. What's a sonata?"

"It's like a song for musical instruments. You don't sing it, you play it."

"How do you write that?"

"With musical notes..." My heart flipped inside my chest. I wanted to show him, or someone, what I'd been working on, but I didn't dare to risk the exposure. I kept my notebook shut, my secret sonata safe.

He was one of the kids that picked up music easily. Ms. Bryant had him on guitar, because like I already knew the piano, he already knew guitar. I thought it suited his personality quite naturally. He knew how to read music but admitted he'd only ever played what someone else had written. It never occurred to him that someone he knew could write original music. He believed in me. He thought I could write a sonata and wanted to know more about it. I told him about the mornings in the music room and he came more than a few times to listen to me play and work out the movements. Sometimes I listened to him play whatever radio song he was working on imitating. Mostly, though, he came and listened to me, never criticizing or praising; simply listening, accepting, taking the sonata and me as we were, not as we ought to be.

I played for him at church too. At night, when the world of accordions and tourists dreamed, we broke into the AG of LV and I defiled the piano with my non-Christian sonata. The baby grand at Gramp's church sounded so much better than the upright at school. We didn't have to stop for classes, we could play as long as we wanted. Twice that was nearly to dawn on Friday nights; so late I did my paper route before going to bed. Those two pre-dawn paper deliveries, Paul walked with me. If ever Austen's Mr. Darcy did live outside of her imagination, it might have been in young Paul Ingersoll, only he never professed his love.

He shared my sonata secret and encouraged it. We broke into the church together. I had a partner in crime. He never ratted me out, the way Gio did. He never picked fights with me either. He liked to listen to my work and I very much liked to write for an audience; even if it was only made up of one sullen eighth grade boy. I loved having someone want what only I could give. Every time he asked if he could meet me early at school or we could sneak into the church, he was telling me I mattered to him. He wanted me, and every time I played for him, I was giving myself to him, trusting him with my most intimate parts. It was never romantic or sexual back then. Maybe he liked me and couldn't say so for some unknown reason. But I like to think I filled some need inside him the way he did for me.

We never talked about much more than the music we shared, but Paul will forever be one of my heroes for two very important reasons, one of which happened several months after our secret, silent friendship bloomed. The other, not until years later, and ought to be saved for a different place in my story. In eighth grade, he saved me from every prepubescent girl's worst nightmare.

CHAPTER 44

SINCE FIFTH GRADE, girls had been getting their periods. Halfway through eighth grade, I was still bloodless. I wondered if I was a freak. It seemed like every girl but me had started to bleed. I stopped expecting it. I figured that maybe I was a boy with girl parts, afterall, everyone always said Gio and I were so much alike. Somehow, along the way I adopted the idea that I wouldn't ever get a period. It explained a lot actually, why I never really clicked with girls the way they seemed to click with each other, why I preferred throwing newspapers to babysitting, why I didn't make sense to anyone. I never talked to anyone about body issues, I came to the conclusion on my own.

I don't remember any cramps or hints I was about to become a "woman," it just happened, and Paul saved the day. We were leaving English class, and for some reason he walked right behind me... I mean *right* behind me. My first thought was that he was going to tell me something private, so I turned to face him but he told me to keep walking. Paul wasn't much of a talker so we didn't converse while we walked down the hall but, he stayed right behind. I trusted him and obeyed his directive but I was so confused. Was he going to tell me he liked me? Was it his way of letting me know? Or maybe he had a knife and was going to stick me? Maybe he liked the way my hair smelled? Maybe he was messing with me like Gio would have? I didn't know what was going on and he wouldn't tell me anything. It was the longest three minute walk of my life.

He herded me toward the girl's bathroom, with a protective, strangely pleasant hand at my waist. My body shivered at his touch. He took off his grungy flannel and handed it to me as we approached the door, and told me to go to the bathroom. I was befuddled, I didn't have to go and told him so.

"Go to the bathroom Gia," he insisted. His expression left no room for argument. I didn't know if he was going to follow me or what. Maybe my dream with DJ wasn't DJ after all but Paul. I obeyed, despite the fear and other feelings stirring inside me.

I walked into a stall, hung his flannel on the chrome door hook, unbuttoned, unzipped, sat myself down on the toilet seat and I saw what his fuss was all about. My parts were right after all. I was a woman. My dear friend Flow had come at last. There was blood; dull, dark, and not at all like what I expected, soaking through my underwear and into my pants. It would have been clearly visible as I bent to get my bag off the floor. Paul saw it and saved me from another year of mortal embarrassment. I understood the reason for his flannel suddenly and with gusto embraced the new grunge fashion movement. I finished off the day with toilet paper stuffed in my underwear and Paul's shirt wrapped tightly around my waist. We never talked about it. He never made fun of me for it. He simply thanked me when I gave him back his washed flannel the next morning.

Although it shouldn't have been, feminine hygiene was another cross I carried alone. I couldn't possibly call my Mom from school and risk someone hearing. Vickie-Jean, Nonna, Aunt Maria and Dad were non-options, because they were working and because none of them ever talked to me about it anyway. I didn't want to be the one to bring it up. I was on my own. On the way home I stopped at Dan's and prayed the cashier wasn't Jonathan, the usual guy, but one of the ladies instead. I grabbed the smallest box of tampons I could find, thinking of concealment more than anything. I figured the less evidence I had to deal with the better for me to keep my secret. It was Charity at the counter, not Jonathan. My heart was pounding, my eyes darted left and right as she put the box in a bag. I grabbed savagely and shoved it, with dramatic flair, into my backpack and rushed out of the store sure the whole world had seen my purchase.

My next stop was the library on Highway Two. I had no clue how to get a tampon inside me but I knew there were books on everything. I hoped they had at least one on women's issues because

I had officially become a woman ... and I had issues! I found what I needed and I read it in the aisle, flipping to a dog-eared page on hair care when anyone else came near. I gleaned everything I could and replaced it on its shelf, checked-out a Nancy Drew mystery, and went home to shove a plug, not a finger, into a place that a baby could now come out of.

It was horrible trying to figure out how to get that thing up inside me without eliciting a gross fuzzy-kind of pain. It wouldn't go in, no matter how hard I pushed or shoved, the stupid thing wouldn't fit. I read the pamphlet in the box but it didn't help with placement at all; but I worried for months after that I was getting TSS. Finally, with much pain and frustration and two wasted tampons, I got one to stay. I contemplated pads because of the pain but there was too much waste, and I couldn't risk my parents knowing I had started my period so I struggled through months of pain and difficulty until I realized the most wonderful fact about the feminine body. A vaginal canal rests at a forty-five degree angle when standing! The pictures in that library book showed it the whole time, but like a convoluted math problem I couldn't see the parts clearly. Forty-five degrees. It wasn't straight-up ninety degrees. I'd been trying to push the tampon 'up,' but 'in' was much more appropriate. Once I figured that out, all I had to worry about was making sure my regular monthly flow was anticipated and how to dispose of the evidence. Everything worked itself out in sweet time and only Paul ever knew my period had come.

CHAPTER 45

CHURCH, LIKE WAKING in the morning, like throwing papers, like hearing the piano every time I thought of my mom was part of me. I had to go. Sunday wasn't Sunday without church, neither was Wednesday or other days when events were planned and I was expected to go with Nonna, or be in my room when the parents shut down the shop.

Church had little to do with actually knowing Jesus. Jesus was a name I said (but never in vain, God forbid) to fit in and stay up late. Jesus was a guy whose admirable life and death and resurrection were the focus of talk at church. I always fit in at church because I was Gramps' and Nonna's grand-daughter so I liked it there despite the condemnation. I talked the talk, like any sports fan can talk all they want about their favorite player's stats. I could speak it and I knew the facts, the plays, the history of Team Jesus, but I never personally met the Man or the God. Church was never more than something routine to do and somewhere safe to go to socialize and be a part of a group.

Our church was remodeled in the early eighties with a Bavarian facade, to fit into the Leavenworth theme. Age itself had settled into the basement cinder block walls. It announced its presence in cold, whispered drafts of moldy dampness mixed with subtle undertones of earth, coffee and paint; always leaving the impression of age and longevity. Except for the baby grand on the stage, that long-gone smelly basement is the place I remember best. The Assemblies of God had a Wednesday night program they used to call *Royal Rangers and Missionettes.* I don't know what came first the Boy & Girl Scouts of America or the AG Royal Rangers and Missionettes but the idea behind both were basically the same. What was different was the major element of scripture memorization and AG indoctrination we got on Wednesday nights. *All have sinned and fallen short of the glory of God*, reminded me over and over how bad, evil, stupid, naughty, dirty, wrong and dumb I was. I liked being around the kids and because the church group was smaller, I enjoyed church much more as a social event than school. There were too many kids at school with too many friends to keep track of. I was a mark for bullying at school, people considered me weird, but there at church, even if I was as awkward as ever, I was one of the regulars, which, by default, made me fit in. All I had to do was show up all the time and I belonged and I was accepted.

Especially after Gio left, church was a safety zone away from Vickie-Jean's malice and school's stresses. It was a predictable schedule of pre-planned events. Dad and Vickie-Jean only went on Wednesday and Sunday nights in the off season. I went to church every Sunday, morning and night and Wednesday too. Nonna, the chauffeur came around and gathered up me, Martin, Alex, cousins Billy and Andy and even drove way down to Wenatchee for Gio, unless it was horribly snowy. Good old Nonna, always persnickety, but the most faithful of fuddy-duddies, would make the trek down to Wenatchee on Saturday nights and get Gio. She also used the time for "big shopping" in the big city, because there were many things our Little Leavenworth town didn't have. Gio always stayed with our grandparents, never again in the loft, and was always in the car when Nonna came around bright and early on Sundays for the rest of the Gianelli crew. Sometimes, if I was still out throwing papers and missed the ride, I had to meet up with them at Nonna's house.

The boys and I stayed with Nonna and Gramps most all day on Sundays and rode with Nonna to take Gio back home before the evening service started. Seat belts were a nice idea back then, but they weren't required and so most days the five or six of us climbed up and down the back seat of her Cadillac. Nonna played her Jesus tapes, we sang along, and before we knew it, we were at church or Canyon Number Two dropping Gio off! Aunt Maria had Billy and Andy go home with her after church, but Nonna dropped Martin, Alex and I off late at the loft. She and Gramps, captains of the AG of LV ship, were always the last to leave. After all the long talks and whisper conversations died away, after the last parishioner hugged or hand-shook good-bye, after the church was dark and quiet and my parents were already in bed, the three of us made our way up the evil stairs and into our respective beds.

Missionettes met on Wednesday evenings and though I memorized the entire Preamble to the US Constitution with a hundred percent accuracy, I never did well memorizing verses at church. I only earned one badge. I guess I didn't have it in me to memorize how good Christians were supposed to be because I already knew I wasn't good. I knew what I had already done, and had been forced to do, disqualified me. I was a whore. I was a fool. I was a liar. I was already going to hell. I knew what I was capable of, the meanness inside me was getting worse every day and the rage growing within made for a bad, bad person. To memorize reminders of how bad I was inside would have put me over the edge. There was no room to store verses from the Bible in my evil mind. Nonna made me feel bad enough with her *tsking*, to have it coming from inside as well.

In spite of the guilt and shame, church was more like home to me than any house had ever been. People, kids, "friends," and acquaintances came and went because of the natural ebb and flow of life in a tourist town, but the building never changed. People in church said God didn't change either. Whether that was true or not, at least I knew the rules and religion, the motions and the emotions were consistent. I knew the songs and the behaviors that went with church. I even knew lots of the Bible, which I read compulsively, obsessively every morning after my paper route. I had to read three chapters a day. Had to, like the imaginary "mowing" of the side of the road. It was the law in my head and I could not turn from it.

I suppose cliques existed at church, but I fancy Gramps' church was more like the .5 gang. There was an "us against wickedness" mentality but Gramps and Nonna treated anyone that came into church like one of "us." Sometimes the message was confusing. Nonna would tell us how horrid smoking was and if she ever found out we smoked it would be the end of us, but she would embrace Miss Chrissy, a chain smoker, that made her way to church once every couple months with never even a wrinkle of her nose. The bar she set for our family was unattainably high, but she never let her standards alienate anyone who wanted to visit.

CHAPTER 46

THEIR 'ALL ARE welcome' philosophy bred a culture of love and acceptance despite the whispers behind closed oak doors and fire and brimstone that bellowed from the pulpit. We really didn't have to live up to any social code of conduct at church. Sin was shunned but people were accepted. As awkward, unwanted and out of place as I felt everywhere else, it was a delight to fit in somewhere and still be able to be me. For whatever reason, there were no ".1" kids at our church. Maybe it was because Gramps and Nonna had as many impoverished minimum-wage workers and Latinos as affluent store owners that attended. Maybe the rich stalk those rich kids came from refused to lower themselves to mingling with "the help." Maybe they weren't the kind to go to church anywhere. I never did figure out quite why, but I was glad that church was safe from the Priscilla's of Leavenworth.

Through the years kids would fade in and out as their parents chose and then left the church for one reason or another, but there was a regular club of middle school church rats. Of course, me and Billy and Gio were perennials. Andy and Martin were barely old enough to count but because they were there as much as the rest of us, they were the tag-a-longs in our gang. Alex, a little Dennis the menace, was really too young to belong, but he somehow managed to make his presence known. There was Carlie, the assistant pastor's daughter, a favorite of mine because she was there so often and because she read the Bible too and together we could waste a whole hour of the sermon finding different naughty bits in the Bible.

My favorite were the metaphorical oral sex parts. I'd seen too much porn to miss the implication no matter how figurative the writer was trying to be. Sometimes it made me think that if it was in the Bible maybe it wasn't so bad. When Lester watched it, it felt wrong despite the arousal, but it didn't feel dirty in the Bible. It felt romantic. Solomon and his princess, lovely not lusty.

Carlie and her younger brother Kevin, went to the Christian school and she was naturally a good girl who truly loved the Lord, and the worst she ever did was sneak out at Preacher's Kid church camp to hold hands with a boy...she did get the first French kiss in our group. Our gaggle of girls consisted of three others; Hannah (not my sister at Mom's but a different Hannah), Ruth and Lupe. Doe-eyed Hannah was fairly regular. She, like me, has an imperfect childhood, not vanilla good like Max and Carlie. She was somewhat of a story teller too. Not as bad as Bianca, but we could tell when she exaggerated. Ruthie was younger and moved from the other side of the mountains. Once she started coming she was "in" because her personality was electric. She sought out companionship and attention. She was a sensationalist and seemed to be proud of it. Lupe, thin as a twig and surprise baby of her large, locally established, Latino family was totally spoiled and if I may say so, more "white" than any other Latina I knew. Sometimes I felt like she was ashamed of her family's heritage of orchard work, but they were good at it and well respected in the community. She became a best friend in high school. She was a .3 kid in middle school and tried desperately to fit in with the .1s. Our classes never really crossed and our opinions about the rich girls were too different at the time to bond us. She kept a cool distance from us all, but because of her parent's church involvement, she was a regular part of our overall group.

Max was part of the boys' club; his dad was an elder. Max was sweet, soft spoken, well-mannered, kind and gentle and always included everyone. I don't ever remember him angry or upset. The regular girls would take turns having a crush on him because he was the most desirable and attractive of the bunch of boys. Max must have also been wise because I don't remember him ever "going out" with any of the girls. He and Carlie had a grade school boyfriend/girlfriend thing, but as middle schoolers we all knew it didn't count. My boys, Billy and Gio and little tag-a-longs Martin, Andy and Alex made the majority of the boys club but weren't the only ones. There was another boy, Stan, with piercing hazel eyes, who hung out but was really into God. His older sister, Tandy was too. She even had a Bible group at the high school. I tried to get into the Bible group in high school, but by then I was traveling down a path I couldn't take the church lifestyle into so I didn't participate long.

Stan was focused on God. Jesus was more than a Bible character to him. Stan knew God. It confused me how he could always be so serious about his faith. Stan had a bad heart and had the neck to belly button scar on his chest to prove it. He was convinced he was only alive because Jesus gave him another chance at life when he got a new heart from an organ donor. He had to be more careful than the rest of us, but that didn't keep him off the basketball courts. He and Tandy loved sports almost as much as God. Their enthusiasm made God seem more real to me but I never quite connected with Stan or Tandy personally.

Some other kids breezed in and out of the church group too. I think Mario would have been one of us...if he'd lived. He went to Royal Rangers and Sunday school sporadically when we were younger. What I remember most about him was that his skin was a rich, even chocolate brown, much darker than most Latinos. He was not a light-skinned Mexican, he was a deep, dark brown; closer to his Native Central American ancestry than the light conquistadors that mingled with them. He had no blemishes, no sunburns, no freckles or imperfections, just fine, brown with a pink tongue and white palms. His skin reminded me of the dark blacks in the Deep South, but wasn't that dark. I liked to look at him because he was beautiful to behold. I did not like to play with him. He was too much like Gio, goofed around, annoyed people, called too much attention to himself with his antics, and eventually he got himself killed.

Mario's parents were Mexican immigrants that had settled in Leavenworth. They, with his grandmother, grandfather and several extended family members, moved from a Wenatchee apartment complex to a nice, large, fixer-upper house in the residential neighborhood Gramps and Nonna lived in. Mario, was big city, fresh from Wenatchee. I don't think he ever actually ran with a gang, but he implied it, and wore Raiders garb to make his point. He got in fights with other boys a lot. He especially liked to argue with a boy named Juan, a pale Mexican. Almost every day the two of them would holler at each other on the bus ride to middle school. One day Juan jumped Mario as he was getting off the bus at our stop by Nonna's. Juan had brought a bike chain and wrapped it around Mario's neck.

The fight broke out right in front of my bus seat. Again, like with Vickie-Jean beating Gio, I watched, frozen but couldn't process what to do. What I focused on was not the chain around Mario's throat, marring that beautiful skin of his, but the part that Juan had wrapped around his hands. It was biting into his fingers and making him bleed too. Kids started howling and cheering or crying or trying to stop them and there I sat, stiff as a statue; paralyzed but taking it all in. The bus driver ran back and broke up the fight. He had Mario get out with all of us kids that used that stop and kept Juan on the bus, in the front seat, after he confiscated the bike chain. Mario was okay, bruised and bleeding around the neck, but okay.

Maybe that near death experience was what brought him to church regularly, but he came all the time after that. It was hard to tell how much God stuff was getting through to him though because he was so active. He could not sit still and had the rest of us looking at him and not the youth leader more often than not. I'm sure, if he had been around longer he would have become one of us but I can't imagine how his dynamic personality would have changed the group. And we never had the opportunity to find out. Mario never grew up, never grew old, never settled down. He died, like he lived, drawing attention to himself.

CHAPTER 47

OUR LITTLE TOWN was full of rivers and bridges to take risks on and jumps off. The "safe" bridge to jump from was a local summertime favorite hangout on Blackbird Island. We knew it wasn't recommended. We could all read the sign that clearly said jumping wasn't allowed, but we all did it anyway. The water was deep and a pastor from one of the other churches often stood on the side encouraging kids to jump. It was enough to get our adrenaline pumping, but not risky enough to be a real threat. Further up the Icicle River, where the pools and eddys swirled deep and dark, it was much more dangerous. There were no warning signs up there because it was pretty much common sense that kayaks were the only thing that should be plunging into the river's depths. Mario didn't get the hint. The story goes that he bet a couple of buddies that he could jump into, and out of, one of the deep pools while they were fishing one summer day. Well, he made the jump in, but never came out... never came up. The other boys freaked out but eventually got a city vacationer in a summer cabin to call 911. The search took two days. When they found his body it was mangled and mutilated by rocks. The life of the boy with beautiful dark skin over, like the astronauts' lives.

Dad took me to the funeral that Gramps performed. I had my collection of serial killer articles and had seen dead bodies under sheets in some of them. I'd watched killings and seen fake, dead bodies on Mom and Lester's scary movies, I'd been to other funerals; but Mario was the first real dead person I actually identified with. I wanted to go more to see his dead body than to say good-bye. The closed casket opened my mind to imagine how badly the rocks and rapids tore him up. Water was fierce, we knew this living where rivers converged, but the danger had never been so real. We were allowed to go up to the casket to pay final respects, and like many, I went forward. What I never realized about my church mate was that he was a son and a student, a nephew and grandson as well as a wily church kid. I stood there staring at his most recent school picture perched on top of the mahogany casket, imagining his body beneath... soulless, lifeless.

Heaven or hell?

Then my dad was at my shoulder, pulling me through the line and I snapped into reality again. Mario's aunt was behind me bawling and all of a sudden I heard her. She asked God, "Why?" in Spanish. Though I was not fluent, I could understand enough of her words because of Nonna's Italian and growing up with so many Hispanics in the town, "My poor baby! Aye! Such a sweet boy! Why God, why?" She was talking to God and it was sad talk, not at all nicey nice like church prayers for His favor or help, but a desperate cry for an answer.

The answer was simple. He died because he was stupid. He jumped into rapids. It was foolhardy; what did anyone expect but death? But she had a point. Obviously God didn't make him do it but why hadn't God stopped it? God could have sent an angel, or a big strong wind gust to blow him back from the edge. Shoot, He could have inspired one of the other boys to pull Mario back from the rock. Yeah God, why?! I wanted to know why God allowed it too. All of a sudden, I wanted to know why God let any bad stuff happen. Why did He let bad people, like Brad, be born? Mario's aunt said what I never realized I wanted to say, "Why, God, why?"

After Mario died, Denny, the assistant pastor, talked to the entire congregation the next Sunday. He said, with tears in eyes and quiver in his voice that he truly believed Mario was in heaven. I found it hard to believe a person who always disrupted Sunday School, who instigated fights, and picked on people, could make it to heaven. Of course, I found it hard to believe anyone but pastors and their picky wives could make it in. I figured we were all screwed up in some way—even the good kids had to have their faults, except maybe Stan, Tandy, Max, and Carlie. I didn't know how to believe Denny when I knew the stuff Mario did. It was fluffy church comfort. It was the stuff church people always said to make themselves feel better inside after a tragic event. How did Denny know if Mario was in heaven? He didn't have a number to call and confirm that. How did I know he didn't make it? Who could possibly know where Mario's essence, if he had one after death, went? Saying he went to heaven was the same as a piece of candy from Gramps' pocket. It was sweet, nothing more. It wasn't the truth, it didn't fix the situation, it was nothing more than a sweet gift to give people. No one could possibly know who got into heaven, or if heaven was even there. Mario was dead, because he was stupid, and God didn't stop it, and that's all any of us could be sure of.

The winter after that, during a Sunday evening service, Gramps ran up on stage as Denny preached and whispered in his ear. The message shook Denny so badly his knees gave out and I watched Carlie's dad slump to the ground in front of our eyes. Gramps tried to keep him from falling but he couldn't. Max's dad ran up on stage too and got Denny to his feet. Gramps took the mic and announced the news to us all. Carlie, Kevin and their mom had been in a terrible accident on their way to church and the kids were in grave condition.

It was common for the pastors to be at the church before the wives and Carlie's mom was famous for being late. That night had been no different. Denny left to teach Sunday night service, like he did every Sunday night, and fully expected his wife and children to follow behind. Max's dad took Denny out of the sanctuary and we all began to pray for the assistant pastor's family. We all prayed, and maybe I really did try to talk to God that time. I asked like everyone else was for them to be okay, and to heal fast. I have no idea how Gramps finished the service that night. My friend was near death and the only thing I could do was pray to a God I really didn't know.

The news came later that Carlie actually died instantly after being ejected from the car, and seven-year-old Kevin was critically wounded. Another kid dead; another, "Why?" And then, "Why them and not me?" I had a horrible life I wanted desperately to escape; but Carlie had a good life, good, loving parents, happy, no-closet memories. She was good and kind and loved Jesus. Why did she have to go and I stay and live one grueling day after another? I didn't want to live, any God in heaven knew that. It wasn't about "going home," as Christians were in the habit of saying, it was about escaping the memories of Brad and dealing with Lester and Vickie-Jean, Nonna, getting everything wrong all the time, and feeling unimportant and broken and mean and being a general disappointment to God and the human race. I was tired of living, I would have gladly gone, and Carlie was the kid that died. Astronauts with promise and students watching them perished. Kids with parents and aunts crying over their deaths jumped to their demise, and I remained. It was unfair.

CHAPTER 48

CARLIE'S FUNERAL, LIKE Mario's, was in the church we grew up in together, and her reception was in the basement that smelled like age. I wanted to go but would have had no choice in the matter if I didn't want to. She was church family. I was obligated to pay final respects. Again, I wanted to go more to see her than to say good-bye I suppose. We lined up for the viewing and time slowed down the way it had when Lester's fingers explored me. I couldn't have been standing in front of her for more than a minute or two, but I memorized every single thing about her, because I knew it was the last time. She was dead, she was no more, her body was all that remained. Her hair was curled fashionably but she never wore it that way while she lived. Then I remembered the whisper that she'd almost been decapitated. Her neck was barely visible under all the hair. They'd positioned her head on the pillow awkwardly and I imagined I could see a decapitation line, but couldn't be sure.

She was dressed in her Easter dress from the year before. She despised that dress. If she were alive to have had a say in it, she would have begged her mother to let her wear anything but that dress. I wanted to stay with her. I wished I would have called her to come early to church with her dad. I wished I'd spent more time with her and gotten to know her better. I wished she wasn't dead. But she was, and all the wishing and praying in the world wouldn't change how dead she was.

Denny and Carlie's mom were granted an extended leave of absence to be with Kevin at Children's hospital in Seattle. The church continued to pray regularly in corporate prayer for Kevin and for comfort for the family. Updates and praises about his progression started to become one of the regular things to pray about. I got bored of listening to how Kevin was going to be better, even though his sister was dead. Everyone else must have gotten bored too because before long we stopped praying for the family altogether. Kevin had recovered, but the family decided to move to the Seattle side of the mountains. Like Gio's it was a move to avoid pain.

I got bored of prayer a lot. It wasn't talking to God to me, it was going on and on to a questionable being I couldn't see who killed kids who should live and let kids live who wanted to be dead. It was a way to say corporately things we wanted other people to hear but pretend we were saying it to God. People at church could pray for what felt like hours. They would go on and on in their eccentric Pentecostal way. Most of the time we middle schoolers would start with our heads bowed and eyes closed, but as the hype and "Spirit" stirred up, we giggled to each other and passed notes back and forth. The gaping hole Carlie left slowly stitched up, sewing her into the fabric of our minds, accepting she would not go forward with us any longer.

The "Spirit" moved a lot in our Pentecostal pews. The movements, like in a sonata, could be so different, one from another. Some were, literally, laugh out loud funny and more than a few of us kids would have to cover our mouths to keep from letting the laughter out… unless the Spirit was moving us all to laugh, then we joined in the laughter. Sometimes the Spirit moved scary-like, and people spoke out hell-fire condemnation against our nation or another nation or type of people. Other times, when the Spirit moved them, the church got all wired up, drunk as any person I'd ever seen come out of the tents at Oktoberfest, only without the beer to do it to them. If enough people in the church group caught on to a song or a feeling, the whole of the church would ride the wave. The idea was that God, in spirit form, was churning around in the air like a wind. It didn't make sense to me, any more than seeing grown men paint their faces or wear cheese hats for their favorite team did. Whether on TV at football games or in the church pews, it unsettled me to see grown-ups who were well-spoken and normal turn into swaying, hand-raising, sycophants.

It was quite common for people to "speak in tongues" at church. This phenomena was supposed to be a gift from God, the Holy

Spirit, and if a person was given the gift they could instantly speak a different language. The first time it was reported to have happened was after Jesus went up to heaven, after rising from the dead. A lot of his followers were hiding out in a room praying and the Holy Spirit, the Comforter, God the invisible, blew into the room like a great rushing wind. The Spirit ignited like flames on top of their heads and they spoke in different languages. The followers were in a populous city where lots of different languages were spoken. The tongues they miraculously spoke were foreign languages other people around them could understand. The Spirit used the gift to speak to a mass of people at once telling them who Jesus was and that he had risen from the dead.

The Bible story of tongues made sense to me; there was a point and a purpose and people needed to hear something in a language they could understand. It was clearly a miracle from a God who was more powerful, or technologically advanced, than the human race at that time. There was a wind, there was something like fire on people's heads, there were thousands of people who heard about God's Son in their own language and chose to follow Christ in that one day. *One day.*

In my church it happened all the time but I never felt the wind, saw fire or had anyone foreign in the church say they heard someone speak in their language. I heard people talk about people who'd had that happen, but it never happened when I was around. It didn't add up. It didn't seem like a God who was bigger than human trifling would waste time getting people all worked up an hour each week for no good reason. We weren't telling people about Jesus, we were hanging out together in our little building. It made no sense to me.

However bizarre some of their practices were, I was one of them and I participated. I sang the songs, I raised my hands, walked up to the alter steps in shame or awe depending on the movement. I got caught up in the moment more than anything. It didn't get me closer to a God I didn't know, but at least I looked the part and I don't think, with my background as a preacher's grandkid and church regular, anyone questioned if it was real; they all assumed I knew their God.

I even spoke in tongues. It was a special club, and I had to be forced into it, but I did it. I got my tongues at a church camp the year after Carlie died. She went every year but I'd only gone the year before; that's how I knew she snuck out with a boy and got her first French kiss. I paid for camp, like I paid for my keyboard, by myself, with my own money and I paid Billy to do my paper route while I was gone. I have never in my life felt as much peer pressure as I did at church camp. The goal was to get everyone to do it, and 'it,' was speaking in tongues. They said if we didn't, we were missing out. I read the Bible and never found where it taught that. I didn't like it the leaders told a room full of kids a lie and said it came from the Bible. But the pressure to perform, and please leaders, and conform to the culture around me was so strong, I played the part.

CHAPTER 49

MOST KIDS DRANK the kool-aid and spoke in tongues that first night. But, like the tongues in church, the tongues at camp weren't like any foreign languages I'd ever heard on the streets in Leavenworth. No one spoke the tongue of Italian or Spanish or any Roman language I could recognize. I never heard anything that sounded Japanese or otherwise oriental. There were no Russian tongues. It sounded like gibberish. When I questioned one of the leaders, he called them the tongues of angels. I thought they sounded like idiots and I didn't want to sound like that. I imagined it like the Bible story. I wanted to get a tongue and then find out there was a missionary from, say, Swaziland there who heard his own language. That would have made me believe, but that didn't happen, not once in all the thousands of times I personally heard people speaking in tongues. If there was no point to speaking a different gifted language, why must I have it?

The next night of church camp, the kids who spoke in tongues the first night were allowed to stay in with the main group. I don't know what they did because I was honest when the leaders asked who still hadn't received the gift. I raised my hand and they singled all us honest kids out. They ushered us to a different room, for more prayer to receive the gift. They brought in a special pastor and older high-school camp counselor kids who were "filled with the Spirit" (which, in AG talk, meant that they spoke in tongues—to the exclusion of all the other ways the Spirit could fill a person). They prayed for our poor souls. I think I had to go back the third night too.

The room was open, with a low ceiling; the preacher man stood on a small podium talking endlessly, telling us what we had to do to get the gift. We had to let go and allow the Spirit to move us. I tried, I really did. I'm not convinced even if I had known God then, if it would have been any easier for me. It wasn't working and I wanted to know what the other kids got to do while we had to pray to be filled.

There were a couple dozen of us at most who had yet to receive the gift… and admitted it. We didn't get to be together. Instead we were circled around by other Christian kids and staff members who were touching us, formally called, "laying on hands." Some touched the head, some the shoulders or back, but never anywhere else, that would break the church propriety laws. Others would speak over us in their special tongues from outside the touching circle. All of them were praying, swaying and crying to God to bequeath the gift onto the poor souls who hadn't yet received it. Breath, hot and sometimes nasty or minty depending on the person, bombarded me. Hands messed in my hair, sweat through the back of my shirt. A thick, meaty hand had a vice-grip at the side of my neck and shook me with the prayers of the owner. The pastor man kept saying it was a gift. God had already given it to us, all we had to do was open it. He analogized it like a parent who gave his kid a car the day he got his license. The kid accepted the car and the keys and kept thanking his parents for the gift but never put the key in to start the car. My key was in, my imaginary car was humming, but my mouth said only English.

After all the pressure and desire to fit in and not stand out among the church people too… and with all of the hype, and hearing one after another of the other late bloomers start belting out what had all the noise of nonsense, I began to make it myself: "Skinny marink a dink a dink, skinny marink a dooooo." Well, not really that but basically voicing imperceptible sounds. I made my mouth move and what seemed like baby babble came out. I felt nothing but the hype and the rush of pleasing the crowd around me. I didn't feel any closer to God and I was pretty confident there was no foreigner there who spoke baby babble. I was a liar and fraud, but so were they, so I did it and tried to convince myself it was really the gift.

Another thing about church started to bug me too. Even though Gramps and Nonna welcomed everyone, there was an air of exclusivity about the whole thing. Kind of reminded me of how mean girls behaved. As a church body, we were a big happy group of AG people and the church camps were full of kids from other AG churches. Our name brand was Assemblies of God and we had a logo, placards and rules for our club. There was no room in the AG way of knowing God for Baptists, Catholics, Foursquare, Methodists, AME, Presbyterian or any other one of the Christian denominations. The Assemblies of God was the only way, as if it didn't matter what the Bible said, unless we followed the Bible the AG way, even when their way didn't sound like what the Bible said (and I knew what the Bible said because I read it). If I wasn't doing it the AG way I wasn't doing Christianity right. Each brand kind of did the same thing. We all spoke tolerance, but we all knew our brand was best.

We all said we served the same God and that it was us, the whole church, against the spiritual forces of darkness in this world and spiritual realms but, why then didn't *we*, the people in the different churches, hang together? We made jokes about other denominations; we competed with other church's food banks to prove our people gave more. I wondered why we didn't work together and make a community food bank for all the needy instead of the needy in *our* church. It seemed to me, even in middle school, that the churches were messed up. Either that, or God was messed up, or people were making up their own stories and there was no God at all.

It was hard for me to believe there was no God because God had been preached as reality all my life. But if there was a God, why had He let Brad defile me? Why had He let my mom get together with Lester? Why did no one believe me about what he did? Why did the Challenger explode? Why did Carlie die? Why did Vickie-Jean beat Gio? Why was Gio so ornery? Why did Mario jump? Why didn't I like Vickie-Jean? Why did my mom have her moods? Why had I been mean to Melody, Gina and Bianca? Why did people who supposedly loved God not accept other people who claimed to also love God simply because of the church they went to? If there was a God, why were things the way they were? It was almost easier to *not* believe in God than to believe in one that sat back and let it all play out. And so my quasi-faith faded to black and was soon replaced with a new religion, the religion of harmony, hedonism, hormones and teen spirit.

CHAPTER 50

THE SUMMER BEFORE high school I had a change of heart where boys were concerned. Other than Kate and my make believe crushes on real or fantasy people, I'd never really been into boys. I was more like one of the guys than one to be infatuated with them. Besides, men scared me and boys were premature men in smaller clothes. I knew there were men who took what they wanted whether the girl wanted to give it or not. I knew it from Brad, and Lester and the movies, and in a way I even knew it from Dad. Hadn't he discarded Meredith and the other girlfriends when he was done with them? Men used women, and boys wanted to be men. I didn't want anything to do with them.

That was before puberty.

That summer, as I made my shop deliveries, I started to notice things about boys I never considered before. Maybe it started earlier, with Paul and the long walk to the bathroom, when he followed behind me, so close I could feel his warmth, when his hand touched my waist and that shivery, tingly thing happened. I'm not sure what triggered it but all of a sudden I liked boys. I liked their stature, especially the muscular ones that had strong lines my eyes could trace. I liked loud boys, troubled boys scared me, ornery boys annoyed me, quiet boys bored me, but the ones who were outspoken were fun to watch and tease.

I liked the way boys smelled. It was different, stronger, more brutish than girl smell. I liked it when they put on cologne to hide it. They weren't hiding anything; I could pick out their young man scent under the cologne, but most colognes somehow made it better. I wasn't a fan of certain musky colognes, though, and even the most attractive boy would turn my stomach if he smelled wrong. I've wondered if I disliked it so much because maybe it's what Brad used. After Gio moved away he started to socialize with new people in Wenatchee. He more than made up for my lack of social graces. He had a knack for making friends and meeting people and Mom and Lester had far less stringent rules about friends coming over. On a hot, humid, flash-flood Monday, the kind that caused the lightening to start the forests on fire, I rode the bus down to Wenatchee, and my bike up the canyon road and we had friends over to play games at the orchard house. I'd invited a same-aged girl who lived further up the canyon road named Laura to come over. We'd enjoyed a casual friendship over the years and Gio had quite the crush on her. Gio invited one of his friends, Titus.

I didn't recognize the set-up nearly as soon as the other three did. At first I was annoyed because Laura and Gio were way too friendly with each other. Gio was tickling her and she was giggling like an idiot—it annoyed me so much when girls did that. Then it occurred to me that my brother was a player and was making a move. I wondered when that had happened and how Laura could be falling for it. I couldn't believe it; it was so ridiculous. He was my brother, and he was one of the most annoying creatures on the face of the earth. How could anyone fall for him? Yuck!

Their little flirting game entertained me as we played a modified game of football around the trees until I realized Titus was totally making a move too. His game wasn't for Laura, it was for me! I hadn't really paid too much attention to him before he tackled me while we played and held me down a little too long. His body against me, on me, sweaty, brutish. His face near mine, bright green eyes searching my own. I laughed and shook myself from his grasp but looked back to smile at him before I ran to retrieve the football. For the first time in my life, other than in my solo moments of self-stimulation, I was aroused but not one bit afraid. It was the most exhilarating feeling of my life. Pure good, a rush of sweet, sexual tension with no anxiety. I was hooked! I knew in that moment why girls got boy-crazy. It wasn't scary or bad but... it was... addicting! As the afternoon wore on and the summer storm forced us inside, Gio's attentions focused more and more on Laura and I realized

Titus was doing the same thing to me and I was giggling like a ridiculous school girl myself. I thought it odd that a boy would be flirting with me, no one in Leavenworth ever had, but I liked it and played along.

Titus morphed from Gio's friend into a strong, funny, crush-worthy guy in the course of the afternoon. He was an attractive boy, a light black and white mix, with curly hair that couldn't decide if it wanted to kink or be wavy. He wore it long, under a ball cap and errant curls bristled around the rim. His parental combination of genes gave his skin a slightly yellow hue. He almost looked sickly because of the yellow, but he was spry and active. I thought his hair, unlike his yellowish skin, was a perfect combination of both of his cultures, curly without being kinky and raven-black. As the day wore on, I wanted to touch it and see if it felt more like white hair or black. The curls peeking out moved easily in the wind. I never had a chance to, though. It's not something I'd go back to redo, but I still wonder how his hair felt. He was not a muscular boy; he was a bean pole, thin and very tall. I liked his height, it made me feel safe. I was tall for my age but I barely came up to the base of his neck. I had to look up to see into his face, which felt nice.

We played games at the dinner table and watched normal movies, probably the Breakfast Club or Terminator or something like that. I don't know how long we were actually together and let the tension and emotion build while Mom slept and Lester worked in the orchard, but it was thick enough to let Gio convince me to stay the night. At Gio's incessant suggestions, I finally called Billy and begged him to cover my route the next morning. I didn't want Laura to stay over with Lester there so she got permission for me to spend the night at her house. Something inside me felt guilty that I left my baby sister, who was nearing the age I was when Lester fingered me, alone with him, but I wasn't going to stay. By evening, when Lester came in, and the thunderstorm mostly subsided, we were all ready to go for a walk. It was sweltering outside, not at all like the usual dryness we were used to. The crickets and frogs sung to us and Gio and Laura separated from Titus and I. We tried to avoid each other, walking down different rows in the orchard but kept bumping into each other. A little game of chase would ensue before we separated again, and on one such occasion he bumped into me and I moved closer to him instead of shying away. We traveled to the edge of the orchard, where the canyon walls stretched to the stars. I was barely familiar with the fringes of the trees in daylight, let alone on dark nights. Sultry, shivery feelings mixed and stirred inside me. I wasn't afraid of him, I knew I could count on him to keep me safe from the darkness.

I wanted to kiss Titus and I know he wanted to kiss me—he was a boy and if I knew anything it was that all boys wanted to use girls physically. Some are just brought up right enough to not take what isn't freely given. I realized I was likely willing to give him whatever he asked for. I didn't have my virginity, but there was plenty of "me" to give him, but I wanted him to initiate it. I didn't want to push it and have him mistake that for an invitation to do more.

CHAPTER 51

HE HELD MY hand in his as we climbed up the canyon. His hand was long and warm, dry and hard wrapped around mine. Mine were soft even with all the hitting I'd done with them, and weak compared to his strong ones. Having him hold my hand in his big, all-encompassing fingers made me feel little like everything else did, but for once I did not feel insignificant. When he held me with his big hands my littleness felt like a good thing, like I was supposed to be little and soft and vulnerable to contrast all that he was growing up to be; big and strong and unbreakable.

I felt like he would keep me and protect me and I felt like that was what was supposed to happen. Men were supposed to keep me safe, not ignore me or use me as they pleased. Real men protected and provided and didn't push for or take what I didn't give or offer. Titus was no man, yet; he was a boy, but he was a gentleman. He didn't go to church—I know because I asked. I don't know if he had a Christian influence in his life to be good or if it was solely his parents training or his own personality but he was a good boy. That night we walked hand in hand to the ridge of the canyon, and we talked. He talked about stuff I'd never heard a boy mention around me before. He talked about real stuff: feelings, family, fears. He was a real person, with real feelings and was sharing them with me. It was an honor to hold his thoughts and feelings the way he held my hands. He was offering himself to me and I received him. It never dawned on me that boys and men had feelings too. All I ever heard them talk about was stuff they did or wanted to do and things they liked, like sports and cars and work.

Titus was sharing his soul. He was as safe with me as I was with him, maybe not so much with *me* but alone with any girl that made a boy's openness possible. Guys felt things too, but they kept their feelings secret most all of the time. I was happy to have been included on Titus's secrets. His life wasn't easy. He was frustrated by his mixed color and how he didn't fit in. I knew how he felt. I never looked at him as a kid again; he was real to me after that.

He didn't take anything I didn't offer, and I was so new at the boy thing that I didn't know how I could have offered myself to him without being overt. There were a few times, coming down from the canyon that he would stop our descent and pull me close, really close and point out a constellation. When he held me, it was a full body connection and we touched from legs to shoulders. His long, skinny arms wrapped around me and kept me inside his slightly sweaty smell. I was safe in his embrace, away from the cares of my worlds. I rested my head on his chest and soaked up his strength, heat and heart beat while he poured out who he was in snippets of stories about his childhood or attempts at becoming a man like interviewing for a job earlier that day.

His words were, or at least seemed, totally honest and from his heart; his body was completely into me. He was hard, I could feel that much even if he tried to hide it. I was waiting for him to do what aroused men did in my life and in the movies: to take, to demand. He didn't. I didn't understand how much self-control he truly must have possessed not to act on his urges. I knew he wanted more. I could feel it and smell it and see it in his eyes in the moonlight, but I didn't know how to tell him it was okay without doing something, and I'd never had to do anything with Brad and Lester for them to take me. I leaned into everything he did, waiting for him to take so I could give.

I lived in fear of a moment alone, in darkness with Lester every second I was around him. I feared him touching me, or sneaking in and spoiling me, but there I was hoping that Titus would do all the things to me I didn't want Lester to do and more. I couldn't figure out how my body could want from someone so desperately what it feared from another. I couldn't figure out what more to do to let Titus know I wanted him to touch me closer, harder and more intimately. I wanted him to kiss me and lift me up and onto himself, like in the movies. I wanted him to but Titus was polite, he was a gentleman and would not.

I might have mistaken his lack of initiation for weakness, except for a run-in we had with a group of orchard workers at the edge of the trees. Three pescadores were near a supply shed. They spoke broken English and smelled like whiskey. When we came up on them, Titus's entire countenance changed. He squeezed my hand and guided me slightly behind him. No longer open or vulnerable, he was dangerously cautious. I swear I smelled his mood change. He went from amorous to brooding instantly. All of a sudden there were three bigger, stronger men in a dark place and my new friend was putting himself between me and them. I was afraid but he didn't let go of my hand as we passed them. They made comments about the pretty girl. He wasn't silent, he told them to not even look at me. He was like a real-live hero. The moment dragged out far too long in my head and now in my memory. In all seriousness, he made it clear I was not up for anything they might be thinking, nor was he going to let it happen.

We walked on further away from the orchard house and I started to balk that we were going the wrong way. He told me to be quiet and keep walking. We were going further away from my house, but also out of the orchard, toward the canyon road. The encounter ruined the mood but there was no mistaking his strength after that. He was not weak. He was what a man was supposed to be and he was only a boy. He was strong and patient, protective and self-controlled even when tempted.

We found the road and followed it back toward my house and met up with Gio and Laura a short while later. Together, the four of us walked to Laura's. I don't know where they went or what they did. I don't know what they imagined we did, but know I was a new girl. That night, as I laid on Laura's floor, I felt feelings that made me happier than I could ever remember feeling. Titus was a wonderful introduction to the wonderful world of what men should be like. Alas, he lived in Wenatchee and I in Leavenworth, but our short-lived fairy-tale romance in the orchard will forever live happily ever after in my memory.

CHAPTER 52

HIGH SCHOOL DAWNED with sweet memories of a mixed boy from Wenatchee still buzzing in my head, and a swarm of small town boys that had once been invisible or insignificant were all of a sudden way more interesting than ever before. My high school wasn't old but rich with Leavenworth history. The school building was much larger than the middle school and upperclassmen were practically grown-ups. They looked older and hairier and not at all like kids. I was a waif of a girl with an awkward, bewildering social footprint. I didn't find myself in the "in" crowd to say the least but the bullying wasn't nearly as big of a deal.

Most of the rich, popular middle school girls tried out for cheer leading, or the drill team. Lupe made the drill team too. Other school and church kids found spots in band, or choir, or on some kind of sports team. I was made for jazz band but the teacher told me it was only open to upperclassmen. Tandy's Bible group was early in the morning and messed with my paper route and, on top of that, was mostly innocent girls talking about maintaining their innocence. It seemed like everyone had a place but me. I sucked at sports, had no coordination to get myself on a drill or cheer team even if I'd had the social clout or desire to be voted into it, my voice was a nightmare to listen to. It was hopeless.

Then, by sheer luck, I found a place to fit in. I didn't have to try out for anything or be voted onto or accepted into a club, I was "in" because of my family. The wrestling coach, Steve Harris, went to Gramps' church and needed a couple statisticians for the team since his had all graduated. My cousin Billy was on the team and the coach knew I didn't have a life. It started out as simple as that. I showed up at practices to watch and learn the moves, and how the wrestlers scored points and how to mark them in the stat book. Kate, the other placeless person in high school, came too.

The boys on the team, upper and lower classmen, noticed us and we noticed them. Kate and I would comment to each other about the ones we liked. We looked them up and down and got a kick out of watching them be dumb to show off. The wrestlers came in all shapes and sizes; I decided my favorites were thick, stocky, muscular, strong and chiseled. Some boys were scrawny, wiry things, some were squishy and chunky—for some reason Kate seemed to crush on them more than the muscular boys. Most of the guys on the team were delicious to behold and we loved to watch them work out and practice. Before Coach Steve showed up they'd always show off. It was fun to be one of the centers of attention. It was something I'd never experienced before. It was different outside of practice, which confused me, in the halls Kate and I barely existed to them, especially the upperclassmen, but at practice they all totally knew we were there.

One boy on the wrestling team, Tyler Weeks, took a special interest in me at practice. Tyler was full of life and energy, never able to sit still and always saying something inappropriate at the wrong time. He was a trouble maker, I think, because of his energy level and somehow began his first year of wrestling his junior year of high school. Most wrestlers started their freshman year, like Billy, and stayed all four. Maybe Tyler's late arrival was an administrative or parental plan to keep him busy and out of trouble. Whatever the reason, there we were, together almost every day. I can't say that I spent much time noticing him in particular. He wasn't really that attractive and he didn't know many wrestling moves, so he got pinned a lot. It made him look weak, despite his muscular build. I didn't like weakness in males. He did have an amazing body though; broad shoulders, defined back. He could have been in one of the body builder magazines from behind. He was thick on top and tapered down perfectly to a strong, toned butt, quads and calves. If I could look only at his body instead of the complete package, I probably would have noticed him a lot sooner than I did.

Coach Steve let me warm up and exercise with the boys if I wanted to, which I did a few times a week. I didn't exert myself too much because sweating would never do in front of the boys, but I did enough to show them I was fit and flexible. Before coach showed up I wrestled with the guys, sparring and rough housing, partly because it was what I was used to from years of living in a male dominated culture and partly to flirt. Kate was more of a bystander. I knew the boys thought it was fun to have me out there with them because they acted differently. Maybe I didn't matter in the halls at school with fifty thousand other more beautiful and popular girls around, but when there were only two of us at a practice, I was quite the attention getter, and I loved to have the boys take notice of me. I existed in their eyes. I was alive. At some point in time, Tyler noticed me, at least at practice, and made his move.

I knew way too much about sex and giving head and the way things worked physically but I was innocent at actual boy and girl flirting games. I flirted with him, not to tease or tempt, but because I liked the attention. I didn't understand the point of it, but I liked it. It seemed to me that a boy, like the men in my life and movies, should grab me and take me. Titus, wasn't like that but Tyler was a whole different story. He took me by force... in a sexy way that didn't frighten me one bit! I was waiting for Billy by the bleachers, my back resting against the wall, talking to Tyler about who knows what, passing time. He stood next to me, close, sweaty and hot, smelling more like hard work than his favorite cologne. He probably only pretended to listen to what I was saying. His muscles were tight and red from the work-out, his hair damp at the ends. Tyler wore glasses, but kept them off for practice. His face was bare and clean shaven and I was looking at his stubble while I babbled about something.

Before I could think, he wrapped his hand up in my hair at the back of my neck and pulled me toward him. I had no time to react, but tried for a second or two to push myself away from him. He wasn't having that. His mouth was on mine almost as fast as he pulled me to him. It took a couple of seconds for me to realize that Tyler Weeks was my first kiss!

CHAPTER 53

HIS KISS WAS amazing, he knew how to do it good, or maybe he was the only one I had to compare with so it was going to be good no matter what. All I know is as far as kisses go, none ever compared to his, and after that, I compared them all to him.

In the moment, mixed in with all the shock, surprise swam in my head at how soft his mouth was. He was a powerful, hard boy, but his lips were warm and soft and smooth. His tongue was gentle and agile moving all over inside my mouth, teaching me what to do. I've always been good at learning and soon enough we were playing together instead of him controlling the kiss. It was a long, slow, strong and artful moment in my life. All of my auxiliary senses kicked in, I could touch him, smell him, taste him, feel him all over me. I didn't want it to stop but of course it did, when Billy came around the corner and coughed to get our attention.

One of my favorite things about wrestling were the tournaments. We had to get up painfully early, in the dark, which for me meant getting my route done earlier than normal. There were a few times we left the night before and stayed in hotels, Kate and I always got to stay together and usually Coach Steve's wife stayed in the room with us. It was the administration's attempt to make sure there was no fooling around between boys and girls. But kids will be kids and we found ways around roadblocks. The team would meet up at the school and Coach would drive a school van or, if there were enough wrestlers, we rode in a bus.

Tournaments were full of testosterone and sweat; it was heaven for horny teenaged girls. At tournaments, the boys had one goal in mind, that was to win—for the best of them, and to "fight hard" for the boys who knew they would never be winners. They defeated themselves by saying they were going to try their best. The boys that set their sights on victory seemed to be more victorious in my estimation. The wussy boys annoyed me. I couldn't even figure out why they came to wrestle if they already expected not to take first. They should have tried for first. Why did they try at all if they already believed they weren't going to take the prize? Wussy boys confused me.

The tough guys didn't talk much at tournaments and to try to coax any of them into conversation about anything other than food or their opponents was worthless. The winners (whether they took first or not) were focused on the task at hand and that was the next match. Girls hardly even mattered to most of them at the tournaments. I liked it because finally, when they were in their zone, they realized there was more than boobs and butts. There was something sexy about their focus on the match. The girlfriends who came learned to give their guy space when he was in his zone. They were little men and it was a pattern I recognized. I was used to preoccupation; it was the only way I knew my dad. There was always something on his mind. We waited for him, all of us: Gio, Vickie-Jean, Martin, Alex and I, like the girlfriends waited for their boys, but Dad was always in the zone, seldom took a break for us. Tyler took breaks for me at tournaments, the breaks were actually self-serving back rubs when he was finished with a match, if I was available, which I wasn't often because I had to track the other wrestler's matches.

It was best I stayed busy and occupied being a stats girl and with Kate because I knew I was nothing more than a wrestling accessory, not a person to him. I was a side dish to his life. One time he said he would take me out on a date, but Steve made it too difficult for him because he told my dad. To my surprise, my dad didn't say "no," only that Tyler would have to "run the deck" to earn a date with me and that date would be supervised. The "deck" was how the firemen worked out. Dad had a set of cards and each card stood for a type of exercise. Dad said most firemen did about twenty cards at a time. I knew no matter how good Tyler's fitness and energy level was, I was not worth a whole deck of cards to him. I was a back massager when he finished a match, a time passer when we made out on the bus, but I wasn't wanted or needed. Had he paid me any attention outside of wrestling I might have thought differently, but there was never more. I was his wrestling girl. For all I knew he had a school girl and a town girl to complement those parts of his life. His kisses, though, made me willing to endure that small spot in his life.

Being used as a wrestling girlfriend was better than other things I'd been used for. I was happy with as much as he gave me. I was a good student, if nothing else, and I was learning from a teenaged seduction artist. I wanted to know how sexual exploration felt without fear. It was kind of liberating knowing there was nothing but a physical connection between us. That meant he never had to be disgusted with who I was, like other people were. It meant he never noticed my pain or how I was mean sometimes, or my insecurities. Tyler taught me how easily I could be turned on and how little fear played a part in normal intimacy. Shame was a different beast, but somehow the feel good of making-out with him outweighed the shame.

On dark bus rides I learned how it felt to have his hands on my chest, fondling me, under and over my clothes. I wouldn't let him do more than kiss and touch under my shirt the first time Kate couldn't make it and he asked me to sit with him. I was content right there. Those touches were safe. The only other person who touched me below the belt line had done so without permission and it scared me. I didn't want to be scared by Tyler. I held him at bay, and he accepted the limitation, even if he did try to get in my pants every opportunity after.

The other thing that worried me about going too far with Tyler was the way my body reacted. Masturbating had always been the means to an end of an urge or compulsion, or boredom. By the time I did it, my body was already ready to orgasm, it just needed me to help stimulate the process. I never knew that passion could wet me so thoroughly. The first time I felt fluid leaking out from inside while we made out, I thought I'd started my period and was determined not to let him put his hands inside me and be the Carrie of Leavenworth. I couldn't have that. The first bathroom break we made I checked, fully prepared to stuff dimes into the hygiene machine. There was no blood, though, only this odd slippery egg-white-ish stuff. I wiped as much away as I could and made a toilet paper panty-liner, in case my period did come. I had no one to ask about it so for the remainder of the bus ride, Tyler tried to gain access and I kept denying him. The worry about him finding the toilet paper or blood (that never appeared) or that he'd make me feel with his hand inside me the way Lester had, was enough for me to keep him out.

After a couple intense make-out sessions, I figured things out. When he turned me on, my body prepared to receive him and I got soaking wet. It made sense. I decided it must be a natural part of the process. I was ready to see what it felt like as much as he was ready to get in there.

CHAPTER 54

IT BOTHERED ME that Coach Steve didn't stop it. I fully expected him to call me up to the front of the bus every time Kate couldn't make it, but he let me sit with Tyler. Coach Steve went to church, he knew what was right and wrong, and he knew I was younger than Tyler, and he had to know what was going on. He had the chance to stop it but he didn't. I would have been mortified to have him call me up, but I would have obeyed. I guess, maybe, it disappointed me that he didn't defend my honor. He called my dad about going on a date with Tyler, but he sat in the front of the same bus while we were clearly going at it in the back without batting an eye. Was he intimidated by what Tyler or I would say? Was he oblivious? Did he not care? I didn't know but Coach Steve lost some respect from me because of it.

Part of me felt like a whore about the whole thing. It wasn't a private, intimate place to be making-out. The other wrestlers knew what was going on even if it was all happening under a blanket. Worse than that, I didn't like Tyler for any other reason than the way he made me feel. I wanted to know more about the physical feelings his hands and mouth could give me than what his parents were like or how he was doing in school. He wasn't a good wrestler, and I didn't care for his personality as it reminded me too much of Gio.

All I wanted was to feel the rush and arousal like I did watching the movies. I wanted the release I used to give myself, but knew he could give me better. I wanted him to touch me the way Lester had and this time make it my choice to have someone's hands fondling me. It was my choice; I wanted this boy to do that to me, and I think I thought, that letting him in would wash away Lester's touch. It didn't. The memory of Lester's finger exploring and inserting inside me stayed, but Tyler's touch was nothing like his and was at least proof there was more to my vagina than what Lester had defiled. Tyler's fingers found places that made me go wild and he had to cover my mouth with his to keep me quiet. I wanted to beg for more, but I didn't have to because he knew, or at least, it seemed like he knew, what he was doing to me.

Deep down, I knew I was only a conquest to him, but for me I found another sweet addiction, lust, and I wanted more of it. I was innocent to the regular stuff. I never felt the work up to consummation of passion, I never knew foreplay, only men forcing, taking. I didn't, I suppose, even realize a girl was supposed to get anything out of the interaction. Brad and Lester certainly weren't in it to give me pleasure, but get themselves off in some sick, twisted way by touching a little girl like that. I liked the way Tyler used me; he wanted to see me aroused and feel me climax around his fingers. He whispered his approval in my ear and got off by how he could make me feel. When he brought me to orgasm, he watched me and soaked it up, smiling like he won a match; victory and conquest was his. He always smiled at the end and kissed me good and soft when I calmed down. I liked that it was something we were sharing but no one else was a part of. It didn't matter if a wrestler caught a peek at us over their seat. Only Tyler felt when I orgasmed, because we were quiet. Even though I didn't like him for much else, I loved him in those moments that were ours alone.

After he calmed me down and reprieve swept over all of me, his kiss intensified once again and the whole process of him bringing me to climax would start all over again. I liked it, I loved it; being touched by someone I wanted touching me, giving my body permission to feel, to enjoy, to submit to him. I loved how he made me feel. I didn't care that I was another notch on his score card except that I would have liked to matter, but I didn't expect to matter so it didn't matter.

At home, in my room, I tried more than a few times to mimic the way Tyler made me feel. It was nothing I could do for myself, it was only by another hand, by getting caught up in someone else's pheromones that the feelings would come. I was using him as much as he thought he was using me. We couldn't go too far on the bus and the boy wouldn't talk to me outside of wrestling so I was pretty sure there was nothing more we would ever do. If there was, by some chance anything more he wanted to do, anywhere, ever, I already knew I'd be up for it.

I knew from church and the Bible that I was supposed to be a virgin or I was a fornicator. Thing was, I wasn't a virgin. Sadistic men took my choice to save myself for marriage, so it didn't matter how far I let Tyler or anyone else go. If I had the choice, I honestly believe I may have waited for my wedding night because of the religious way Dad and Nonna had brought me up. But I was unclean and defiled because of Brad and Lester. The littlest sin was as bad as the greatest, so what did one more guy touching me matter? What did five hundred matter if I was already dirty? There was no point in pretending I was good if I wasn't. The way I was raised sin was sin. I decided then and there when Tyler was touching me, if I was bad already, I might as well enjoy it.

All I wanted to do was keep my sexual secrets to myself (not a problem since no one wanted to listen to me say a man molested me). No one cared enough to ask how serious Tyler and I were, because I never let on there was anything, because really there wasn't, other than his explorations of my body and that wasn't appropriate conversation. As far as I knew, Coach Steve didn't tell anyone I was making out on the bus with one of his wrestlers. The worst the wrestlers and Tyler could do was exaggerate what he did to me, and it didn't matter if they did because I was no one of significance. I was an underclassmen, I wouldn't earn him any popularity points, and it wouldn't affect me greatly because I was too meaningless for it to matter. Some teenagers think the world is all about them. I knew it was not all about me; I knew I didn't count. No one would care if I gave myself away on my wedding day or to a thousand different guys. It didn't matter, because I didn't matter, but still, I kept my secret.

I liked the way it felt to be turned on. The church made it seem evil, Lester and Brad made it seem scary *and* evil, the movies made it seem violent, scary and evil, but Tyler made it feel soft, sensual and good. Maybe the reason Brad, Lester and even Tyler messed with me was because I really was a whore doomed to hell and they knew it. Good girls, I perceived, from the way they talked in church, didn't like the way I liked to feel. Good girls didn't let boys touch them. Good girls said no. Had they never molested me, had I never seen those movies, I don't know if I would have ever started masturbating, but I might have still fallen for Tyler's kiss... or I would have slapped him for daring to take a kiss from me. Would I have let the course go the way it did even if Brad and Lester had never existed in my life? I do not know. All I knew was that I liked Tyler's kisses and didn't want to say no after knowing how good it could feel compared to how badly the others made it feel. I am left to wonder how much what they did to me really affected what I allowed others to do to me. The point is, I never had the chance to see what I'd do without their influence. I was already bad. I had nothing to lose.

I had one confidant, Kate. She knew what I let Tyler do, and we made believe I really liked him and he really liked me and we were a couple. We pretended her boyfriend was another boy on the team, Neil, and because of their jock status, we were popular. It never happened but it made the fantasizing fun. Kate and I had fun goofing off together at school and wrestling practices and talking for hours over the phone, on a line I paid for with my own money, but I could tell things were changing. We still talked and shared life together, but even with wrestling practice, we started to drift apart.

CHAPTER 55

IN FRESHMAN HOME Economics class, Leslie Reynolds stepped in and broke Kate and I up. Kate and I, we were a team. It was me and Kate forever, at least in my head that was how it went. We were going to have our weddings together, have kids together, be family friends and do things together...Never mind she never went to church and that other than our make believe fantasies and wrestling life we had little in common, we were supposed to be together for life. In that class, though, there were freshman girls she knew from eighth grade that I did not. Leslie was one of them. I knew from the moment she and Kate talked for the first time that they had been good friends and she had never told me.

Kate and I would never be the same. We sat at a table together, but Leslie and Kate talked. They knew the same bands and music, the stuff I wasn't allowed to listen to at home so I couldn't relate. They giggled to each other about this and that and had other classes together too. They were together more and it was natural they bonded. I never gave Leslie a chance because I was jealous. Besides, we had nothing in common. She was a punk rocker with long earrings and oodles of eye make-up. She was loud and abrasive and enjoyed drawing attention to herself and I tried to blend in to avoid causing pain to others or myself. People looked at her because of her flare and persona. I didn't like her. Wrestling season was winding down and Kate's calls stopped coming. It was always me trying to connect. I knew she was leaving me, I just knew it.

My rages couldn't be kept a secret anymore, or I should say, something inside me didn't want to keep them a secret. I wanted attention, I wanted to matter to someone. I wanted to stick out more than Leslie. I'm sure part of the reason I switched my pain of choice was to try and capture Kate's attention. It was also difficult to explain the perpetual scabs to Tyler when his hand drifted over my thighs, which happened now and again. I started punching cinder-block walls. My first one was a sea-foam green wall in the Home Ec. Room. That's how I know Kate was part of the reason. I don't remember anyone noticing, but what I noticed was how good the pain felt. The scratching made a sound when I did it. Hitting the wall made no sound except my bones cracking; it was an internal sound, like my pain. The wall was far too solid to resound because of my fist hitting it. Something about that thrilled me. It was proving once again my littleness. A hit that could break knuckles and bones in my hand, couldn't even make a sound on the wall. The other nice thing about hitting was I could feel the pain coming, with scratching it was slow and gradual, almost like a frog in a warm pot brought to a boil. My body would acclimate to the pain and only really feel the result of the scratching after I was finished. With the hitting, the pain was instant. It wasn't as messy either. Scratching left pus and blood and scabs, nice reminders of how I felt, when I was feeling really bad, but seriously inconvenient. I had to be ever on guard for exposure when I wore shorts, and my pants were always sticking to the open or healing wounds. I had to watch out to make sure pus or blood didn't leak or leave wet marks. A hit was quick, so much quicker than having to wait for the pain of the scratches and less messy. I was left with a bruise, mostly faint and bloody knuckles but nothing like the annoyance of scratching. After that first hit and the high I got off of it, I found walls to punch all the time.

No one noticed at home. Gio would have said something to get me in trouble, had he been there, but he wasn't. Martin and Alex were too little to notice anything but their toys. I played my keyboard in my room so no one had a good reason to look at my hands. Once, I added a particularly colorful bruise and wanted to see if anyone would notice. I wore short sleeves and did my homework at the table after Dad and Vickie-Jean came up from the shop. The bruises could often be obscured with long sleeves, but they were hard to miss with nothing covering them. They were dark purple towards the knuckles and faded to a sickly yellowish-green near the back of my wrist. I had a few knuckle scabs, and my hand was swollen. When I looked, I thought the markings were pretty obvious. I thought they would get some sort of comment, but nothing except, "It's late Gia, head to bed." In their world, my pain didn't exist. I didn't exist. I was the last remaining shred of evidence of Dad's life before Vickie-Jean and I knew that if ever I left and never came back, I would not be missed in the slightest.

I don't know what I would have done, had they noticed. I honestly don't because I was testing my hypothesis that they wouldn't notice. I was right. Had they noticed, some of the issues festering in my soul could have been addressed, but then again, we were Gianelli's and I knew us. We didn't deal with problems, we made them whispers. Maybe they whispered together about it and wondered why I was doing it, but we never once talked about any of the injuries I inflicted on myself. We didn't talk about what I did at wrestling tournaments, or how I felt about Gio moving, or how my social life was. We never talked about anything.

After the first real battering to my hand, I loved to watch my bruises. They colored and faded and decorated my hand. Bloody knuckle scabs healed way faster than my legs too and were fun to watch suck together into a smaller and smaller scab without the outside of the scab going anywhere. I was fascinated by the healing process as much as the destructive part of it. I could feel reminders of the pain when I touched the bruises or scabs and I could see how long it took my body to mend. Some of my knuckles, like some of my soul, never had a chance to heal before another blow would come. No one noticed, even when I hit walls in front of them, no one saw me. The school was too big for teachers to care, students too self-absorbed to try to figure the awkward girl out.

I didn't have to hide hitting because no one took an interest in me anyway. I think I remember hitting a wall something like ten or fifteen times in a class. It was in Home Ec. and my intention was to counteract some monologue Leslie was going on and on to Kate about. I piped in over her, "How many times do you think I can hit that wall before it hurts too much and I have to quit?" People guessed numbers and watched but no one freaked or stopped me. It was nothing to anyone, I was nothing to anyone.

No matter how hard I hit walls, it didn't get me noticed, it didn't stop my insides from rotting and it certainly didn't stop Kate from being friends with Leslie and spending less time with me. I imagined she was weirded out by the hitting and that's why she wasn't talking to me as much. It was easier to let her go that way, thinking it was something I was purposely doing than to think it was because I was less important than Leslie.

I guess, knowing her departure from my life was eminent, like Mom's, like Meredith's or any of the billions of Dad's girlfriends before Vickie-Jean, like Mario, and Carlie and Gio too, I looked for a reason to leave Kate before she left me. If it was going to happen, I wanted to be in control of the leaving. I wanted to have a say in when she would go. I refused to be surprised by it and look like an idiot left to wonder when or why she left me. I didn't know, though, how to leave her and even if I wanted to, even when she was leaving me. I felt like I had a loyalty to be best friends with her for the rest of my life. She never picked on me or made me feel like garbage the way other people had. I had no good reason to stop being friends with her. I knew how it felt to have someone not want me in their life, and I didn't want to do that to her. I figured a slow fade, though painful, was best. I would let her leave me in her own time.

My task was to figure out how to survive in high-school without a friend like Kate. I knew how to be an outsider and how to tear people down because I didn't quite fit in. I'd learned that sticking with a "pack" like the 8.5 kids or wrestlers, kept me from feeling completely alone and I'd learned having even one close friend made all the difference. I decided I ought to make another friend. I guess I should have learned how to make friends in elementary school but ninth grade was my time. It seemed like something I ought to try to do, because punching walls for attention was making it difficult to play the piano, and not really winning me any friend points with Kate.

CHAPTER 56

I FOUND THE first opportunity to make a new best friend around the end of wrestling season. My church friend, Lupe, and I had classes together. I can't remember which classes but we already knew each other and she had a higher social ranking because of the clothes she wore and things she was allowed to do. She got on the drill team to make a name for herself at school. With my lack of coordination the option wasn't open to me, but for some reason she allowed me into her school life. I suppose it was because we had church and school in common, and the drill team was full of preppy mean girls so I was a safe person for her. Like Kate and Leslie, we started doing more together. I liked how she trusted me and was determined to honor her trust in a way I hadn't with Bianca. My goal was to fit in and have a friend, not to ostracize anyone. Lupe accepted me at school like she did at church and I had a new friend!

I never disagreed with anything she said. She could have said she was going to kill her parents in the middle of the night and I wouldn't have done anything about it as long as we could stay friends. It felt good to belong even if to just one person. I wouldn't risk losing her by telling her she was wrong about what she was thinking. Except for Billy the rest of our group wasn't in high school yet. Carlie would have been, but she would have continued at the Christian school, I'm sure. Lupe and I were freshmen in our church group clique, and that was probably the deciding factor in her really latching on to me in high school.

Lupe and I started staying at each other's houses and talking on the phone all the time. She told me about her crushes and crazy dreams and I listened, thinking she was so much better than me. I couldn't figure out why she liked me. To this day I don't know what it was. Maybe I wasn't as awkward as I felt I was and she had no problems with me. I always felt like I might tarnish the cool persona she was trying to convey to everyone. She didn't avoid me and that was one of the first times I felt accepted by someone I perceived as "better than" me. I was petrified, though, of losing her friendship so I never questioned what she did or why she was doing it. I was convinced doing so would make her leave. I knew she would have no problems discarding me if I begged to differ with any of her attitude. And did she have attitude!

I felt sorry for her parents. She was mean to them. The first time I heard her talk back to her dad I was floored. I couldn't imagine talking to my dad that way. He would never tolerate it, and yet, her dad mumbled something like, "That's not very nice," and left the room. I probably would have talked back to him too. It was really a weak counter point to his mouthy daughter. I was expecting him to march me to the car and drive me home because of her disrespect. I asked her if she was going to apologize to him or if she got in trouble for talking like that. She looked at me like I was nuts and laughed and said, "No, this is my house, not his."

After wrestling season, Tyler was nothing but a sensual memory, Kate and I barely spoke, school was a blur of following social norms to fit in and I was disengaging from life in Leavenworth. I saw Paul now and again but we didn't have any classes together and he had a Gothic girlfriend. I hung out with Lupe, listened to her talk about who she liked and her master plan to get on the cheerleading team. I went to Mom's when I could fit it in my schedule. I snuck in to church by myself. I hung out with the gang at church. We still hung together, but it was another eminent split I could feel and see. I was the one breaking away. We did a lot of church activities that year, more than ever before. I saved my paper money to get out of the house and do stuff with the group because church activities were one of the few things I was allowed to do. After feeling the freedom of tournament weekends away from the shop, I took any chance I could get to leave because Vickie-Jean, in my opinion, was getting more horrid by the day. I wonder, though, if it was her or me being horrid. All I knew was that I couldn't stand living with her one more year.

The older I get, the less wicked Vickie-Jean seems but back then, alone, without Gio, after Brad and Lester, she was the meanest person in my life. I felt, and had felt for a long time as if I was a nuisance in her otherwise perfect life. She had her Gallery and pictures in places from sea to sea, she had her boys and her remodeled retail building and her this-and-that. She successfully managed to beat Gio right out of Leavenworth and had me stuffed up in an attic unless she needed me for grunt work. All she had left to get rid of was me completely and then my dad would be all hers. She never had anything nice to say to me, never did anything with me, and had me do so much work every day before I could do anything else, I felt like a slave.

The only time I remember her touching me after Gio left was when she put her arm around me at church one time during an alter call. I had gone up to repent for my sin and she had the nerve to come up and pray over me. She asked the Lord to remove my spirit of rebellion.

My spirit of rebellion?! She had no idea the pain I was dealing with. Spirit of rebellion? How about spirit of sexual abuse that had damaged my mind and none of my parents helped me deal with? How about the spirit of hoping he doesn't sneak into my room? How about the spirit of Nonna telling me I messed up...again? How about her and Dad's spirits of emotional disconnectedness? How about the spirit of watching a wonderful super-Christian like she was presenting herself to be, beat a little boy down the steps? How about the spirit of making me work for hours for nothing every day? What about all those spirits, did they count for anything? At that moment apparently the only thing she could find to pray about was, surprise, surprise, how bad I was. I wanted to beat my head on that altar step so bad. I wanted to gouge my eyes out, flip myself around and scream till my voice was gone to everyone there that I was the devil himself, but in a church like mine, actions like that would get me called demon possessed. That would only ostracize me from my group, and I needed them, especially since I was fitting in at school because of Lupe.

I'd never hated Vickie-Jean more. She was evil, she was mean and she had no idea the pain I was dragging around, and didn't care about any of it, except that my "spirit of rebellion" was bothering her. How dare she! That was the moment I made my decision to leave, and I also decided that if Lester tried anything, I would kill him! It was time anyway, for all his orneriness, I missed my twin too much. And Hannah. My little sister, Hannah, was in a princess dress-up phase. She was the age I'd been. If I didn't have a protector, at least I could be one for her.

I moved out at the end of that year, but that altar prayer, whenever it was, was when I packed up emotionally and left my dad and Martin and Alex. She was dead to me, she didn't count. She was nothing but a wicked step-mother that I needed to escape from. I started to double-up my Lester avoiding tactics against her, listening for where she was in the house and moving about when she was in a different area. I did everything on my work list, dodging and moving, leaving things half-finished when I heard her coming. I never got everything right. She would call me to re-clean this, or re-fold that. I turned into a robot, she input the instruction, I spit out exactly what she wanted. I tried to keep an emotionless expression but I'm sure she saw the disgust.

CHAPTER 57

I STAYED OUT as late as I could after school and broke into the church to play my sonata alone more nights than not. I skipped the bus and walked home and stopped off at the library where I spent most of my free time if the church group wasn't doing anything. I read author Robert C. O'Brien that last half of the year and would consume books similar to, "Rats of NIMH," and "Z for Zachariah," like candy. One book could occupy me at the library or in my room for hours on end. When I was too hungry to stay out anymore or knew I'd get seriously busted if I was gone longer, I started for home. I took the long way home and walked through town making eye contact with people who looked at me, mostly boys and young men. Some smiled, winked or nodded, others looked at me like a notch they wanted in their belt, a few looked more scary like Lester, but no one ever approached me.

I came home one day later than I should have from the library and got a huge lecture from Vickie-Jean the Evil Queen. All I could think in my head was that I was at the stupid library, *the library!* And she was flipping out because I wasn't there to watch her children when Nonna dropped them off. She must have grounded me or something, because that started the late night calls to my mom and Gio. I started sneaking down to the church and calling them to cry about how bad things were. When Mom was home and I got to talk to her, she always asked if my dad knew I was out that late. She *said* she was not okay with me being out, but she was fine with it. I know, because she never told Dad I was sneaking out. She would help me pass time by talking to me about Gio and the other kids. Gio and I could talk until his cordless phone battery died late in the night but Mom would talk with me for a while, let me pour out my heart about how much I hated it with Vickie-Jean then would finally tell me I needed to go home and go to bed. She promised me I would be with her soon enough and I needed to stick it out until the end of the year. I did what I had to do and made it through one day after another.

In my mind, Vickie-Jean had no chance of redemption and it seemed like it got worse every day. Once, in church, instead of sitting with my friends I sat with her. I'm not sure if it was a punishment or if it was because I had work to do and didn't want them distracting me. I was working on a science assignment, book in lap, and she kept jabbing me in the ribs with her finger, trying to get me to quit doing work and listen to the sermon about how horrible we all were and how much we needed to confess our sins. I whispered to her that I had work to do and wasn't hurting anyone. She made silent, sneering eyes at me and gestured toward the door for me to leave the sanctuary. I knew it was all coming down, and boy did it!

I followed her out to the car with my best "bad attitude" I could come up with. She went off once again about how bad I was, how I should be doing nothing in church but listening. I went off on her about maybe if I didn't always have to clean the apartment for her top to bottom and watch her kids after Nonna dropped them off while she flirted with tourists and gallery owners I could do my work, but I didn't have the chance because I was doing the things she was supposed to be doing. Then, I asked if my dad knew what she did to the New York gallery man to get her pictures featured. That was the question that unleashed her.

Her hand flew from her side. She slapped me so hard and fast across my face that her nail scratched my eye. The sting felt good and I smiled back at her. She was a good hitter. I'd seen what she could do to Gio and I figured I was in for it, and braced for the next blow. It never came. Probably she regretted the way she had dealt with Gio and learned restraint but at the time I thought the only thing that saved me was the fact that we were at church and any one of the people she tried to impress so much could have seen us.

"Go ahead, Vickie-Jean, hit me again! I can take it!" I could feel the welt from her hand searing my face. "You might as well finish the job, finish me. Isn't that what you want to do anyway? You want me out of the picture, right? Well, you got it! You already ruined my life, YOU made Gio leave and now I'm leaving too!"

I told her she was vile and mean and I had no idea what my dad saw in her, that she didn't measure up compared to the ladies he used to date and that he only married her because she got pregnant. I told her the fancy clothes she bought for herself and the little boys couldn't cover up the nasty inside her. I told her I didn't even think Martin and Alex were my dad's kids because she was always so flirty and touchy with men in the store. Everything, everything I'd been holding in about her and Dad, and maybe even me, came out. I think I might have even brought up the abuse that happened to me and asked how come they didn't do anything about it. She was horrified, it was all over her face. She had no words, and now I feel really bad about how hurtful mine had been. She left the little boys at church with Nonna and Aunt Maria and drove in a fury to the store.

The shop was full of happy tourists on that bright spring day and the look on Dad's face told me I was inconveniencing him. He came to the back while Vickie-Jean took over the counter, "What is your problem? What's wrong with you, Gia?" I laid into him about his lovely wife.

"What's *my* problem, Dad?! Do you know how much work she makes me do? I couldn't even do my school work because of how much work she gave me to do this weekend! I wasn't being disrespectful in church I was making a wise use of my time, the way you always tell me to do. She was poking me! Do you know she beat Gio and that's why he left? She was the reason Gio left and... I'm leaving too! She ruined the family we had, and you let it happen." Then I brought up the past on him too and asked why he didn't save me from Brad.

He stood stunned for a second, like she had, "That has nothing to do with your behavior right now."

CHAPTER 58

"YEAH IT DOES," I said, "It has everything to do with it! Maybe if you guys would've helped me instead of make me your slave, I wouldn't be so messed up!!" I couldn't control the tears, they poured out of my eyes. I had had it! I pushed my swollen, bruised knuckles in his face, and pulled up my skirt for him to see the darkened scratch scars on my legs. I told him I tried to be perfect for them and Nonna and it was never, ever good enough. "I clean your store and house, I watch your perfect boys. I do everything you guys tell me to and YOU HATE ME! Other people in town like me but my parents hate me! I can't do anything right for you two!"

"Knock it off, Gia! Get up to your room. I'll come find you later. Don't you dare come down." Later was hours after church was over and the shop had been locked up for the night and the brothers were put to bed and he and Vickie-Jean whispered so quietly I couldn't hear them through the vent. He came up and acknowledged that he knew bad things had happened to me but that it was no excuse to say the things I said or do the things I was doing to Vickie-Jean. He said I needed to stop hitting walls and hurting myself. Then he told me he loved me, as if that was going to fix it all, and told me dinner was in the microwave for me.

Nothing was fixed, nothing was resolved, except that I was more set to leave than ever. If I was avoiding Vickie-Jean up to that point, it was nothing compared to the remaining time I was there. I tried not to talk to her at all, or even look at her. I was done with her and her high class photos and fake personality. I was sick of her boys getting the world on a platter and me being her slave-maid. I was done with life there; Lester fingering me up was nothing compared to the constant hell my life was with her. I couldn't wait to get out of there. All I had to do was make it until the end of school. All I had to do was stick it out a little longer. It was a test and trial. The rages, my sonata, paper route and attic room were the only ways I made it through.

On one of my home-avoiding excursions through and around town, I ran into a group of choir boys from Seattle while walking one of the shopkeeper's dogs. Their all boys choir was singing in the gazebo in the center of town later that day and they were exploring in the meantime. I think they noticed the dog, Pepper, first. He was a large, beautiful Great Dane. I took him on walks all over the trails on Black Bird Island. He was well-mannered but still a challenge to manage being well over my full weight. I had fun walking him and loved the attention he always drew. The boys were joking around about how a little girl like me could walk a big dog like that. They were all my age, although Boston, the one I spent the most time with, seemed older somehow. They asked me to show them the city and I took them on a tour only a local could give. Boston and I were flirting, but it was pretty innocent all around. My guess is they were probably fairly good boys. They were performing with a respected group, and I don't ever remember any of them being untoward. They didn't swear much, another mark of well-raised stock. They had the tough guy persona, but they were good boys.

Boston was that deep, dark black that fascinated me so much on my trip down South and I swear his dark eyes could see right through me. I could tell he liked me, and I reciprocated his advances.

"How bad do you want to kiss a black man?" he asked with the slightest hint of trepidation in his voice. It was adorable, I could tell he was nervous, but he was trying.

"I don't know, I don't see any men around," I joked back, but leaned toward him. The other boys heard and had a good laugh at his expense. "I want to kiss you, though," I said loud enough to help him save face. "I have to take Pepper back home. You can come with me if you want..." Oh, he wanted to. He gladly accepted and the other boys took the hint. We broke off from the group and walked alone toward Pepper's house. I couldn't stop staring at his lips. They were dark-rimmed and looked soft and lickable. They faded to pink and the inside of his mouth was the same color as mine. His hands felt somehow different. I can't say for sure why or how, but different, drier, thicker, more sturdy. His hair and skin was, of course, different. I held on to his arm as much to feel the brown under my fingers as to stay close to him. His mouth transfixed me. I wondered about kissing him. Would his lips feel different, like his hands did? Would his kiss feel the same way Tyler's did, or would it too be different? The closer we got, the more delicious anticipation swirled inside me.

We didn't talk like Titus and I had. Titus confessed his heart to me, Boston only talked about the trip and choir and asked about my skills on the piano. We dropped off Pepper and I led him back down to the river, to the trails along its banks. We walked up a hill and he pulled me into a secluded spot next to some popular trees. For a slight moment, I questioned what I was doing, and hoped he really was a good boy and not like Brad or Lester. I came up with a plan to scream and fight my way out of his grasp if that was the case and then evacuated that thought from my mind.

He pulled me closer still, into his rich, black arms and blocked out the rest of the world. The river rushed behind me, his face, strong and confident, hovered over me. He leaned in, and sure enough, those big, dark lips of his were soft, so soft and he kissed me. Tyler had ruined it for him. Boston didn't measure up. He wasn't a bad kisser by any means, but Tyler was my first and he was a master with his tongue. Boston didn't stand a chance compared to him, but it was a most pleasant kiss. I thought about what we must have looked like, him swooping down to meet me, dark wrapped around white, connected, close, blending together. What I can say is Boston's mouth felt like mine. His kiss was good, and we enjoyed a fantastic afternoon together that summer. For one day, for one moment, I was his girl and his memory of Leavenworth would always have me in it. Something about that made me proud. I'd always be with him, and he with me.

He was my only summer fling with a tourist. No other visiting boys made an attempt to take me on walks alone. No local boys showed interest in me either. None of the church regulars wanted to change the dynamic within our circle of friends. I was a girl doing my best to pass time away from home until school was over.

CHAPTER 59

I DETACHED FROM everything in Leavenworth. I stopped doing errands for shop-keepers, Billy took over my paper route, I made sure Coach Steve knew Leslie would take my spot as stats girl next wrestling season. I counted down the days in my head. Lift off was upon me. Despite the anxiety about living with Lester every day, I was glad to leave because I had no good reason to stay anymore. Dad knew I was going and tried to keep me. Like any addict, making a deal, again he tried to get me to believe this time would be different, and he really would spend more time with me, and do more with me.

He took me, just me, for two whole days, to Silverwood. It was a passionate pomedoro attempt to prove his promise that things would be different. I enjoyed every roller coaster, ice cream cone, and laser tag hit of the trip. I especially noticed how he avoided the merch shops. He usually shopped other novelty town merchandise shops to see how they did things and which vendors they used. It was common to wait on him for hours while he talked to shopkeepers about small town retail business. He didn't do that. He wanted me to stay. I think, even though he heard the words I said at the store when I'd confronted him and Vickie-Jean, he must have thought it was only his not being there that was the reason I was moving because that was all he had for me as a promise. If I stayed, he promised to spend more time with the family and less time managing the shop. He never asked for more information about what Vickie-Jean did to Gio or the abuse I said happened to me. He only promised to spend more time with the family.

Our last trip together was wonderful; a bright red, two day pomodoro adventure ticking by slowly, sweetly. It was good-bye.

He knew it. I knew it. My dad was my hero, a real-life hero that made mistakes. I wanted him to come blazing into my life, cape-on, chest puffed, fists clenched ready and able to squash the bad guys and defend me against mean, abusive people. But he was only a man, doing the best he could with a broken, bitter teenaged daughter. We soaked up the time together. I didn't have to compete with tourists or brothers. I didn't have to contend with a woman as driven to succeed as he was. For a precious, fleeting moment in time it was me and my dad.

If only it could have been like that forever, then I would've wanted to stay with him; but I knew he didn't mean it. He was lying, to me and to himself. Maybe he couldn't see it, but I knew the truth. Years of broken promises were stacked against that glorious trip. If I gave in, changed my mind, life wouldn't change. Vickie-Jean would still hate me, Nonna would still tell me I did everything wrong. Gio would still be gone. I would still be misunderstood. I couldn't change my mind. We had our fun and then headed home. We never talked about the problems; just that he didn't want me to go. I knew nothing would change.

I wasn't staying. I had enough of Vickie-Jean's high-class, name-brand life that I wasn't a part of. I had enough pretending at church that I was a good kid, like the other kids. I had enough of everything that Leavenworth had ever offered to me. Lester seemed manageable compared to the conditions I felt like I had to endure in Leavenworth. He hadn't touched me in years, but Hannah was getting older and needed to be watched over. I promised myself he wouldn't dare try it again and if he did, with me or Hannah, I would kill him. I didn't think about how the anxiety of being with him day in and out would affect me. I didn't think about how Mom's music moods would annoy me. I had no way to know what I was getting in to. All I knew was I couldn't stay in Leavenworth one more year.

The day came. School let out for the summer. I packed my suitcase and boxes into the back of Mom's car and said good-bye to a half-way decent life, to tourists, to Nonna, to bus rides with boys, and church and the God of the Bible. A new god was about to rule over me, a new slave master be the boss of me.

My addiction laid before me.

ALSO BY LUCY H. DELANEY

Catching Tatum (Road to Love – Book 1) After a high-school romance left her heartbroken, Tatum turned love into a game; the boys either followed her rules... or they were out! Everything was fine until Cole and Justin decided to play. Will Tatum's rules help her navigate two very different men, or will she strike out at her own game?

Waiting on Justin (Road to Love – Book 2) Amidst tragedy and despair, Justin and Haylee seek an answer to the age-old question: can love endure the harshest of climates and passage of time? A touching and poignant story about a love worth waiting for.

Finding Jordan (Road to Love – Book 3) Jordan's life was great. She had an amazing job traveling the world, and a super hot romance with a blue-eyed guy who was almost too good to be true. But, just one night and just one decision was all it took to put both in jeopardy and leave her with a secret that could ruin everything.

Scandalous Affair - Nate appears to have it all, but he is torn between two sexy, powerful women. Chelsea, one of Hollywood's hottest leading ladies, has warmed his bed for years. Sofia, has beguiled him for far too long but she wants him to leave Chelsea for good. Is it a choice between two women or a tale of something more dramatic than a Hollywood love triangle could ever be?

Made in United States
North Haven, CT
27 February 2024

49286923R00139